Entropic Angel

And Other Stories

*To Pat + John,
with best wishes,*

[signature]

Entropic Angel

And Other Stories

Gareth L. Powell

NewCon Press
England

To Pat + John,
with best wishes

Contents

Introduction

Aliette de Bodard

What I love about Gareth's stories is that they're always large-hearted.

It's very easy, when writing science fiction about large-scale changes and cool new inventions, to forget that these happen to people, whether human, post-human or alien. What I like about Gareth's work is that, while he writes big idea stories, he also never loses sight of the people at the heart of them. They're not always *nice* or comforting people, but then that's the way people are, too.

His characters are survivors, whether by design or by accident; and the question Gareth repeatedly asks is who gets to survive – who deserves to survive – and what is the cost of doing so. An equally important theme in those stories is memory and the memory of things we have done, and the possibility of atoning or making up for them, no matter how much time may have elapsed (and this is science fiction, so 'time' can cover many centuries, or the entire span of millennia from the 21st Century until the end of the universe!). Many of the stories are explicitly about escape: from a dead-end childhood with all too familiar pathways into the future, from the responsibilities of family to a dust-choked world, from an unimaginably brutal war where all the dirty tricks of history are used to create bloodthirsty monsters. Gareth doesn't shy away from consequences, either: the price to pay for survival or redemption or escape is often prohibitively high, and there's always a question of whether it's all worth it, a darkness at the heart of them which makes them all the more strikingly realistic.

Let's come back to big ideas. In these stories you will find a multitude of them: time-hopping soldiers hunted by their instructor, the earth devastated when caught in a fight between two different alien races, AIs creating fleeting superstructures that are mined for wealth...

Gareth L. Powell

Gareth excels at not only imagining them, but rendering them in vivid details that make the reader feel as though they, too, are alone at the end of the universe and adrift without a sense of purpose, or walking in the dust of a forgotten planet and struggling to breathe. They show us different worlds and different pathways, whether at the scale of a life or at that of all of history; and the whirlwind, memorable journeys they map for us are always worth taking.

Aliette de Bodard
Paris
January 2017

Ride the Blue Horse

We were breaking into shipping containers the day we found the blue horse.

My friend Dan had convinced me we should give it a shot. The stacks were dangerous, but since getting the sack from the call centre we were desperate.

"I heard of a guy two towns over," Dan said, rocking back and forth on his heels in the call centre parking lot, "who cracked a container of canned fruit. Peaches, cherries, and mandarins – stuff you just don't see any more. It made him rich."

"How rich?"

"Rich enough to leave town."

We had to walk to the freight yard, and it took us the whole day. Heat shimmered off the empty road. The place had been abandoned since we were kids. With the big ships gone, it just hadn't been economical to keep open. And once the port authority stopped dredging, it only took a couple of years for silt to choke the harbour. All that was left now were these rusting container stacks, and the wiry little green fireworks of grass that had smashed their way up through the shattered tarmac.

The perimeter fence had been smashed down in several places.

"Are you sure there's going to be anything left?" I said.

Dan gave me one of his looks. He was still wearing his call centre clothes, dark jeans with a white shirt and black tie, and his top button was undone.

"Look at the size of this place. It's about a bazillion square kilometres. There are literally thousands of crates." He stepped through the fence with the sprightly confidence of a door-to-door evangelist. "The ones at the edges may have been looted, but I'll bet you there's still plenty of good shit further in."

"You'd better be right."

"Of course I am." He clapped his hands together and rubbed them briskly.

"Now come *on*, Spelman, let's hustle."

As it turned out, he was right. But we had to open six crates before we found her.

The first three were full of plasma TVs, electric kettles, and other unusable junk. The fourth was empty, and the fifth strewn with the discarded rags of a shipment of long-forgotten immigrants.

At that point, I was ready to give up for the night. The sun had gone down and the sky was ripening towards the colour of a day-old bruise. Dan convinced me to continue.

"Just one more." He slapped the side of the next container in line and the metal made a deep booming sound. "Come on," he said, "I've got a *great* feeling about this one."

Unfortunately, Dan injured himself as we were prying off the lock. The crowbar slipped, and the end of it gashed his palm.

"Goddammit!"

"Are you okay?"

"Just peachy." I watched him suck the wound. Thankfully, it didn't seem deep. We both knew we didn't have enough money to get him a tetanus shot.

With his hand still in his mouth, he kicked the door.

"Get this sucker open, Spelman."

"Yes, sir." I stooped to retrieve the fallen crow bar, and carefully popped the lock.

The door opened on rusty hinges.

"What have we got?"

I frowned into the gloom.

"Some jerry cans and kit bags... and something wrapped in a tarpaulin. I think it might be a car."

Dan pushed past me.

"Well, there's no need to sound so disheartened."

He crouched in front of the covered vehicle and pulled at the edge of its shroud.

"Voila!"

The cloth came away and he stood there like a conjuror awaiting the applause of the crowd. I looked at what he had uncovered.

"Pretty car."

"Pretty?" He dropped the edge of the tarpaulin and walked around to the driver's door. His fingertips brushed the blue-painted bodywork. "You don't even know what this is, do you, Spelman?"

"Nope."

He shook his head sadly, as if disappointed in me.

"It's a 1960s Ford Mustang with a V8 engine and four-speed manual gearbox." Dan was quite the student of classic Americana. Plus, his dad had once owned a garage out near the Interstate. He opened the door and slid behind the wheel. "And the keys are in the ignition."

I walked over and kicked one of the jerry cans. The dull thump told me it was full. I unscrewed the lid.

"This is petrol. And these bags are full of camping supplies and dehydrated ration packs."

Dan was beside me in an instant.

"Put all of it in the trunk."

I raised an eyebrow. "You think it's worth something?"

"Are you kidding?"

He helped me load the car, and then we both climbed in.

"You know what this is?" He gave the steering wheel an affectionate pat. "It's somebody's cache. It's their end-of-the-world back-up plan, only they never came back for it." He laughed. "Just imagine for a moment, some wannabe Mad Max trapped in a departure lounge in Washington or Buenos Aires, knowing the planet's going to hell but being unable to reach all the gear he's so carefully squirrelled away."

He pulled a pair of sunglasses from the glove box, and admired himself in the rearview mirror.

"So," I said, "how much do you think we can sell it for?"

He looked aghast.

"Where's your imagination, Spelman? This might be the last functional car in America. Do you know how far a blue horse like this could get us on a full tank of gas? At least two or three hundred miles. And then we've got the refills in the trunk."

"And when they run out, then what?"

"And then we've got all this neat camping gear, and these rations. I'll bet they're super tasty. They'll keep us going until we find someplace." He put his hand on my shoulder. I could feel warm, sticky blood soaking through my t-shirt. "We can hit the road right now, and never come back to this ungrateful crap-hole."

My skin prickled the way it did before a thunderstorm.

"Not… ever?"

"Nope." He lit the headlights and we blinked against their sudden brilliance.

"One question." I fastened my seatbelt. "Do you actually know how to drive?"

He turned the key in the ignition. The engine coughed twice, and then bellowed. The metal walls amplified the sound. I caught a whiff of carbon monoxide. Dan released the parking brake.

"No, I can't say I do." With his bloodied hand, he crunched the gearstick into first and eased up the clutch. We began to roll forwards. "But really, how hard can it be?"

~

I wrote the entire first draft of this story on a Thursday afternoon. I know it was a Thursday, because I remember that the commission came in on a Wednesday evening, and the submission deadline was the Friday of that same week!

The commission for "Ride the Blue Horse" came from Medium.com, and the finished story eventually appeared as part of a climate fiction special, alongside contributions from Margaret Atwood, Bruce Sterling, Paolo Bacigalupi, Tim Maughan and others.

Although the two main characters are only lightly sketched, I'm still very fond of them. I drew them from my experiences as a call centre operator in the early 1990s, using my younger self and the people I worked with in that 'graduate's graveyard' as models. Wherever they end up in that car, I wish them well in their travels.

I've performed this story several times in readings at various events, and it always seems to go down very well with the audience. I read Dan as an over-caffeinated, over-enthusiastic force of nature, and Spelman as his slightly dopey, long-suffering sidekick.

Given that it only took me a couple of hours to write, I was particularly delighted when "Ride The Blue Horse" made the shortlist for the 2015 BSFA Award.

Lift Up Your Face

She was the only kid he knew who didn't look down her nose at him. They were both outsiders in a Welsh border village, where rifts and enmities ran beneath everything like festering seams of smouldering peat, and the children in their local primary school class stifled beneath the weight of generational feuds stretching back to the misdeeds of their great-grandparents – whole histories in which neither Lee nor Kerri had a part to play.

Neither of Lee's parents had been born in the village. His father was from Swansea, his mother from London. They were both college lecturers. Even in the holidays they had work to do, books to read. Having successfully bred once, they seemed disinclined to repeat the experiment. Lacking siblings and scorned as a 'blow-in' by the other children, it was inevitable he'd wind up in the orbit of another outcast – in this case, the farmer's daughter from the house on the hill.

She lived with her father in the farmhouse high above the higgledy terraces of the village. He was an ideological farmer, a city boy driven to the country by a need for self-sufficiency and a fear of urban collapse. Their house had solar panels, a composting toilet, and a wind turbine whose blades rattled as they spun. The cellar held enough tinned food for a year. Growing up readied and prepared for an environmental or political apocalypse, Kerri was as different to the pinch-faced village girls as June is to January. She had six freckles on her nose, comb-resistant tresses of off-blonde hair that danced and played behind her ears, and eyes as bottomless and unreadable as the sky-polished surface of a tarn.

In the summer, when the tractors droned and grumbled in the fields and the high-hedged roads were full of walkers heading for a day's ramble around the brown bracken foothills of the Brecon Beacons, the two of them would sit in the shade of the ruined tower in the paddock to the west of the village, their backs resting against the coolness of the stones. The tower and a few crumbled walls were all

13

that remained of a twelfth century castle, and constituted the village's one and only tourist attraction. They scuffed their feet in the dirt, watching newly shorn lambs nose among the fallen stones; read superhero comics; and listened to music on their mobiles. Kerri liked anything with a beat and a bit of aggression. She was also occasionally a bit mean to him, and teased him the way girls sometimes do; but she let him hang around with her, and together they explored the hills, her father's farm, and the ruins of the castle.

And then, on one particularly hot and drowsy August afternoon, when they were fourteen years old and stretched out in the shadow of the old tower, she saw a helicopter and burst into tears.

They'd been lying in companionable silence, looking up at the dome of sky suspended between the hills on either side of the valley, and Lee had been thinking about the stars and how they were all still there, on the other side of that blue curtain, and how it was only the fact that they were hidden during the day that let mankind forget what a precarious and insignificant ball it lived on, adrift in a vast eternity of night. How different, he wondered, would we have been as a species if, throughout history, the stars remained visible during the day? Would we still have bothered to raise monuments and build skywards like the builders of this castle tower; or would our spirits have been crushed beneath the weight of the universe? Personally, he rather liked the idea of having that constant reminder. At home, he'd filled his bedroom walls with old Hubble photographs of rosy nebulae and colliding galaxies, and pictures of Mars and Titan torn from the pages of *National Geographic*. His dream was to one day program his computer with a complete and accurate scale model of the solar system: a simulation he could explore at his leisure, with every comet, rock and asteroid accounted for and in their proper orbits.

He and Kerri both had computers, of course; but where Kerri was content to play games and mess around on the Internet, Lee wanted to know how his worked. At school, while the other kids flocked and clustered, he sat in the corner and read programming manuals and computer magazines. It wasn't enough for him to know how to use the desktop his parents had given him; he wanted to delve into its code and build his own worlds and amusements. Because, he thought, what would be the point of owning such a remarkable machine if you weren't going to pop the hood and tinker with it, and exploit its full potential?

Sometimes, he wondered if he was the only person in the village with a drop of curiosity in his head. He couldn't understand how the people around him could go on ploughing the dreary furrows of their lives when all around them, just beyond the surrounding hillsides, the entire universe seethed with drama and potential. On clear nights, he'd sit at his bedroom window and watch the vault of Heaven wheel overhead, imagining himself as an old man, withered and gnarled; a lone scholar huddled over a lamp in the topmost nook of the castle's tower, custodian of the world's few remaining books of science and literature (and superhero comics); curator of knowledge and learning that would otherwise be lost to the ravages of the weather, and the indifference of the barbarians outside.

He was about to open his mouth to ask Kerri if she ever thought about the stars during the day, when he heard the eggbeater thump of an approaching helicopter and a grey military transport chopper battered its way down the length of the valley, sashaying from side to side as it tracked the course of the river that wound across the valley's meandering floor. He and Kerri watched it pass overhead, so low they could read the number painted on its underside and feel the *thudthudthud* of its rotors in their chests.

Lee sat up to watch it clatter off. When he turned to Kerri, he saw that tears were sliding down her cheeks in translucent stripes.

"What is it? What's the matter?"

She let her gaze fall from the dwindling helicopter and angrily wiped her eyes on the back of her wrist.

"Shut up."

"But –"

"You wouldn't understand." She turned away and sniffed.

Lee glanced nervously around the paddock.

"Are you okay?"

Kerri pulled a crumpled tissue from the pocket of her denim shorts and snuffled wetly into it.

"I heard about Mike, okay?" she said.

Lee blinked, then frowned.

"Mike?"

Kerri gave him a look.

"Mike *James*. You know, Glyn's older cousin. He lived with his ma on Forest Street."

"Oh, him." Lee remembered the kid as a red-haired, thick-knuckled bully, maybe four or five years older than them. "Didn't he join the army?"

Kerri climbed to her feet. In the week since the start of the school holidays, the sun had tanned her scrawny legs the colour of weak tea. She brushed grass from her palms.

"Yeah, and now he's dead." Her lips whitened as she pressed them together. Then her face collapsed like a sagging cake and she stood there, hands at her sides, sobbing.

Lee scrambled up. His heart beat with an odd sort of panic. He didn't know what to say. He wasn't used to girls crying. Tentatively, he reached out and touched her shoulder.

"What happened?"

"H-he was in Afghanistan and he d-died."

"How?"

Angrily, she brushed a strand of hair away from her eyes. "Does it matter?"

Lee withdrew his hand, and used it to adjust his glasses.

"I don't understand why you're so upset."

Kerri hunched her shoulders.

"I've never known anyone who died before."

"But, he was a dick."

"That doesn't mean he deserved to die!" She crossed her arms over her chest and walked away.

Lee watched her go.

He could feel the sun on the back of his neck. The air held the farmyard scents of scorched grass and sun-warmed dung, and his insides felt empty, hollowed out by an inexplicable sense of aching loss.

He didn't see Kerri for the whole of the next week. She wouldn't answer her phone or reply to his texts. When she finally came to find him, he was surprised at how much she'd changed. She'd chopped her tangled locks into a Warhol mop, and wore a denim jacket at least three sizes too large. A pair of sunglasses perched on the end of her nose. The small, round lenses shimmered with the iridescent peacock sheen of an oily puddle.

"Where have you been?"

A shrug.

They were standing by the tower, in their usual spot. She pulled a soft pack of cigarettes from the jacket, and tapped one out.

"When did you start smoking?"

She pushed the cigarette between her lips, and pulled out a disposable plastic lighter.

"You don't know everything about me." Her thumb clicked the little wheel and, with her hands almost imperceptibly trembling, she held the flame up to the cigarette's tip.

As she sucked the cigarette into life, Lee watched the smoke curl around her face and hair, grey and blue in the sunlight. He could feel his heart twitching in his chest, panicky with the sense that he was witnessing an act of perverse and irreversible self-mutilation.

Kerri looked over her glasses at him and smiled. Then she offered him the pack.

"Do you want one?" She waggled it, daring him.

Lee shook his head. "No way."

"God," she laughed, "you're so immature."

She leant her denim shoulders against the stone tower, and crossed her legs at the ankle.

Lee looked down at his clothes. He wore a red superhero t-shirt and a pair of knee-length cargo shorts that his mother had bought him. He felt his cheeks flush. Kerri was right; he *was* still a kid. And, at some point over the past week, she'd become something else. She'd gone on without him, leaving him behind. The little girl he'd known had left, displaced by something taller and leaner, with awkward, self-conscious limbs and eyes that glittered with an aggrieved and surly hunger.

He swallowed hard. A pair of bright white butterflies danced between the fallen stones like scraps of windblown paper. A lorry ground its gears on the main road out of town.

"So, what do you want to do?" he asked, struggling to keep his voice level.

Kerri looked at him. Then she pulled out her mobile and started thumbing through her text messages.

"You do what you like. I'm waiting for someone."

"Who?"

She huffed, exasperated by his questions.

"Him."

Lee turned to see Glyn James, Pete Evans and Geraint Hughes climbing over the stile at the village end of the paddock. Like Kerri, the three boys held their cigarettes curled self-consciously in their hands. They spat the smoke from the corners of their mouths like curses.

"Oh shit. What do they want?"

"Glyn probably wants his jacket back."

Lee looked at her with wide eyes.

"You nicked it?"

Kerri laughed. "No, he lent it me. He says he's taking me to the disco at the church hall tonight."

"But, but," Lee waved his arms, lost for words. Glyn James was in the year above them at school. When he wasn't playing football, he was finding new and inventive ways to make their lives a misery. "He's a *dick*."

Kerri's eyes narrowed into slits. "You said that about his cousin. Maybe you'd like to see him dead, too?"

"I never said that."

"You didn't have to."

Lee felt his eyes prickle. "Why are you being like this?"

With a shrug of her shoulders, Kerri pushed herself away from the castle wall.

"Like what?"

"I don't know." He waved a hand. "Different."

"You wouldn't understand; you're too immature." Angrily, she tugged at her cuffs. Then she turned to face the approaching boys. "All right, Glyn? What's happening?"

Glyn took a last drag on his cigarette, and then flicked the butt into the weeds. He spoke around a mouthful of smoke.

"You coming up the hill?"

Kerri swallowed. "Yeah."

"Good." He turned to Lee, and his lip curled. "Hey, *pidyn*," he growled, "keep away from her, yeah?"

Kerri tugged his sleeve. "Ah, leave him alone, Glyn, he's not so bad."

Glyn shook her off. "I don't like him. He's always hanging around." He held his fist in the younger boy's face. "Go on, fuck off. We're going up the hill, see. And we don't want you following us." A finger jab to the chest. "Got that?"

Lee knew enough local slang to know that 'going up the hill' meant they were heading for the old quarry. It was the place the older kids went to snog and fumble. Porn mags, old syringes and used condoms carpeted the floor of the rusty corrugated iron shed at the far end, in the shadow of the rock face.

He stuck out his chin.

"I can go where I want."

For a moment, the older boy looked surprised by his defiance. Then he shoved him hard against the tower's stones, and slapped him across the face.

Lee's glasses fell to the floor.

Glyn drew his fist back, ready to throw a punch, but Kerri caught his wrist. She pulled him away.

"Come on, you said you'd leave him alone if I did what you wanted."

Glyn shook her off. He ran a hand across his hair and looked her up and down. Then he smirked.

"All right, then."

Lee knelt to retrieve his specs.

As he cleaned them on his t-shirt and slid them back onto his nose, Kerri led Glyn across the field to the lane. The other two boys slouched along behind, grinning at each other around their cigarettes. Occasionally, one or the other would turn and flip Lee an obscene gesture.

Miserably, he watched them go. His fists were knotted at his sides. His throat felt tight and his eyes were burning. His face stung where he'd been hit. Mercifully, he managed to wait until they were out of the paddock before he started to cry.

He didn't want to follow them. He knew no good could come of it, yet he couldn't help himself. Tears rolling down his cheeks and fogging his glasses, he stumbled forward on traitorous feet, unwilling and yet somehow compelled. With each step, he winced, cringing inside at the prospect of the hurt to come; but still he trudged onward, inexorably drawn to the lip of the quarry by a slow gravitational inevitability.

Instead of following the lane, and risking a beating at the hands of Pete and Geraint, he took the steep, rocky path that followed one of the streams up onto the hills, and looped around to the top of the quarry.

The quarry itself was a deep bowl-shaped depression scooped from the hill's flank. Its sides were steep slopes of scree tangled with brambles, brown, tinder-dry bracken, and yellow-flowering gorse.

When he reached the edge, he dropped to his stomach and wriggled forward. From up here, he could see everything, from the old black gates with their desultory curls of barbed wire to the rust-red roof of the corrugated iron shed. Bees droned back and forth on incomprehensible errands. An old, burned-out car lay swamped in a patch of nettles, the glass long-gone from its windows, fading layers of graffiti carved into its paintwork and sprayed across its roof and bonnet. It all lay spread before him, pinned and sweltering beneath the weight of the hot, still air.

Kerri stood by the door of the shack. She'd taken off the borrowed jacket, and it lay draped over a rock. Her sunglasses were still in place, and she had a cigarette dangling from her teeth.

Glyn stood in the doorway. His two lieutenants, having been dismissed by their leader, were in the process of sauntering back down the lane in search of fresh mischief. As Lee watched, Glyn circled Kerri's waist with his slab-like hands and bent to plant his lips against her throat.

Lee felt that kiss like a rail spike to his chest. His eyes filled with tears, and he dropped his forehead onto his arms.

He'd thought they were friends and comrades. How could she have gone over to the enemy and so thoroughly betrayed him?

He lay there for a while, immobilised by his dejection. He couldn't watch, but neither could he bring himself to leave.

Down in the valley, the village huddled around its ruined castle. He thought of running for help, but whom in that ill-disposed encampment would he ask? He had no other friends. His parents were both at their respective jobs, and Kerri's father was at work in his fields on the opposite side of the valley. If he tried to reach any of them, whatever was going to happen in the quarry would be long over by the time they could get here. There was, he realised for the first time in his life, nobody who could help him. Never had he felt so completely and wretchedly alone.

Without wanting to, he looked back down into the quarry. Glyn had his right hand on Kerri's t-shirt, cupping her left breast. His other hand held her upper arm. He whispered something in her ear, and then stepped back, pulling her into the shadowy interior of the corrugated iron hut.

No!

Tears ran down Lee's face. He clenched his fists and drummed his feet against the grass. He took his glasses off and rubbed his eyes with his knuckles.

How could this be happening?

He rolled onto his back and looked up at the blue vault of the sky. The air seemed to shimmer with the heat. Flies and other insects buzzed back and forth.

Unbidden, his mind filled with obscene imaginings, and he held his fists to his head and moaned. He felt hot and sick and sweaty, and his guts seemed to be squirming around with a life of their own. He knew with a clear and anguished certainty that, after this afternoon, nothing would ever be quite the same. A threshold had been irrevocably breached and there would be, and could never be, any turning back.

Lee heard laughter coming from inside the hut. Urgent whispers. The unzipping of clothes. Without knowing quite how or why, he found himself standing at the top of the steep scree slope with a rock in his hand.

"Stop it!"

His hand whipped around, sending the rock arcing down into the quarry. With appalled fascination, he watched it fall towards the hut's iron roof.

Clang!

The sounds stopped. Lee swallowed but stood his ground. Red-faced, Glyn came running out into the light. He had his shirt off and his jeans were hanging open. He held them up with one hand while using the other to shade his eyes.

"You!" He shook his fist at Lee. "You little bastard. Just you wait 'till I get up there."

"Leave her alone!"

"Or what?" The older boy zipped and buckled his jeans. "What are you going to do, throw stones?"

Behind him, Kerri appeared in the doorway. Her sunglasses were missing. She held her blouse closed. Her skin looked cold and white in the sunlight.

Glyn turned to her.

"Get back in there."

"You leave him alone."

She tried to push past, but he blocked her way.

"Go on, get back inside."

Glyn was a good head taller than her. He reached big hands for her shoulders but, with a laugh, Kerri skipped back through the doorway.

"Go home, Lee," she called. "I'm all right. Everything's fine."

Lee felt himself flush with heat. He could hear the laughter in her voice. His palms prickled. Without thinking, he scooped up another, bigger rock, and threw it with all his strength.

As soon as it left his fingers, he saw its trajectory, inevitable and unstoppable. It was a black asteroid tumbling through empty space, moving with infinite slowness. Lee felt his blood pulse in his ears once.

Twice.

Three times.

Intent on following Kerri, Glyn, perhaps warned by some tingling instinct, glanced up.

The rock caught him across the bridge of the nose. The thump of the impact seemed to echo off the hills. The force of it snapped his head back on his neck. For a long, sickening moment, he remained standing, face raised to the sky, mouth open. Then he fell to his knees, and then onto his front. His jaw hit the dirt floor with a crack and his head lolled over to the side. His legs shook once, and were still.

Kerri came up the slope. She was fastening her jeans and zipping her jacket. Straightening her spiky hair.

She put her hands on either side of Lee's face, and her eyes burrowed into his. First one, then the other, as if somewhere in the black mirrors of his pupils she might find an answer that made sense of what had just happened. Her fingertips were like talons against his scalp. Then, with a cry of exasperation, she let go and flopped down beside him. He watched her light a cigarette.

"Nobody ever finds out about this," she said, speaking around the smoke. Her hands were shaking so hard she could hardly hold her lighter. "Do you understand? You can't tell anybody."

Lee wasn't really listening. He couldn't even feel the sun on his skin. In his head, he was standing on the battlements of the old ruined tower while the world fell apart beneath him. He felt like a husk, as if his insides had been scraped and hollowed by a flint axe, and his skin wrapped and sewn around the resulting void.

Everything was wrong.

He had become one of the barbarians.

~

I'm not sure this story qualifies as science fiction, but it was written using all the tools of the genre – applying a genre sensibility to life in the Welsh Marches rather than on the surface of an alien planet. It's not a happy story, but I tried to make it truthful. I wanted to give it the heft of a real memory. Like the narrator, I grew up in a small village, and I wanted to fill the story with all the painful awkwardness of adolescent love; with days spent playing over the fields, far from adult supervision; with the smells of hot earth and sun-baked cowpats, and the far-off bumbling drone of a tractor.

Sunsets and Hamburgers

1.

My first thought is that I don't remember dying. They tell me nobody does. It's like trying to catch the exact moment you fall asleep; when you wake, it's gone. You may remember feeling tired, you may even remember starting to fall asleep; you just don't remember the transition, the actual moment when you passed from one state to the other.

And then they resurrect you.

One minute you're nowhere, nothing. The next you wake up coughing and thrashing in a tank of blue gel.

2.

My stomach's full of gas and my bowels full of water. My brain feels like melted polystyrene. Every thought hurts and every breath is an effort.

The robot doctors try to reassure me. Everything's going to be okay, they say.

And then, just when I'm beginning to wonder if the worst is over, they take me out and show me the sky.

What's left of it.

3.

The doctors tell me that I've been dead for billions of years. They give me pamphlets to read, films to watch.

Billions of years!

I'm struggling to imagine it. Every time I get close, I get breathless and my hands start to shake.

4.

I have a few confused memories: faces, names of places, that sort of thing. I have an image of a sash window on a grey and rainy autumn afternoon, and bass-heavy ska playing somewhere off down the dull street. And after that, there's nothing. I fall to my knees and begin to weep.

The doctors comfort me. They're pleased with my progress.

5.

There's something dreadfully wrong with the sky. They try to explain it but I have trouble understanding.

When I was alive, I worked for a financial software company. I worked in their marketing department, writing letters and making calls. In my spare time, I liked sunsets and hamburgers, movies and bottled beer.

It's something to do with black holes, they say, pointing at the blank sky.

Like everyone else, I skimmed through A Brief History of Time once or twice, but I've got to admit I'm struggling with this one.

6.

Today, the robot doctors introduce me to Marla. She has feathers in her hair, and her clothes are made of vinyl.

They show us to our new home. It's small but comfortable; reassuring, in a simple, everyday kind of way. There's a kettle and a toaster, a stereo and a CD collection. There's even a TV.

'You can stay here as long as you need to,' they say.

The porch looks out over a sandy beach. Wild palms sway in the offshore breeze.

7.

We've been here a couple of weeks now. The pamphlets are starting to make sense.

The sky's dark because the galaxies have flown too far apart and the stars have exhausted themselves. In order to survive, the remaining people huddle close to the embers of the left-over black holes.

8.

We're sitting on the porch watching breakers crash and slither. It's late in the evening and there's music drifting out from the kitchen.

Marla's upset.

The doctors have given us a new pamphlet.

Throughout history, it says, love has served a serious evolutionary purpose. It compels us to look after those around us, and to allow them to look after us. This is the root of community, and the groups that survived and prospered were those with the most love.

It goes on to explain how they matched our personalities, made sure our genetic traits complemented each other. Apparently Marla and I are over ninety-eight per cent compatible.

And they want us to have kids.

9.

When I was a student, I used to like to spend the afternoon in a city centre bar reading the newspaper, doing the crossword and watching the world go by. It was like meditation, the mind roaming free: the rattle of coins in the fruit machine, the hum of the pumps and refrigerators, the low murmurs of the bar staff.

And when I finally left the bar, just around the time most people were finishing work for the day, I'd stumble out with my senses heightened. Suddenly, everything seemed significant; I'd want to write poetry or paint something, just to capture this perfect feeling. But I never could. My efforts never stood up to the critical light of the following day.

Sometimes now at night, when I wake up beside Marla, I have a similar feeling; everything feels sharp and unreal and meaningful, as if I'm waking up in a movie and everything's somehow symbolic.

If I keep my eyes shut it passes, after a while.

10.

Babies cry out in the night. We nudge each other awake. There's a noise outside. Marla sees to the children while I go out to investigate.

Those damn trilobites have been going through the bins again. They skitter around the beach in the dark, some of them as big as my foot.

Overhead, there's a fine selection of moons.

11.

We've been here for a year now. Every morning there's a cardboard box of food waiting for us on the kitchen counter. Some days it's mostly fruit, other days it's fresh bread and cold meat. Today, it's a jar of instant coffee and a pack of Silk Cut.

When I unscrew the lid on the jar and tear the cellophane from the pack, the sticky familiar smells hit me like an adrenalin rush.

The coffee smells like heaven. Before I've time to think, I've made myself a steaming cup. And damn, it does taste good. It's like visiting a town where you used to live, or finding a fiver in the pocket of a pair of jeans you haven't worn for a while. The cup feels natural in my hand, comforting.

I drink about a quarter of it before I have a strange feeling in my stomach.

I leave the cigarettes where they are, but I can feel them watching me.

12.

Every now and then I have a doubt, like a shadow moving in the corner of my eye.

Have we been seduced by the sand and palms into believing we're living a perfect life, here on the beach, with the kids?

They're growing up strong and clever. They have their mother's looks and their father's restlessness.

But I can't help feeling that we were pushed into having them, that we were selected to breed the same way you'd select a couple of pedigree cats.

Is that why they brought us back? To have kids?

Has something so catastrophic happened to humanity that it needs to resurrect untainted individuals from the past to repopulate the Earth? Are our descendants all shooting blanks?

13.

One day it hits me.

When they brought us back, they must've made alterations to our minds. I don't know how or why, but I think they tailored us as they resurrected us.

I look at Marla and know the urge I have to make babies with her is stronger than anything I felt in my former life. Back then, I used to panic if you put me in the same room as a baby. Now, I can't seem to get enough of them.

How can I talk about any of this with Marla? She's already three months gone with our fifth.

'You'll stop loving me if I get any fatter,' she says.

14.

The doctors have disappeared. They don't answer our calls. The hospital is deserted, empty. It's almost as if they've fulfilled their task and taken their leave.

Marla doesn't like it. It gives her the creeps to be suddenly alone.

15.

They left us a final pamphlet, pinned to the door. But it doesn't make for happy reading.

It tells us how vicious wars erupted as the final stars began to gutter. It tells us that huge reserves of life and power were burned as various factions competed for survival. Stealth ships slipped like sharks through the woven fabric of the universe. Titanic energies were squandered in futile attacks.

And now here we are, in our cabin by the sea. A little bubble world, a few miles in diameter. Fragile and lost in the encroaching darkness.

16.

We're close to the end of everything. Beyond our snow shaker bubble of greenery and life, the universe is a sterile wasteland. There may be other survivors in other galaxies, but they're irretrievably lost to us now, pulled away into the expanding darkness so that not even their light can reach us.

Eventually, the black hole that provides the energy for our heat and light will evaporate. We'll have a few years left after that, but they won't be quality time.

We'll go down with the dying universe. We'll see the final wisps of the Milky Way torn asunder; we'll feel the ground begin to rip beneath our feet, feel our bodies begin to break apart.

And what happens after that? On the face of it, time would appear to end.

But I have a hunch, a feeling, that the doctors brought us back to do more than simply witness the death of creation.

If that's all that they wanted us to do, why did they encourage us to have so many kids?

17.

In my former life, I used to read science fiction now and then. One evening, in bed, I try to explain the attraction of it to Marla. Beyond the sand, the sea stirs restlessly.

I want to tell her about the joy of imagining strange new worlds filled with bizarre and dangerous creatures, of watching mighty armadas blow hell out of each other, but she flicks her hair dismissively and I know I'm not getting through.

Through the window, two of the brighter moons linger on the horizon, one gold and the other amber. Their reflections shimmer on the dark water.

I tell her that my grandfather dreamt of going to sea, of finding fortune and glory in mysterious far-off lands. It wasn't my fault that by the time I hit my teens the few remaining earthly frontiers were already full of holiday show camera crews and Australian gap year students. There were no mysterious lands left, save those that lay in the books I read.

"I guess what I'm trying to say is that all my dreams seem to be coming true," I say. I want her to understand that before I came here, the local library was my only frontier.

She looks at me for a long time, and I honestly can't read her expression. Then she turns over and wraps the sheet around her shoulders.

My legs are left sticking out. I get goose bumps.

18.

Marla says I think too much. She thinks I'll poison the kids by telling them that there's no point to their dreams and ambitions, by telling them that the universe is ending.

But deep down, I know there's hope.

19.

I'm sloshing through the surf, wondering why the doctors have gone to so much trouble to replicate coffee, cigarettes, and a tropical paradise, why they resurrected a breeding pair of *Homo sapiens*.

And then the three juggernauts appear in the sky.

They must each be half a light year in length. As we watch over the next few hours, the effect of their mass scrambles the remains of our solar system, but not before their shuttles swoop down and snatch up our little bubble biosphere from the ashes.

20.

It's still half dark when I rise at noon and take my coffee out onto the porch. The kids are playing in the gloomy sand. It feels like the high end of summer and the air's stale and used. A vast vault arches overhead. Lights in its roof look like brightly burning stars. Around us, on the cavern's floor, we can see the glow of other collected bubbles; they shine green and blue in the gloom. I wonder who they contain, and if we can reach them.

21.

This will be my last diary entry.

These giant ships seem to be arks, of a sort. I can't tell you where they're going, or what we're going to do once they get there. I can't even tell you why we're here, alive, at the end of time.

All I can do is repeat the same conclusion that every man or woman has reached since the dawn of time: I don't know why we're here, or how long we've got, but we're here.

And we're going to survive.

~

Gareth L. Powell

This was my first experiment with what Rudy Rucker calls "Transrealism" – taking chunks of autobiography and treating them as science fiction. I was working for a software company at the time, so I tried to imagine what would happen to somebody like me (but not necessarily me) if they found themselves having to deal with such science fictional tropes as genetic engineering, suspended animation, galactic drift, the end of the universe, and the extinction of the human race. I also wanted to talk about what it means to be part of a family, and speculate on the role of love in the evolution and survival of community – which seems a lot to pack into one very short story, but I think it works. Of all the stories I've written, this one remains one of my favourites.

Entropic Angel

For four days it snowed. On the fifth day, the angel came. As light dawned, the Reverend Christina Pike saw it squatting like a gargoyle on the tallest of the village's wind turbines, its shoulders hunched over and its radiant face raised to the sky.

An hour later, that turbine failed. A few minutes later, the one next to it did likewise. Watching through binoculars from the window of the vicarage, she said: "It's an angel all right."

Around her, the hastily-convened members of the village council muttered to one another. They knew what lay in store. They'd seen the lights dim around the Estuary as each of the other towns fell in turn to the depredations of the angelic host. With their own eyes, they'd watched civilisation sputter like a dying candle. They'd spoken to refugees and army deserters and knew things were bad all over, that without power they were doomed to freeze, and that nothing could be done to save them.

Pike lowered her binoculars.

"Maybe I could talk to it?" she suggested, but the council leader, a retired colonel, shook his head.

"Far too dangerous, vicar, I won't hear of it."

And so Pike stayed by the window, watching helplessly as, one by one over the course of the day, all the turbines on the wind farm slowed and screeched to a halt, until by sunset nothing moved and, stripped of their electricity, the houses of the village fell into darkness and silence.

The children cried. The men and women built fires in their hearths and sat around them bemoaning their fate. Some offered prayers to appease the lace-winged angel. Others tried to hide from it. Some even contemplated sacrifice as a means of driving the angel away, but were stymied by their lack of conviction. They had nothing in their village worthy of sacrifice but goats and children, and they weren't strong enough to make offerings of either.

Sitting around the stone hearth in the vicarage behind the church, as the untapped winter wind blew in from the Severn Estuary, the adults argued long into the night; and all the while, silhouetted against the night sky, the angel remained as still and solitary as it had first appeared.

Then, at seven in the morning, as a bone-coloured Moon fell behind the Welsh hills in the west and a new day peered from behind the Mendips in the east, something stirred. By that time, most of the villagers had retired to bed and only a handful, Pike included, still clutched coffee mugs around the embers of their fires. They had heard of other communities blighted by angels. They were tired and desperate. Even so, not all of them heard the throaty roar of the approaching engine at the same time.

It came on like the buzz of a bee, starting as an irritation well below the threshold of conscious register. One moment they weren't aware of it, and the next they were rubbing condensation from their windows, craning their heads, looking inland for the source of the sound.

And there it was!

It came moving through the snowy, hedge-shrouded lanes like an angry ghost – a black and chrome motorbike eating up tarmac that hadn't felt the tread of a pneumatic tyre since the first snows fell.

Some of the villagers bolted their doors. Others took up arms and hunkered down, ready to repel an invasion of marauders. Only the Reverend Pike went out to welcome the newcomer, flanked by three of the village's hardest and most unimaginative residents.

An unarmed and careworn woman in early middle age, Pike stood at the porch door, her palms spread out to either side in a gesture of helplessness and trust. The three toughs took up positions around the graveyard, skulking behind stones, pitchforks and meat cleavers at the ready.

With her breath steaming, Pike watched the bike growl through the half-frozen ford below the village, and followed it as it negotiated the shattered concrete at the lower end of the lane. The rider sat high in the saddle, a tall man and rake thin. In place of a helmet he wore a leather cap with fur lining, and mirrored goggles that gave him the look of an aviator. A crossbow rode with him, strapped to the outside of one of his side panniers.

He prowled up past the shop fronts and market stalls until he reached the gate of the churchyard, at which point he pulled over and killed the bike's engine.

For a long moment, he sat astride the machine, looking up at the dark spires and stilled blades of the wind farm. From the Estuary, the winter morning breeze brought the smell of salt and the half-hearted gurgle of waves pawing lazily at the muddy shore.

Keeping her hands in plain sight, Reverend Pike walked through the slush on the path through the cemetery. The man watched her approach. As she neared, his hand strayed towards the hilt of a knife jammed in his belt. His skin looked smooth beneath the goggles and his lips were red with lipstick. Pike guessed him to be somewhere in his late thirties or early forties.

"I see you have a visitor," he said.

Pike glanced at the occupied tower. The angel still hadn't moved, although she noticed there were now streaks of black, like oil, staining the turbine housing beneath it.

"It arrived yesterday."

The tall man pushed his mirrored goggles up onto the front of his fur cap. His eyes were pinched into slits, as if constantly squinting into the sun.

"Would you like me to kill it for you?"

Pike gave a snort that was half amusement and half derision.

"Kill an angel?"

"That's what I said."

He kicked the bike onto its stand and climbed off, movements slow and stiff. Pike folded her arms and watched as he brushed dust from his worn leather coat. His fingernails were painted the same carmine shade as his lips.

"What's your name, stranger?"

The man put one hand on the small of his back and straightened with obvious effort. "Most people call me Kenya, Reverend. Kenya Vick."

"No one can kill an angel, Mister Vick."

"I can."

He opened the bike's side pannier and pulled out a short black metal tube about a hand's-breadth in diameter, which he clipped to his belt. Then he unstrapped the crossbow.

Pike shook her head. "You can't shoot it." She'd seen people try before, many times. Whatever you threw at an angel passed through it as if passing through smoke. It just made them angry.

"Says who?"

"Says everybody."

Kenya Vick regarded her with an unblinking eye. "Well, I ain't everybody."

He walked a few paces, as if testing the frozen ground. Reverend Pike ran her tongue over her teeth. She was nobody's fool.

"How much?" she said.

Kenya stopped walking. He hefted the crossbow in one hand.

"A smoked goat haunch, four bottles of wine, and a dozen boiled eggs."

Pike blinked.

"We don't have much. That seems expensive to me."

Kenya turned to her. He blew into his hands and rubbed them together. "Do you have children and old people here? It's only October and the temperature's already below freezing. How are you going to keep them warm, with fires and lamps? Wouldn't you rather have radiators and electric light?"

Pike bowed her head, acknowledging his point. She glanced back toward the church, to where a small crowd had joined the three heavies she'd left lurking there, many armed with knives and farm tools.

"I'll relay your terms to the village council," she said. She pointed a stern finger at him. "You stay here."

The council meeting took place in the church. Kenya Vick waited outside, leaning on the dry stone church wall. The local children, wrapped in coats and scarves, eyed him and giggled nervously. Dogs sniffed his Cuban-heeled boots. As the sun thawed the morning, he pulled off his fur cap to reveal shoulder-length dreadlocks, which he tied back with a red scrunchie from his coat pocket.

At length, the church doors opened and the Reverend appeared, blinking against the light.

"It seems you have a deal, Mister Vick. We can't run our refrigerators without electricity, and so when the weather gets warmer we'll lose all the food we've stored for the summer. We'll starve." She glanced back over her shoulder. "But even so, I should warn you that there's a small but vocal minority that considers what you're proposing to be a blasphemy of the highest order."

"You included?"

She folded her hands. "I'd rather not answer that."

"Surely you don't believe they're actually angels, from God?"

Pike turned her head away. When she spoke, it was scarcely more than a tired whisper. "Sometimes I don't know what to believe, Mister Vick."

Kenya snorted.

"They're not angels, Vicar, they're vermin. They're parasites. Somehow they leech the energy from mechanical processes. The wind still blows but the sails don't turn."

Pike held up a hand. "You have your deal. You don't need to convince me."

Kenya pushed himself up off the wall. "These things are sucking us dry. They gum things up. They feed off our energy. When the power stations and wind farms are gone, they'll move onto water wheels and solar panels, then battery-operated torches and clockwork toys."

He held the crossbow down and used a crank to pull back the bowstring.

"And when the machines are gone, what do you think they'll eat then? They'll turn on us," he continued. "Do you know how much energy the human body uses in a day?" He locked the string in place and lifted the weapon, sighting it on the winged figure on top of the mast.

"We have to kill them before they kill us," he said.

Pike had her arms folded.

"That's as maybe, Mister Vick, but do you mind if I ask what makes you think you can kill the creature, given that I've never heard of anyone doing such a thing?"

Kenya reached down to his belt and popped open the tube he'd clipped there. Inside, it bristled with crossbow bolts.

"Look at this," he said. He drew one out and held it up for her. It was black and metallic and as he turned it the morning light made rainbow oil slicks up and down its length.

He pointed at the angel squatting on the now-stained wind turbine cowling.

"It's made from that stuff they extrude," he said. "It's some kind of polymer. You can put it into moulds and bake it."

"And it kills them?"

Kenya slipped the bolt back into its quiver. "It's the only thing that does."

Kenya wanted to wait for noon. He said it was the best time for an attack, as the angel would be at its drowsiest. He spent the time tinkering with his bike and oiling his crossbow. Pike brought him a cup of hot nettle tea.

"I have a couple of questions," she said, "if you'll indulge me?"

"Go ahead."

She unfolded her arms. "Is Kenya your first name or a nickname?"

The thin man blew steam from the mug and squinted at her. "What difference does it make?"

Pike shrugged. "None, I suppose. It's just that as the local vicar, it's my job to know everybody else's business."

Behind her, the villagers milled around in the lane, their boots tramping the snow to dirty slush. Most of their knives were sheathed now. They were curious but wary, afraid they were being conned.

She said, "And if you fail, I'll need to know what to carve on your tombstone."

Kenya pressed his reddened lips into a hard line. For a moment, she thought he wasn't going to answer.

"I went to Africa once," he said, "back before the angels came, when the Internet still worked and planes still flew. I went to get in on all that fake software they had going on back then, figuring I'd make some cash bringing it back home on the sneaker-net." He took a breath. "Instead, I spent six weeks sweating my ass off in a Nairobi jail and came back with a gut parasite that made me shit like a fire hose, pardon my French. I lost half my body weight and I threw up once an hour, every hour for a fucking *month*."

Pike suppressed an unexpected smile. "I see."

"You have any more questions?"

She looked at his lipstick and nail polish, and the scrunchie holding back his locks.

"Maybe later," she said.

When both the hands of the clock tower pointed to twelve, Kenya remounted his bike. To his surprise, Pike climbed on behind him.

"What are you doing?" he asked as she hugged herself to him.

She leaned around. From her cassock she pulled the polished bronze crucifix from the church altar.

"If you're wrong about the angel, you're going to need some spiritual back-up."

Kenya shook his head.

"Stand clear," he said to the villagers blocking the lane. He let the brake off and revved the throttle. The bike leapt forward like an eager horse, slipping and fishtailing on the icy tarmac. With Pike holding on tight, he steered for the concrete farm track leading up the hill to the wind farm on the cliff top.

The sun shone white from a milky sky. The air smelled of the sea. When they reached the wind turbines, he skidded to a halt.

The track ran straight and cold for a mile back down to the village, undulating gently. Goats picked at the frozen grass, tails flicking. The cries of gulls could be heard across the fields, and a far off church spire showed the spot where the next village nestled in a dip overlooking the patchwork, snow-covered Levels.

From up here, he could see Pike's house behind the church. She pointed it out to him. The vicarage was a low red brick affair with black iron window frames and a tiled roof slumping in the middle as if tired. The gravel drive had been worn down to mud in several places. Brown wisps of ivy crawled around the front porch, and the wan light winked off a cluster of old CDs that had been strung up to keep the birds off the flower beds.

Turning the other way, he looked out over the waters of the Severn Estuary. To the north, the broken spans of the twin Severn bridges sagged into the brown water like the spines of gut-shot dinosaurs. To the south, the flour-dusted hills of Devon lay like clouds on the horizon.

"Okay," he said to the vicar, his breath swirling, "get clear and don't interfere."

He watched her walk a hundred yards back down the track, then he gunned the bike, coughing out clouds of exhaust. Six times he pushed the engine as far as it would go, red-lining the rev counter, making as much racket as he could. Then, calmly, he climbed off and left it running. He didn't look back. He walked around behind the base of the turbine's tower and found himself within ten metres of the cliff's edge.

An overgrown coastal path followed the line of the cliff, separated from the drop by a tangled hedge of bramble and thorn.

He knew it would take the angel a while to stir itself, and so he settled down in a crouch, with his back against the warm metal of the tower. He took a quarrel from the quiver on his belt and placed it into the crossbow's groove. The weapon was an antique. He'd taken it from the wall of a stately home in Dorset. It suited his purposes. Guns, tanks and other complex weaponry tended to fail when close to an angel's entropic influence. The old crossbow fared better.

He glanced up but the angel still hadn't moved. With time to kill, he took a compact mirror from the pocket of his leather coat and touched up his lipstick.

An hour later, the angel still hadn't moved. It didn't so much as twitch until two o'clock in the afternoon, when its head slowly turned away from the heavens in order to look down at the ticking-over bike. It stayed that way for a further fifteen minutes and Kenya started to worry that the old machine would run out of fuel before the creature became sufficiently interested.

When fifteen minutes had passed, the angel stretched its wings as if waking from a deep sleep. With aching slowness it raised itself into a standing position and stepped off the turbine's cowling.

It fell like a vulture, circling down in a controlled glide. Still watching, Kenya stepped back, retreating almost as far as the cliff path. His knuckles were white on the crossbow. His pulse fluttered in his chest. There was something awe-inspiring about the creature's grace and power. It came down with the insouciance of a predator, its dark lacy wings like unfurled rags of night-time cloud, and landed on the bike's fuel tank with enough force to flatten the suspension and tip the machine onto its side like a wounded antelope.

Immediately, the headlight dimmed and the engine stuttered and dropped a note. The angel's wings fell over its kill, tips almost touching the grass. Seen from this close, the thing looked less human than you might have thought had you only seen it on top of the mast. What looked like eye sockets at a distance were merely indentations in the smooth, leathery skin; the nose a simple ridge of bone; and the mouth a toothless slit. It had two sinewy arms, and hands sporting six vicious-looking claws.

Moving behind the turbine mast, Kenya double-checked his crossbow. He knew he'd only have time for one shot and he had to make a clean kill. Although angels moved sluggishly when not feeding, like cheetahs they were capable of incredible bursts of speed when angered.

Satisfied that the weapon was ready to fire, he took a deep breath and stepped out into the open – just in time to see the Reverend Pike marching toward the creature brandishing the brass cross from the church altar.

"Our Father," she bellowed, "which art in heaven –"

At the sound of her voice, the nightmarish angel turned in her direction. The slit of a mouth opened and it let forth an angry, mewling screech that stopped the woman in her tracks.

Seizing his opportunity, Kenya ran forward. He got as close as he dared and pulled the trigger. The glistening black bolt flew forth, but at the last instant, the creature raised itself and instead of delivering a killing blow the shaft pierced the angel's thigh. The screech turned to a howl of pain and indignation. The angel staggered and fell from its perch on the bike, landing in a thrashing heap on the snow.

Kenya didn't stop to watch. He knew he'd only wounded the beast, and was already fumbling with the crank that drew back the bowstring.

"Shit. Shit. Shit."

Across the field, Pike stood rooted, watching the angel rise slowly to stand on its good leg, wings flapping to steady its balance. The cross drooped uncertainly in her hands.

"Run!" Kenya yelled. She looked at him but he was too far away to interpret her expression. "Run you idiot!"

Defiantly, she raised the cross and thrust it at the advancing angel.

"Hallowed be thy name," she called, her voice carrying over the sound of the bike's spluttering engine. "Thy kingdom come, thy will be done –"

The beast's outstretched wings towered over her, black and ragged. Kenya bit his lip. What was she playing at? Why wouldn't she run?

He got the string pulled back and locked it into place, ready to fire. As he did so, he realised with horror that Pike was buying him time to reload, putting herself at risk in order to give him a chance to finish the job.

Moving as quickly as he could, he whipped a bolt from his belt and slid it into place.

Too late!

Uncoiling like a spring, the creature took a swipe at Pike. She screamed and tried to dodge but its claws raked the bronze cross with a force that dashed it from her hands and sent her spinning into the grass.

As the angel prepared to pounce on her, Kenya sprinted up behind with his reloaded crossbow at the ready. Alerted by the sound of his boots clumping on the frozen soil, the angel spun to face him – but by then there was less than a metre between it and the weapon. It screamed and lashed out, wings beating the air. Teeth bared, Kenya fired. He saw the quarrel pierce the angel's chest an instant before the dying beast's claws skewered him through the side, sinking into his waist up to the knuckle. He fell to the ground. For an instant, the angel stood over him in triumph. Then the black wings drooped. The creature's knees went out from under it, and it crashed down beside him, twitched twice, and was dead.

"Kenya!"

Pike crawled over to him on her hands and knees in the snow.

"Kenya, are you all right?"

He coughed. He couldn't move. He felt as if he'd been sawn in half.

"I wanted to make sure I hit it," he said. "Stupid. I got too close."

Pike ripped her cassock and wadded it into a pad, which she pressed against his wounds to stop the blood. Her breath clouded in the cold air. She kept saying his name, over and over again.

"Shut up," he said.

At the foot of the hill, a few of the braver villagers were starting to move in her direction, rakes and knives at the ready. They wanted to see the fallen beast. She watched them approach.

After a while she said: "That wasn't one of God's creatures, was it?"

No answer. She looked down.

"Kenya?"

By Christmas Eve, the village had been changed almost beyond recognition. After the midnight service, as the other villagers hurried home wrapped against the cold, Reverend Pike wheeled Kenya to the door of the church and together, they looked out from the porch at the electric lights burning in the windows of all the houses on the lane.

"We fixed the last turbine this afternoon," she said, "while you were having your nap." Between supervising the repair work and organising the church service, she hadn't had much time to speak to him since helping him out of bed earlier that morning.

In his wheelchair, Kenya twisted to look up at her. "Did you get all the black stuff off the cowling?"

"Every bit, just as you said. I scraped most of it off myself."

"Good." He settled back. "Tomorrow I'll show you how to heat it. We should have enough to make another dozen bolts."

Pike gave his shoulder an affectionate pat. She smoothed the blanket covering his useless legs. "You take it easy," she said. "You're not as strong as you think you are."

As the night's first flurries of snow whipped sideways across the graveyard, she straightened up and applied her lipstick. Then she closed and locked the church door and turned up the collar of her new leather coat, ready to take him back to the warmth of the vicarage.

"Do you really think we can do it?" she said to the scrunchie on the back of his head. "Do you really think we can turn this little community into an army?"

Still looking out at the cottages and the lane, he gave a slow, thoughtful nod. "If you can build more crossbows, I can teach you how to shoot them. You've got a fair bit of food stockpiled, and if we can trade enough leather from the other villages hereabouts, we can make body armour."

Pike smiled, gripping the handles at the back of his chair.

"We can, can't we? We can do all that."

"Sure."

She leaned forward to plant a kiss on the top of his dreadlocked head.

"We know how to kill them now, thanks to you, my love. When spring comes and the snows melt, we'll march out to the other villages. We'll spread the word."

The clock in the tower struck one. Gently, Pike pushed Kenya out into the graveyard. Her nails were painted red like his, and she had a brand new crossbow of her own slung on her back. She trod lightly down the path, humming the tune to 'Onward Christian Soldiers', as

Gareth L. Powell

the thickening white flakes fell like static from an unforgiving sky.

~

When I first came up with the idea for this story, I conceived it as a quasi-supernatural spaghetti western set in a near-future Somerset, featuring angels, wind farms, crossbows, and lone transsexual drifters wearing hair scrunchies. I used a fictional village on the banks of the Severn as a setting, because it doesn't hurt to write what you know, and chose a female vicar as heroine because I'd never seen it done before. My own feelings about Christianity are complicated and tend more towards the atheistic end of the spectrum. But for this story, I thought who better to confront a false angel than a woman of God.

Red Lights, and Rain

It's raining in Amsterdam. Paige stands in the oak-panelled front bar of a small corner pub. She has wet hair because she walked here from her hotel. Now she's standing by the open door, holding half a litre of Amstel, watching the rain stipple the surface of the canal across the street. For the fourth time in five minutes, she takes out her mobile and checks the screen for messages. From across the room, the barman looks at her. He has dark skin and gold dreads. Seeing the phone in her hand again, he smiles, obviously convinced she's waiting for a date.

Outside, damp tourists pass in the rain, looking for the Anne Frank house; open-topped pleasure boats seek shelter beneath humped-back bridges; and bare-headed boys cut past on scooters, cigarettes flaring, girlfriends clinging side-saddle to the parcel shelves, tyres going *bop-bop-bop* on the wet cobble stones. Paige sucks the froth from her beer. On the other side of the canal, a church bell clangs nine o'clock. As it happens, she *is* waiting for a man, but this won't be any sort of date, and she'll be lucky if she survives to see the sun come up tomorrow morning. She pockets the mobile, changes the beer glass from one hand to the other, and slips her fingers into the pocket of her coat, allowing them to brush the cold metal butt of the pistol. It's a lightweight coil gun: a magnetic projectile accelerator, fifty years more advanced than anything else in this time zone, and capable of punching a titanium slug through a concrete wall. With luck, it will be enough.

She watches the barman lay out new beer mats on the zinc counter. He's just a boy, really. Paige should probably warn him to leave, but she doesn't want to attract too much attention, not just yet. She doesn't want the police to blunder in and complicate matters.

For a moment, her eyes are off the door, and that's when Josef arrives, heralded by the swish of his coat, the clack of his boots as they hit the step. She sees the barman's gaze flick past her shoulder, his eyes widen, and she turns to find Josef standing on the threshold, close enough to kiss.

"Hello, Paige." He's at least five inches taller than her; rake thin with pale lips and rain-slicked hair.

"Josef." She slides her right hand into her coat, sees him notice the movement.

"Are you here to kill me, Paige?"

"Yes."

"It's not going to be easy."

"I know."

He flicks his eyes in the direction of the bar, licks his bottom lip. "What about him?"

Paige takes a step back, placing herself between the "vampire" and the boy with the golden dreadlocks. She curls the index finger of the hand still in her pocket around the trigger of the coil gun.

"Not tonight, Josef."

Josef shrugs and folds his arms, shifts his weight petulantly from one foot to the other.

"So, what?" he says. "You want to go at it right now, in here?"

Paige shakes her head. She's trying not to show emotion, but her heart's hammering and she's sure he can hear it.

"Outside," she says. Josef narrows his eyes. He looks her up and down, assessing her as an opponent. Despite his attenuated frame, she knows he can strike like whip when he wants to. She tenses, ready for his attack and, for a moment, they're frozen like that: eyes locked, waiting for the other to make the first move. Then Josef laughs. He turns on his heel, flicks up the collar of his coat, and steps out into the rain.

Paige lets out a long breath. Her stomach's churning. She pulls the coil gun from her pocket and looks over at the barman.

"Stay here," she says.

She follows Josef into a small concrete yard at the rear of the pub, surrounded by walls on all sides, and lit from above by the orange reflection of city lights on low cloud. Rusty dumpsters stand against one wall; a fire escape ladder hangs from the back of the pub; and metal trapdoors cover the cellar. Two storeys above, the gutters leak, spattering the concrete.

Josef says, "So, how do you want to do this?"

Paige lets the peeling wooden door to the street bang shut behind her, hiding them from passers-by. The coil gun feels heavy in her hand.

"Get over by the wall," she says.

Josef shakes his head.

She opens her mouth to insist but, before she can speak or raise the gun, he's closed the distance between them, his weight slamming her back against the wooden door. She feels his breath on her cheek, his hand clasping her throat. She tries to bring the gun to bear but he chops it away, sending the weapon clattering across the wet floor.

"You're pathetic," he growls, and lifts her by the throat. Her feet paw at empty air. She tries to prise his hand loose, but his fingers are like talons, and she can't breathe; she's choking. In desperation, she kicks his kneecap, making him stagger. With a snarl, he tosses her against one of the large wheeled dumpsters. She hits it with an echoing crash, and ends up on her hands and knees, coughing, struggling for air. Josef's boot catches her in the ribs, and rolls her onto her side. He stamps down once, twice, and something snaps in her left forearm. The pain fills her. She yelps, and curls herself around it. The coil gun rests on the concrete three or four metres away on the other side of the yard, and there's no way he'll let her reach it. He kicks her twice more, then leans down with his mouth open, letting her see his glistening ceramic incisors. They're fully extended now, locked in attack position, and ready to tear out her windpipe.

"Ha' enough?" he says, the fangs distorting his speech.

Paige coughs again. She's cradling her broken arm, and she still can't breathe properly. She's about to tell him to go to hell, when the back door of the pub swings open, and out steps the boy with the golden dreads, a sawn-off antique shotgun held at his hip.

"That's enough," the boy says. His eyes are wide and scared.

Josef looks up with a hiss, teeth bared. Startled, the barman pulls the trigger. The flash and bang fill the yard. Josef takes both barrels in the chest. It snatches him away like laundry in the wind, and he lands by the door to the street, flapping and yelling, drumming his boot heels on the concrete.

"Shoot him again," Paige gasps, but the young man stands frozen in place, transfixed by the thrashing vampire. He hasn't even reloaded. Paige uses her good arm to claw her way into a sitting position. The rain's soaked through her clothes.

"Shoot him!"

But it's too late. Still hollering, Josef claws his way through the wooden door, out onto the street. Paige pulls herself up and makes it to the pavement just in time to see him slip over the edge of the bank, into the canal, dropping noiselessly into the water between two tethered barges. She turns back to find the boy with the shotgun looking at her.

"Is he dead?"

She shakes her head. The air's tangy with gun smoke. "No, he'll be back." She scoops up her fallen coil gun and slides it back into her coat pocket. Her left arm's clutched against her chest. Every time she moves, she has to bite her lip against the pain.

The boy takes her by the shoulder, and she can feel his hands shake as he guides her into the pub kitchen, where she leans against the wall as he locks and bolts the back door.

When she asks, the boy tells her his name is Federico. He settles her on a bar stool, plonks a shot glass and a half-empty bottle of cognac on the counter, then goes to close the front door.

"I'm going to call the police," he says.

As he brushes past her, Paige catches his arm. "There's no time, we have to leave."

He looks down at her hand.

"I don't *have* to do anything," he says. "Not until you explain what the hell just happened."

She releases him. He's frightened, but the fear's manifesting as anger, and she's going to have to do something drastic to convince him.

"Okay." She puts her left arm on the bar, and rolls up the sleeve, letting him see the bloody contusions from Josef's boot, and the splinter of bone, like a shard of broken china, sticking up through the skin.

"What are you doing?"

"Shush." She takes hold of her wrist, forces the arm flat against the zinc counter, and twists. There's an audible click, and the two halves of broken bone snap back into place. When her eyes have stopped watering, she plucks out the loose shard and drops it with a clink into the ash tray. With it out of the way, the skin around the tear starts to heal. In less than a minute, only a red mark remains.

Federico takes a step back, eyes wide, hand pointing.

"That's not natural."

Paige lifts the half-empty bottle of cognac with her right hand, pulls the plastic-coated cork with her teeth, and spits it across the bar.

"Josef heals even faster than I do," she says. "You blew a hole in his chest, but he'll be as good as new in an hour, maybe less."

"W-what are you?"

Paige takes a solid nip of the brandy.

"I'm as human as you are," she says, and gets to her feet. The stiffness is fading from her limbs, the hurt evaporating from her ribs and arm. "But Josef's something quite different. And trust me, you *really* don't want to be here when he comes back."

"But the police –"

"Forget the police. You shot him, that makes it personal."

Federico puts his fists on his hips.

"I don't believe you."

Paige jerks a thumb at the back door. "Then believe what you saw out there." She stands and pats down her coat, making sure she still has everything she needs. Federico looks from her to the door, and then back again.

"Is he really that dangerous?"

"Oh yes."

"Then, what do you suggest?"

Paige rubs her face. She doesn't want to be saddled with a civilian, doesn't want to be responsible for anybody else's well being; but this young man saved her life, and she owes him for that.

She sighs. "Your best bet's to come with me, right now. I'm the only one who knows what we're up against, the only one with even half a chance of being able to protect you."

"How do I know I can trust you?"

She looks him square in the eye.

"Because I'm not the one who's going to come back here and rip your throat out."

Paige lets Federico pull on a battered leather biker jacket two sizes too large, and they leave the pub and splash their way down the cobbled streets in the direction of the Red Light District, and her hotel. As they walk, she keeps her eye on the canal.

Federico says, "Is he really a, you know?"

"A vampire?" Paige shakes her head. "No. At least, not in the sense you're thinking. There's nothing supernatural or romantic about him. He's not afraid of crosses or garlic, or any of that bullshit."

"But I saw his teeth."

"Ceramic implants."

They cut across a square in the shadow of a medieval church. Federico has the shotgun under his jacket, and it makes him walk stiffly. The rain's still falling, and there's music from the bars and coffeehouses; but few people are out on the street.

"Then what is he? Some sort of psycho?"

Paige slows for a second, and turns to him. "She's a guerrilla."

"I don't understand."

She starts walking again. "I don't expect you to." Her right hand's in her coat pocket, gripping the coil gun. She leads him out of the square, across a footbridge, and then they're into the Red Light District, with its pink neon shop fronts and narrow alleys. Her hotel's close to Centraal Station. By the time they get there, they're both soaked and stand dripping together in the elevator that takes them up to her floor.

"In a thousand years' time, there's going to be a war," she says, watching the floor numbers count off. "And it's going to be a particularly nasty one, with atrocities on all sides."

The lift doors open and she leads him along the carpeted corridor to her room. Inside, the air smells stale. This has been her base of operations for nearly a month, and she hasn't let the cleaner touch it in all that time. She hasn't even opened the curtains.

"The vampires were bred to fight in the war," she says. "They were designed to operate behind enemy lines, terrorising civilians, sowing fear and confusion." She shrugs off her coat and drops it over the back of a chair. "They're trained to go to ground, blend in as best they can, then start killing people. They're strong and fast, and optimised for night combat."

Federico's standing in the doorway, shivering. She ushers him in and sits him on the bed. Gingerly, she takes the shotgun from his hands, and places it on the sheet beside him; she then drapes a blanket around his shoulders.

"After the war, some of them escaped, and they've been spreading backwards through time ever since." She crosses to the wardrobe, and pulls out a bottle. It's a litre of vodka. She takes two teacups off the side and pours a large measure for him, a smaller one for herself.

"They're designed to survive for long durations without support. They can eat just about anything organic, and they're hard to kill. You can hurt them, but as long as their hearts are beating and their brains are intact, there's a chance they'll be able to repair themselves, given enough time."

She puts the bottle aside and flexes the fingers of her left hand – there's still an ache, deep in the bone.

"That's important," she says. She kneels down in front of Federico, and takes his hands in hers. "The next time we see Josef, we've got to kill him before he kills us. And the only way to do that is to do as much damage as possible. Stop his heart, destroy his brain, and he's dead."

She takes one of the teacups and presses it into Federico's hands.

"Sorry," He says, accepting the drink, "did you say that this war is *going* to take place?"

"A thousand years downstream, yes."

"So it hasn't happened yet?"

"No."

He frowns.

"Who are you?"

Paige reaches for her coat, and pulls out the coil gun. "I'm a fangbanger, a vampire killer."

"And you're from the future too?"

Paige stands.

"Look," she says. "All you need to know tonight is this: When you see Josef, shoot out his legs. That'll immobilise him, and give us time to kill him." She stops talking then. Federico's clearly had enough for one night. She slips a pill into his next drink and, within minutes, he's asleep, wrapped in the blanket, with the shotgun clasped protectively across his chest.

Alone with her thoughts, Paige moves quietly. She turns out the bedside light and crosses to the window, pulling aside the heavy curtain. It's after twelve now, and the trams have stopped for the night. The streets are quiet. She feels she should congratulate Josef on his choice of hiding place. Amsterdam is an easy city in which to be a stranger; there are so many tourists, so many distractions, that it's a simple matter to lose yourself in the crowd. If she hadn't known what to look for she might never have found him. But then, she's been a fangbanger for a long time, and she's learned to piece together seemingly unrelated deaths and unexplained crimes; to filter out the background noise of modern urban life in order to reveal the unmistakable M.O. of an active vampire. She leans her forehead against the window glass; heart pumping in her chest, knowing it won't take Josef long to track her down. She's been doing this job for enough years, waded through enough shit, to know how dangerous a wounded vampire can be.

At 4 am, the sky starts to grey in the east. Federico's still asleep, and Paige gives up her vigil. She tucks the coil gun into the back of her belt, pulls on a sweater to cover it, and wanders down to the hotel restaurant. She finds the place empty, although cooking sounds reach her from the kitchen as the staff gear up for the breakfast rush. She helps herself to a cup of coffee from the pot, and a large handful of sugar sachets, and takes it all over to a table by the window, where she stirs the contents of the little packets into her coffee. There are sixteen altogether, and she uses them all. Then, leaving the sticky mess to cool, she rests her left arm on the table and clenches and unclenches her fist. Everything seems in order. The tendons move as they should, and there's no trace of the break. It doesn't even ache now. Satisfied, she takes a sip of the lip-curlingly sweet coffee. It tastes disgusting, but she needs the sugar to refuel the tweaked macrophages and artificial fibroblasts that have enabled her to heal so quickly.

Outside the window, it's still raining. She watches the drops slither on the glass. It makes her think of Josef in better times, before he had his fangs implanted. She remembers him as bright and swift and clever; a sociopath, yes, but still her best student. And there it is, her dirty little secret, the inconvenient truth she's been hiding from Federico: the reason she makes such a good vampire hunter is that during the war, before the vampires were deployed against the enemy, it was she who trained them. She was a military psychologist at the time, an expert in guerrilla warfare. While combat instructors taught the vampires how to kill, she showed them a range of nasty tricks culled from a thousand hard-fought insurgencies; from the Scythians of Central Asia to the soldiers of the Viet Kong, and beyond.

She remembers her penultimate briefing in particular.

"The vampire's a powerful archetype," she said to the cadets. "It's an expression of our darker side, playing to our most primal anxieties, from the threat of rape to the fear of being eaten." It was a hot day, and the sun had blazed through the classroom windows. She walked up and down in front of her students, hands clasped behind her back. At the rear of the room, the surgeons waited with their trolleys, ready to wheel the young men and women down to the operating theatre, one-by-one, in order to implant their fangs and night-adapted eyes. "To complete your mission, you must be prepared to kill. You must become assassins – anonymous killers in the night, spreading panic and mistrust." She stopped pacing and turned to Josef. He sat in the front row of the classroom, chin on fist, eyes blazing, and she knew it would be the last time she'd see him before his transformation. "If you do your jobs correctly," she said, "each of you will be worth a hundred troops. You'll demoralise the enemy, eat out his fighting spirit from the inside. You'll have the soldiers worried about their families, the families suspicious of their neighbours. But in order to achieve this, you'll have to move like shadows, and show no mercy. Do anything that needs to be done, be ruthless, and be prepared to strike anywhere, at any time."

She had taught them every psychological trick she knew, and shown them how to exploit the power of myth, how to generate fear and horror from darkness and blood. From their test scores, she'd known they were intelligent. In fact, she'd personally overseen the original selection process, picking only those recruits with the right balance of brains and insanity – those clever enough to survive the mission, but also psychotic enough to become the monsters they'd need to be in order to succeed.

And then later, when the war went temporal, spilling into the surrounding decades, they came back and she briefed them again, only this time on the peculiarities of each of the time zones in which they were to operate, giving them the background they'd need in order to blend into each zone's civilian population.

Sometimes, she wonders if her history lessons inspired their eventual escape into this dim and distant past, far from even the outermost fringes of the conflict. One thing's for certain: since they mutinied and fled to these primitive times, she's had to travel all over the place to hunt them down. She's tracked individual vampires across half a dozen decades, in Los Angeles, Cairo, Warsaw, and London.

Now she's here, in Amsterdam.

And suddenly, there's Josef.

He's standing in the shadow of a doorway on the other side of the street, watching her through the glass. He has his hands in the pockets of his black raincoat. Their eyes meet for a second and Paige can't breathe. Then he's gone, moving fast. Between parked cars, she catches a glimpse of him crossing the street, heading for the back of the hotel. With a curse, she pushes herself to her feet. Josef will know which room she's staying in – a simple phone call will have furnished him with that information – and now he's after Federico, hoping to kill the boy before tackling her.

Paige bursts out into the foyer. Her room's on the fourth floor, so there's no time to take the stairs. However, luck's on her side; this early in the morning the elevators all stand ready, their doors open. She slams into the nearest and slaps the button for the fourth floor. Then, even as the doors are closing, she's pulling the coil gun from her belt and checking its magazine.

Paige kicks her shoes off in the elevator and pads along the corridor in her socks. As she nears her room, she hears the door splinter: Josef's kicked his way in.

"Damn."

She lifts the coil gun to her shoulder and risks a peek around the frame. The room's dark. She can see a faint glow from the curtains. There are shadows all over the place: chairs, desks, and suitcases. Any one of them could be a crouched vampire.

"Fuck."

She ducks back into the corridor and takes a few quick breaths. If Josef's still in there, he'll have heard her already – and there's a good possibility Federico's already dead. She flicks off the coil gun's safety catch. There's nothing beyond this room but window; the chances of civilian casualties are slight. Stepping back, she gives the trigger a squeeze. The gun whines. Holes appear in the door. Splinters flick out. The TV sparks. A chair blows apart.

And there, in the maelstrom: a shadow moves.

She tries to hose him down but he's moving too fast. He hits the wall and pushes off; hits the floor and rolls; and then he's running on all fours, leaping at her throat before she can draw a bead.

Paige rolls with the impact, still pressing the trigger. Scraps of material fly from Josef's overcoat. An overhead light explodes. Blood sprays. His ceramic teeth scrape her neck, grazing the skin. Then his momentum carries him over her head, and she uses a Judo throw to heave him into the corridor wall. He hits like an upside down starfish, arms and legs splayed, and then falls to the floor.

They both lie panting.

The carpet's soft. She rolls onto her side. Josef's lying on his front, looking sideways at her. His eyes are as blue as a gas flame. This is the first good look she's had at him since he left her class, and he looks older and harder than she remembers. His fangs are white and clean. Blood soaks into the carpet from a hole in his side.

He doesn't move as she elbows herself up into a sitting position; but, as soon as she lifts the coil gun, he twists. His wrist flicks out, and a pair of shiny throwing stars bite Paige's arm. She cries out and the gun drops from her fingers. Instinctively, she reaches for it with her left hand, but Josef's anticipated the move. He pushes himself towards her, delivering a kick to her cheek that shatters the bone.

Paige falls into the open doorway of her room. Black spots dapple her vision. She feels Josef grip her leg. His hands work their way up. He's climbing her, using his weight to keep her pinned down. She tries to fight back, but she's still dazed. He swats her hands away from his face.

Then he's on her, his thighs clamped across her hips, his knees pinning her arms. He wraps his fingers in her hair, and yanks her head back, exposing her throat. His fangs are fully deployed. She sees them through the hair hanging down over his face, and cringes, expecting him to lunge for her artery.

Instead, Josef clears his throat

"I don't want to kill you," he says around his teeth. He pulls away, and his incisors slip back into their sheaths. He lets go of her hair and sits up, straddling her. Paige blinks up at him as he smooths back his wet hair. "I just want to talk."

They end up slumped against opposite walls of the corridor. Josef's bleeding onto the carpet; Paige feels as if she's been hit by a fire truck. One side of her face throbs with pain, and the eye above her broken cheekbone won't focus properly.

"You've got me all wrong," Josef says.

She gives him a look.

"You're a killer."

"Not anymore." He lets his shoulders relax, but keeps one hand pressed to the bullet hole in his side.

"But Federico —"

"I haven't touched him."

"He's still alive?"

Josef shrugs. "I can't say for sure. You sprayed a lot of bullets in there."

And suddenly, they're falling back into their old pattern: teacher and student – and she *knows* there's something he's not telling her.

"What's going on, Josef? Why am I still alive?"

He tips his head back, resting it against the wall.

"Because things are different now. *I'm* different." He reaches into his coat and pulls out a photograph, which he Frisbees across to her.

"I wasn't trying to hurt you, you know? Not here, and not at the pub." He dips his chin and looks at her. "Just acting in self-defence, trying to stop you from killing me."

The picture shows Josef holding a child, maybe four or five years old.

"What's this?"

"It's my daughter."

The girl has Josef's blue eyes and blonde hair. She's wearing a red dress.

"Your daughter?"

Josef closes his eyes.

"Yes."

Paige glances at the coil gun, lying on the carpet between them. She wonders if she can reach it before he can reach her.

Josef says, "I don't want any more trouble."

Paige lifts a hand to her ruined cheek, and her lip curls.

"So what? You think it *matters* what you want? So you've gone and got yourself a family, and you think that wipes away all the shit you've done, all the people you've killed?"

She reaches for the gun. Josef howls in frustration, and lunges for her throat. His teeth rip into her oesophagus, and she feels his jaw snap shut on her windpipe. His hair fills her face, and he's heavy on her chest. She can't breathe, and wonders how many others have died like this. How many others, because of her, and what she taught him?

Josef pulls back, his face dripping with her blood and, as Paige gasps for breath, the wound bubbles.

Josef snatches the photograph from her unresisting fingers. She tries to move her arms, but can't. Josef's speaking, but the fangs make it difficult and she can't hear him over the roaring in her ears. Her eyes swivel around in panic, looking for help. The guests in the other rooms must be awake now, and cowering behind their peepholes. Some at least will have called the police.

Then, as she twists her head, she catches movement in the room behind her. Federico stumbles into the light. The boy looks dazed and frightened; there are scratch marks on his face, but he has the shotgun in his hands.

There's a flash, and Josef jerks. Part of his face disappears, bitten off by the blast. Another flash, and he topples from Paige like a puppet with its strings cut, knocking his head against the doorframe as he falls.

Paige slaps a palm over the sucking wound in her neck, pinching the skin together, hoping she can heal before she suffocates.

Federico bends over her. Wordless, she points to the coil gun, and he kicks it over.

"Help me up," she croaks. As long as she keeps her hand covering the injury, her vocal chords still work.

With Federico's hands under her shoulders, she struggles to her feet and coughs up a wad of blood. She feels unsteady, but each breath is easier than the last.

Josef lies in a spreading patch of red-soaked carpet. One of his eyes is completely gone; that side of his face is a gory ruin; but the other seems miraculously untouched, and still beautiful. His hands twitch on the carpet like angry spiders.

Paige plucks the slippery, homemade throwing stars from her forearm, and tosses them aside. She points the coil gun at Josef's heart. Dimly, she can hear sirens pulling up on the street outside.

Josef's remaining eyelid flutters. She knows he's down, but he's obviously not out.

She says, "How many people have you killed, Josef?" Then, without waiting for an answer, she pulls the trigger. The gun whines and his chest blows apart. His heels scrape at the floor, as if trying to escape, and she raises the gun to his face.

"I'm sorry," she says.

She looks away as she fires, and she keeps the trigger depressed until the magazine clicks empty.

When she looks back, Josef's head's gone, and there's a hole in the floor.

The photograph of his daughter falls from his fingers.

He's dead.

She sticks the spent gun back in her belt. For some reason, her smashed cheek hurts more than her torn throat. She looks around to find Federico leaning on the doorframe.

Paige hawks red phlegm onto the carpet. Then she leans down and takes hold of Josef's boot. Gritting her teeth, she drags his body back into her ruined hotel room. Moving slowly and painfully, she retrieves the vodka bottle from the dressing table, spins the lid off, and raises the bottle in a toast to her fallen student. She stands over him for a long moment. Then she takes a deep swallow, which makes her cough.

"Goodbye, Josef," she says. There's nothing else to say. There's no triumph here, no closure, nothing but bone-deep weariness. Solemnly, she pours the remaining contents of the bottle – most of a litre of spirit – over his chest and legs; then she pulls a complimentary matchbook from the desk, and strikes one.

The wet clothes go up in a woof of blue flame. The fire spills onto the carpet, and the room fills with smoke.

Paige opens the desk drawer and takes out another clip of ammo for the coil gun. Then she limps back to Federico.

"I have to go," she says. She has to move on to the next target, the next time zone.

A fire alarm rings, and the sprinklers go off. The shotgun's on the floor at Federico's feet. He's holding the photograph of Josef's daughter. Water's running down his face, streaking his cheeks. His dreads are soaked.

"You're a fucking monster," he says.

Paige puts a hand to the torn flesh of her throat. She can feel the sides stitching themselves back together.

"I know," she says.

And with that, she fades away.

~

I like Amsterdam a lot. The last time I was there, I got caught in a storm and had to shelter in a doorway. It was late in the evening but the streets were buzzing, much as I describe in the story. The tourist boats took shelter beneath the bridges; the dark waters of the canal reflected the lights of the buildings opposite; and thunder rolled overhead like the iron-shod wheels of Thor's war chariot. It was, I thought, the perfect setting for a sci-fi horror tale with the atmosphere of a noir detective story. At the time, I had been toying with the idea of artificial vampires being used as covert troops in a future war, to frighten and demoralise the enemy – and suddenly I had my setting. The night-time streets of Amsterdam were the perfect stage on which to play out the confrontation between monster and creator.

"Red Lights, And Rain" first appeared in Solaris Rising 3, an anthology from Solaris Books, who also published my four novels, *The Recollection, Ack-Ack Macaque, Hive Monkey*, and *Macaque Attack*. It was later reprinted in *The Year's Best Science Fiction: Thirty-Second Annual Collection*, edited by Gardner Dozois (released in the UK as *The Mammoth Book of Best New SF 28*), and in the audio anthology *The Year's Top Ten Tales of Science Fiction 7*, ed. Allan Kaster.

The Bigger the Star, the Faster It Burns

Ed stops at a lonely roadside café on a hot autumn night. He drums his fingers on the counter.

"Hey, how about a coffee?" he says. It's late and he's the only customer. The waitress comes over. She's eighteen or nineteen, with long hair and black eyeliner.

"I'm waiting for the water to heat up," she says. She's got a black t-shirt and there's a biro behind her right ear. She looks over Ed's shoulder. "Is that your car?"

He turns in his seat. He's left the Dodge across two handicapped spaces in the empty car park.

"Isn't it a beauty?" he says.

She looks at the sweeping tailfins and scratches her chin. There's dried egg on her sleeve. "It looks old," she says. "Is it American?"

Ed nods. He's just borrowed it for the weekend. "I'm on my way up to Hereford, to see the crash site."

She looks him up and down. "Are you a reporter?"

Ed shakes his head. "I'm a photographer."

"Up from London?"

"How did you guess?"

She leans her elbows on the counter. "Are you going to take my picture?"

Ed smiles. "That depends. You haven't told me your name yet."

She brushes the dried egg from her sleeve. "Natalie."

They shake hands. "I'm Ed."

The radio at the back of the kitchen's playing an Elvis track. A truck rattles past on the road outside. "I'll get you that coffee," Natalie says. As she pours it, she looks back at him, over her shoulder.

"There's some wreckage at the top of the valley," she says, "I can

61

show it to you, if you like."

Half an hour later they're rolling up the valley in the Dodge, with the roof down. The single-track road smells hot and the stars overhead are hard and sharp. Natalie's finished her shift. Ed's taken his jacket off. He pulls up his sleeve to show her his tattoo.

"I got that in Amsterdam," he says. Natalie wrinkles her nose. Whenever she moves, her jeans squeak on the seat.

"Take the next left," she says.

Ed lets his sleeve drop. He likes her accent. He touches the brake and downshifts into the turn.

Natalie points through the windscreen. "It's just up here."

Ed pulls off the road. Up ahead, caught in the headlights, is the wreckage she promised him. Strewn over the gorse and heather, twisted splinters glint in the moonlight.

He kills the engine. "Does anyone else know about this?"

Natalie shakes her head. "No one comes up here much."

It's midnight. Ed opens his door and climbs out, camera in hand. He can smell the heather. He walks over to the nearest fragment. The metal's smooth and warm to the touch. With a dry mouth and sweaty palms, he starts snapping; knowing the pictures he's taking will make his reputation.

Back in the car, Natalie lights a cigarette. She puts her feet up on the dashboard and lets her long hair fall over the back of the seat. She knows there are armed helicopters patrolling the main crash site to the north. But here in the valley all she can hear is the click of Ed's camera in the hot night air.

Ed comes back to the car with a souvenir from the wreckage: three luminous brass gauges mounted on a broken panel, all smashed, faces starred, each the size of a dinner plate.

"These have to be worth something," he says, and drops them onto the back seat. Natalie says nothing. She keeps her eyes closed. Her hair and clothes still smell of fried eggs. She hears Ed walk around to the driver's side. He gets in and pulls the door shut, *ka-chunk*.

"Thanks," he says.

Natalie arches like a warm cat.

"No bother."

She gazes down into the valley. The lights of the main road snake away like an orange river. She can see the café, and beyond it, the town. She can almost see her house. It all looks pathetically small from up here, and she can blank everything out with her hand, cover it over as if it never existed.

Ed shudders the engine into life, and pulls the car round in a tight circle.

"Where can I drop you?" he says.

The wheels bump over the uneven ground. Natalie leans forward.

"Take me with you."

"What?"

"Take me with you to London." She's never even been as far as Cardiff, but she's feeling wild. It must be the fresh air.

Ed looks at her as if he's looking over a pair of spectacles. "How old are you?"

"Nineteen."

"What about your parents?"

"They won't even notice I'm gone."

Ed scratches under his white t-shirt. He knows that, thanks to her, he's going to be rich, and so he's feeling generous.

He says, "Okay, what the fuck."

He steers the car back down the hill and on to the main road, where he guns the engine and lets the old car wind out to seventy-five. As they scream past the café, Natalie turns her head. She watches it recede into the darkness.

Ed clicks on the radio. Another Elvis song. It's a long, flat drag back to London, but he doesn't care. He's wired, practically jumping in his seat. There's music on the radio, the top's still down, and the warm night air makes him feel like a teenager. It's the first time he's felt like this in years. Beside him, Natalie starts to pat the side of the car door in time to the music. Her hair straggles out, careless in the wind.

They hit London an hour before dawn. On the backseat, the brass gauges glow, brighter than ever. Ed eyes them in the rear view mirror. By the time he pulls up at the kerb outside his house, the glow's spread itself to the dials on the car's dash.

Later, after they've freshened up, Ed introduces Natalie to some of his friends. He takes her on a Monopoly board tour of the Capital. He's trying to offload the brass gauges, but no one will buy them. He tries all his contacts, but they won't touch anything from the crash site. They're scared of the government. All he manages to sell are the pictures – but that's still enough to land him a suitcase full of money.

He brings it back to the car, a stupid grin smeared all over his face like grease paint.

"Let's go shopping," he says. And by three o'clock in the afternoon, they're both fitted out with new suits, shirts and shoes. They keep stopping to admire themselves in shop windows. They're drunk on how good they look.

He takes her for an early dinner at an achingly hip Thai place off the Portobello Road. She's bought a new mobile phone, and while they're waiting for their food, she logs into her social networks, and brags to her mates about her new boyfriend.

"So," says Ed, "we're young and rich in London. What do you want to do first?"

Natalie puts the phone down. They're both tired. She reaches across the tablecloth, and her fingertips brush the back of his hand.

"Take me home," she says. "Take me home, with you."

Ed buys a bottle of wine and they walk back to his flat: a third floor studio, up six flights of stairs. There's a framed picture of Elvis above the fireplace. The fire escape opens onto a flat section of roof, still warm from the day's heat.

"Sit down, make yourself comfortable," he says.

It's getting dark. In the city, night comes all at once. The orange streetlights fire up and the blinds in the apartment blocks across the road go down. Everyone's cooking dinner and watching TV with the volume turned way up. No one's looking out. No one wants to hear what's happening in the street.

But out here on the roof, Natalie smells of flowers. She's wearing a silvery cocktail dress and has her hair chopped into a shaggy mop. Planes pass overhead, one after the other, on approach to Heathrow, their navigation lights like drifting fireworks. After a glass of wine, he kisses her, and she wraps her arms around his neck.

They stay together for the rest of the week, hardly leaving the flat. They live on takeaways and cups of tea. Ed tells her about his ex-wife. She tells him about her parents. They have both forgotten the brass gauges on the back seat of the borrowed car. Neither of them expects their relationship to last.

Natalie's had boyfriends before, back in the Valleys, but nothing serious; symptoms of her boredom rather than cures for it. Ed's the first man to bring any real excitement into her life, and that's why she's grabbed him, the way drowning girls grab ropes.

The next morning, Natalie tries to phone her dad but can't get through. There's a government block on the line; no calls in or out of South Wales. So she takes a shower instead. Ed pops out to buy a paper, and he reads the headlines on the way back to the flat. Three helicopters have disappeared from the crash site. An eyewitness claims they shot straight up into the night sky, glowing like meteors.

On the street, there are stalls setting up, and crowd control barriers being lowered into place. It's the weekend of the Notting Hill Carnival. When he gets back to the flat, he finds Natalie in the kitchen, wrapped in a towel. Breakfast consists of cold pizza from the fridge, left over from the night before. As they eat, he shows her his portfolio of photographs: the landscapes; the portraits; the journalism. She flicks through it all with one hand, a slice of congealed pizza balanced in the other. Eventually, she comes to a shot of the Pleiades.

"That's pretty."

She turns to the next page, which shows the familiar rectangle of the Orion constellation rising above the black branches of an autumn tree. The stars in the belt are cold and blue.

Natalie takes a bite of pizza, and talks around it. "Why's that one red?"

Ed leans over her. Her hair smells very clean. Her fingernail's tapping the upper left corner of the rectangle.

"That's Betelgeuse," he says. He traces the star with his own finger. "It looks red because it's all swollen up into a giant, nearing the end of its life."

"So it's an old star?"

He shakes his head. "No, actually it's younger than the sun."

She raises a quizzical eyebrow and he shrugs. He looks at the framed Elvis picture over the fireplace.

"The bigger the star, the faster it burns," he says.

Accepting this, she flips the page to find another view of the same constellation.

"These are great. How did you take them? Did you use a telescope?"

Ed straightens up. "No, it was a tripod camera on a ten second exposure." He had a telescope, years ago. Not much use for one in London, though; too much light.

He walks over to the window. Three floors below, he sees the borrowed Dodge parked at the kerb. It's a handsome machine, and he's a little bit in love with it. The car's brought a much-needed splash of glamour into his life, and he'll be sad when he has to return it to its rightful owners.

Natalie's still eating pizza, still wrapped in her towel, her bare legs crossed at the ankles. She's cute, and he loves her accent, even though he knows there's no future for them, because they're too different. She's too young and excitable; he's too old and restless.

And he hasn't noticed that down below, the car's floating with its tyres half a centimetre above the road.

The phone rings. Ed picks the receiver up. It's the editor to whom he sold the pictures.

"There are government types sniffing around. They want to know how you breached security at the crash site."

Ed stiffens. "I wasn't *at* the crash site. This was a separate area, a secondary impact."

"Then you should have reported it. They want to pull the pictures."

"Screw them."

"I can't protect you, Ed."

"Then screw you, too."

He breaks the connection. He takes Natalie out into the carnival crowds. Hand-in-hand, they walk the length of Ladbroke Grove, and she can't stop gaping. She's never seen anything like this. There are at least a million people packed into these streets. It's a sea of bodies, bright costumes and police horses. They buy coffee and jerk chicken from a stall. They have to shout to hear each other over the music.

They spend the day wandering, edging their way through the crush. They pause to watch live music on improvised stages; they follow the procession route, marvelling at the stamina of the dancers; and end the afternoon on a wooden table outside a corner pub, drinking overpriced beer in plastic pint glasses.

They watch as darkness falls. The carnival's still in full swing despite the late hour. Everyone's celebrating, even though it's been raining and the pavements are wet.

"What time is it?" Natalie says. She has damp tinsel in her hair.

Ed shrugs. He doesn't have a watch. It's been a wild day, but now he's had enough of playing tour guide.

He pats her leg.

"Let's go home."

Natalie stiffens. She's been having the time of her life. She feels like a caged bird released into the wild, and she doesn't want it to end.

"I'm going to stay here," she says, not looking at him. "I'll meet you back at the flat later, okay?"

They both know she won't. She stands up and brushes down her skirt. Ed folds his arms.

"Don't be like that," she says.

By midnight, she's in the arms of a Brazilian telemarketer from Teddington. They lie together in his hotel room, the open window allowing the deep bass of the street festival to ebb and flow over them, the mingled smells of hashish and fried onions to galvanise their empty stomachs.

"I feel kind of bad about Ed," she says. "I shouldn't have left him like that."

Alejandro rubs a sleepy palm across his face. Although bare-chested, he's still wearing his jeans, and his hair's flattened on one side, damp with sweat.

"You don't have to worry about him anymore," he says. "You have me now."

He lights a cigarette from the pack on the bedside table. Natalie sits up and hugs her knees.

"Do you think he'll be all right?"

There are steel drums playing in the street. She gets up and pulls back the net curtain, looks down at the crowd. She says: "It was just a stupid argument."

Her shoes are lying on the floor by the door. In the orange half-light, Alejandro holds the cigarette pinched between his thumb and forefinger. He takes a small, tight drag and curses in Portuguese.

"Come to bed," he says.

Natalie ignores him. All she wants is to be left alone.

"You know, it was his idea to come here," she says. There are people blowing whistles in the street, and strange lights in the sky. She wraps her arms across her chest. The Valleys seems so far away, and she doesn't know where she is.

"I hope he's all right," she says.

Meanwhile, Ed walks back to the flat alone, hands in pockets. He hates London now. It's so dreary, and he's so tired. He needs to move on, find something new to do.

By the time he gets home, the crowd's started to thin. He sees the old Dodge parked where he left it, and no one seems to have noticed that its tyres are floating a good couple of centimetres above the tarmac. The gauges on the back seat light it up from inside, like a miniature carnival float.

He looks up. A few stars poke through the ragged clouds. He doesn't want to go back to the flat. He's thinking of the crash site and the vanished helicopters, and how bone-achingly bored he is.

The very metal of the car seems to glow and sing. When he touches the bodywork it makes his fingers tingle. He gets in and starts the engine, and the Dodge immediately rises half a metre into the air, much to the surprise of the crowd. He touches the accelerator, and it jumps up another half. Ed gives a fierce grin.

"Okay, here we go," he says. He waves to the circle of astonished onlookers, and mashes the pedal. The car leaps. Foot to the floor, he drives it straight up into the night sky, aiming for the stars.

He drives so far and so fast that he ends up on a planet somewhere out on the edge of the galaxy. It takes him six weeks to get there. He gets a flat near the shoulder of Orion and has to drive the rest of the way on steel rims, but he gets there.

And he never comes back.

~

This story is probably best described as a mash-up of Elvis songs, fast cars, crashed UFOs, street parties, the movies *Repo Man* and *Back To The Future*, and the musicals *Grease* and *Chitty Chitty Bang Bang*... It was an exercise in trying to write a story without a proper plot, in which events progressed from the actions and reactions of the characters, and the technology involved was, to use Arthur C. Clarke's famous phrase, "indistinguishable from magic."

Rise Reviews praised the story's imitation of "the inertia of life, the sort of 'there-is-nothing-here-to-piece-as-plot' storytelling, which accumulates to some hidden meaning."

The day after I wrote the first draft, I read it aloud to a room full of students at Bath Spa University, as part of a lecture on creative writing, and they seemed suitably bemused.

Fallout

1.

Despite what was to come, the day started well. An hour before sunrise they landed the rented jet at a decommissioned RAF base in Wiltshire, near Swindon. It was a cold morning and frost glittered on the grass at the edge of the runway.

Leaving the pilot and cabin crew to look after the plane, they pulled four motorbikes from its hold and clipped dosimeters to their lapels. Then they donned helmets and drove their bikes downhill, through dark and empty villages, to the army checkpoint at the M4 motorway junction. Rusty, concrete-filled oil drums blocked the westbound slip road and a tired sergeant blew into his hands. He wore a long coat and a fur hat with khaki earflaps. The men behind him cradled standard-issue SA80 assault rifles.

"We were told to expect you," he said through his moustache. His breath steamed in their headlights. He glanced at their papers, then back over his shoulder at the unlit, empty carriageway stretching away behind him, into the dead zone. He shivered.

"Rather you than me," he said.

On the lead bike, Ann Szkatula pushed up her visor. She had silver eye shadow and a matching silk scarf. Behind her, the three other riders each had a foot on the ground, engines running, eager for the off.

"Thanks," she said.

Some of the soldiers wanted autographs. Ann sat patiently as the three American boys signed iPod cases and posed for photographs. Then, with the barrier open and the empty road stretching ahead, she led them out onto the carriageway, and up to a steady 110 kilometres an hour. Travelling at that speed, they soon passed the derelict service area at Leigh Delamere, and the Bath junction.

On both sides of the road the countryside was dark. The farms they passed were deserted. There were no crops in the fields and the cattle were long-gone. On the motorway verges, abandoned vehicles rusted, their tires flat and windows broken; and until the white sun rose behind them, the only lights Ann saw were their own.

"Welcome to the West Country," she said over the bike-to-bike intercom. No one answered. They were all too caught up in the desolate splendour of the cold dawn, and the creeping fear of the invisible radiation sleeting through their bodies from the crash site ahead. Beside her, she saw Dustin leaning forward on his bike, his chin almost touching the Honda's handlebars. The other two members of the band were weaving around on their yellow Kawasakis – trailer park kids still adjusting to their new-found wealth.

Dustin was the cute one. With his blue eyes and floppy fringe, he was the face of the group. He sang lead. The other two, Kent and Brad, danced and did backing vocals. Today, all three were wrapped in brand-new matching black leathers.

Together, they swept down to the junction with the M32. It was the main turn-off for Bristol. Ann pulled over and the boys slithered to a halt beside her. Dustin was the closest. He flipped up his visor.

"How much further is it, Ann?"

Ann looked at her dosimeter. This close to ground zero, the ambient radiation levels were more than a hundred times higher than normal – not enough to cause undue concern, but enough to remind her of the need for caution.

"If we carry on for a couple of miles, we'll be able to see the crater. We can't go any further than that, so from there we'll take the A38 right into the heart of the city, where there'll be plenty of empty streets for you to race around."

Four-abreast, they rolled up to the Almondsbury interchange, where the M4 crossed the cracked and shattered surface of the M5. From there, the Severn Valley stretched out before them, a patchwork of overgrown fields and industrial ruin.

Ann turned her engine off and leaned the bike on its stand. They could go no further. A barricade of charred and rusting cars blocked the carriageway. Below, through the morning haze, the irradiated waters of the Severn smouldered like molten bronze. The ruined power stations of Oldbury and Berkeley lay to the north, and directly ahead, the twin Severn bridges stood, their towers partially collapsed and their sagging steel cables slowly unravelling...

The boys took off their helmets and Dustin ruffled his trademark fringe into shape. Brad shook out his white dreadlocks. Ann took a pair of binoculars and climbed up onto the bonnet of a burned-out Volvo. It was hard to make out the crash site itself from this angle, lying as it did in the mud at the water's edge.

"There's some wreckage over there," she said. She handed the glasses to Dustin, guiding him to where the nose of the crashed alien craft lay in the thick estuary mud like a dropped eggshell. Smaller fragments littered the grass for miles around, like twisted tinfoil. As she moved her head, some of them caught the morning sun.

"I heard it was bigger than that," Dustin said.

Ann took the binoculars back and handed them to Brad. "It exploded in the air," she said. "I guess some of it fell in the water."

When they'd all had a look, Dustin gave Ann his mobile camera phone and the three boys posed on the rusted cars as she used it to take pictures of them, with the collapsed bridges and crash site as an apocalyptic backdrop.

Dustin tucked his helmet under his arm and struck a heroic attitude.

"I'm so putting these on MySpace," he said.

They took the A38 down through Filton and Horfield, to the centre of Bristol.

"Watch out for rubble," Ann said as they hit the roundabout by the bus station. The boys ignored her. This was what they'd been waiting for: the chance to go wild. They ripped open their throttles and surged away into the empty streets, dodging potholes and leaning crazily into the bends.

Within seconds, they were gone.

Ann followed them as far as Castle Park before giving up. It was where they planned to regroup. She pulled her bike off the road, rumbling through the unkempt grass to the ruined church. Her front wheel wobbled over the uncertain, frosty ground. When she turned the engine off, all she could hear was the wind in the bare trees and, far away between the buildings, the distant roar of the other bikes.

The church had been gutted by the Luftwaffe in 1940 and then left as a memorial to that distant conflict. There were empty birds' nests in its eaves, strands of ivy scaling its walls. Beyond it, the waters of the old dock were thick with weeds. The few remaining pleasure boats wallowed half-submerged, their sides green with accumulated scum.

Ann stretched the stiffness in her back. After two decades of neglect, the city didn't look as bad as she'd been expecting; the shops and office buildings appeared almost untouched, if she discounted the fire damage and broken windows.

She unpacked her portable gas stove and put a pan of coffee on to heat. She checked her dosimeter: they'd be okay for another hour or so, as long as the boys didn't try anything stupid, like trying to bust their way into one of the shops, where the seriously contaminated dust still lay undisturbed.

She blew into her hands and bent down to stir the coffee. At heart, they were good, all-American boys. But they were young and, like all young people, they thought they were immortal. As the person responsible for keeping them out of trouble, she'd be much happier once they were all safely on the jet this evening. She hadn't wanted to come here and, now they had, she couldn't wait to get away.

She'd been eighteen years old when the alien ship exploded above the Severn mudflats, damaging the nuclear reactors at Berkeley and Oldbury. At the time, she was living near Oxford with her parents, both Polish immigrants. Like so many other families, they fled for the continent when they heard the news. They panicked at the thought of the radiation. Spurred on by memories of Chernobyl, they packed their lives into suitcases and crossed the English Channel at night, crammed onto a dangerously overcrowded car ferry.

Two days later, dirty and hungry, they made it to her paternal grandparents' apartment in Warsaw, where they stayed for the next six months.

There were only two bedrooms. In order to escape, Ann joined the army as a trainee chef. She did two tours in the Middle East. After that, she went into business for herself on the streets of Krakow; selling hamburgers containing vat-grown meat cloned directly from pop stars and celebrities. She nearly got rich. But when her patties turned out to be ordinary pork instead of vat-grown human flesh, she wound up in jail.

When she got out, two months later, she drifted down through Slovakia and Hungary to the pebbly beaches of Croatia. There were British refugees everywhere she went. She'd lived for a while as a busker in Budapest. She drove a cab in Zagreb, and then worked the door at a music club in Rijeka, where she drank Ouzo with the roadies.

Then, at the age of thirty-three, she woke on a tour bus in the unreal light of a wet Italian dawn to find she'd blagged her way into the music business. Now, years later, here she was: babysitting this boy band from an American TV talent show, chaperoning them through their first (and probably last) European tour.

Her job was to keep them clean and sober, and show them the sights. When they were finished here, she'd lead them across country to Stonehenge, and then back to the plane. Tonight, they'd be in Helsinki for two shows, then on to Copenhagen, Prague, Belgrade, and Bucharest.

She wrapped her arms around herself and stamped her feet on the cold, shattered concrete. After all these years, and sandwiched into such an itinerary, being back in the UK, the land of her birth, didn't feel like coming home. In fact, it didn't feel much like anything at all.

Half an hour later, the other bikes rejoined her. Dustin, Kent and Brad were laughing, bubbly with adrenalin, their mid-west accents loud in the stillness of the abandoned city. She poured them coffee and broke out the sandwiches. There were apples in the lunch box. She took out her penknife and sliced them into quarters.

As she handed them around, she heard the echo of another engine. Brad met her eyes. "What's that?" he said, cocking his head, his dreadlocks swinging. Ann shrugged. They were supposed to have the city to themselves. As far as she knew, the army hadn't granted permits to anyone else. She turned in the direction of the sound. As she did so, a tattered Land Rover lurched into view, weaving crazily. It roared along the road toward them, then bumped over the kerb, through the trees, and ploughed to a halt in the long grass.

Dustin took a step forward: "Is it the paparazzi?"

Ann pulled him behind her. "I don't think so."

A rat-faced man and a woman were sitting in the front of the vehicle. Both had black army fatigues and short blond hair. The woman stepped out, a compact silver pistol in her right hand.

She said: "Hello, Skat."

Ann bristled. She hadn't been called that since school in Oxford. She had a gun of her own in her bike's pannier. She'd packed it to scare wild dogs but now couldn't reach it. Instead, she narrowed her eyes.

"Vic?"

The woman held the heavy door open. She motioned with her gun. "Get in the van, Skat."

2.

Inside, with the doors shut, the Land Rover's cab smelled damp. The plastic foam seats were rotten with mildew.

Vic said: "Buckle up." She still had the middle class Cotswold accent that Ann remembered, and she'd taken the rat-faced man's place at the steering wheel. He now stood out on the grass, his gun trained on the three boys.

"Where are we going?" Ann asked.

Vic ignored her. She had the gun in her lap. She mashed the gear lever into reverse and backed out onto the road, then crunched it into first and they rolled off in a cloud of blue smoke, rattling through the city centre, past the cathedral, and out onto the road following the river through the Avon Gorge, towards the grey shores of the Severn Estuary.

As she drove, she said: "You remember me then, Skat?"

"It's been a long time." Ann eyed the pistol in the blonde woman's lap. She hadn't seen Victoria O'Neill since they were at secondary school together.

"I heard you went to Spain and joined the army. And now you're managing this boy band, what do they call themselves?"

"One Giant Leap."

"That's it." Vic shifted gear, coaxing a little more speed from the aged engine.

"After school," she continued, "I joined the army as an officer. I was in Afghanistan for a while. And then I had the bad luck to be stationed over *here* when the crash came."

They passed the abandoned coal terminal at Avonmouth, its skeletal cranes and coal dust conveyors rusting in the open air like abandoned Martian tripods.

"I was on one of the first choppers into the crash site. It was dark and there were fires burning on the water from the spilled fuel, and fallout from the cracked reactors."

"It sounds grim."

"I was only nineteen. But to cut a long story short, I found something in the wreckage. Maybe it was a weapon, maybe not. But I stashed it. I dropped it out of the helicopter as we left."

"And now you're looking for it?" Ann had heard rumours of scavengers selling illegally-foraged artefacts to anonymous collectors.

Vic shook her shaven head. "I know *exactly* where it is. That's where we're going. I memorised the GPS coordinates. But when we get there, I want you to get it for me."

"Why me?"

"Because it's probably radioactive as hell and frankly, I'd rather not touch it."

After a few miles, the Land Rover bumped off the road onto the rough windblown grass at the edge of the Estuary, and the engine died. Across the water, the hills of Wales were brown with winter bracken. The sky was a clear eggshell blue at the horizon, shading to navy at the zenith.

Ann waited until the other woman stepped out of the vehicle, and then popped her own seatbelt. She still had her penknife, tucked safely into her zipped jacket pocket, but Vic had the gun.

"There's a metal detector in the back," Vic said.

Ann walked around and pulled it out. It was a lightweight carbon fibre model with a battery at one end and a magnet at the other. There was a lead-lined plastic container sitting next to it, about the size of a shoe box.

Ann took both around to the front of the van, to where Vic was consulting a portable sat nav unit.

"Try over there," she said imperiously, pointing to a thorny clump of bushes beside a reed-clogged drainage ditch. Ann trudged over and turned the detector on. They were a few miles downstream of the main crash site and the grey mud had a clinging, fishy smell. It stuck to her motorcycle boots. A few dozen yards away, it merged into the thick grey water at the shoreline.

"Why are you doing this? I mean, it's been twenty years, why now?"

Vic scowled. "My reasons don't matter." She pushed the sat nav into a shoulder pocket. "All you need to know is that there's a buyer in the Ukraine who'll give me at least a million for this object."

Ann moved the detector around on the scrubby grass. She knew there had to be a good reason why the other woman hadn't come back before this; perhaps a long spell in hospital or even prison. Whatever the truth, Vic clearly had no intention of telling her.

Instead, Ann said: "Meeting you here, now. It's not a coincidence, is it?"

Vic shook her head. "I've been looking for a way to smuggle the object out of the country. When I heard your boy band announce this little trip of theirs, it seemed like too good an opportunity to miss."

She checked her dosimeter and frowned at what she saw. She waved her pistol impatiently. "Now, get on with it. We *really* don't have all day."

Twenty minutes later, Ann found what they were looking for: a short metal tube, about an inch thick at its widest point, tapering to half that at either end. Reluctantly, she scraped it from the mud with her bare hands and placed it in the lead-lined box from the back of the Land Rover. The thought of it being radioactive made her skin crawl.

"What is it?" she said.

Vic still had the sat nav in one hand, the gun in the other. Her combat jacket flapped in the offshore breeze. "There were four bodies at the crash site, and they all had one."

"Do you think it's a weapon?"

"That would be my guess. It's certainly what my buyer in the Ukraine believes."

Ann rubbed her hands together, trying to brush off the sticky mud. "What were they like? The bodies, I mean. What did they look like?"

Vic shivered. "Trust me. You really don't want to know." She shook her head, as if trying to dismiss the memory. Then she straightened up and motioned for Ann to get back into the Land Rover with the box.

"We came up the river last night by boat," she said as she released the handbrake and eased the vehicle back onto the road. She was trying to change the subject. She looked tired. She was holding the pistol against the steering wheel as she drove, ready to use it if necessary. "Phil's my husband. He found this old heap and got it going." She tapped the Land Rover's steering wheel, as if willing it to keep running. "But tonight, we're flying out of here on your jet."

Ann looked down at the box on her knees. When handling the tube, she'd noticed three touch pads spaced around its waist. Thinking of them now, she wondered what they were for. They were obviously controls of some sort, but there had been no markings or other clues to their purpose.

"You'll never get out of here by road," she said. "The soldiers saw four of us go in, they'll be expecting the same four to come out."

Vic shook her head. "They saw three blokes and a girl go in wearing motorcycle helmets. As long as they see the same number coming out tonight, no one's going to be any the wiser."

When they reached Castle Park, Ann saw Dustin, Brad and Kent sitting miserably around the camping stove on the steps of the ruined church. The blond man – Phil – stood opposite them, his gun held loosely at his side. He looked around in obvious relief as the Land Rover's corroded brakes brought it to a squealing halt.

"You found it?" he said.

Vic jerked a thumb at Ann. "It's in the box."

Walking stiffly, she led Ann over to the stove, where the boys were huddled. Dustin looked up.

"Are you okay, Ann?"

Vic pointed her pistol at him. She made him get to his feet and then shoved him toward Ann. "The two of you get undressed," she said.

Dustin bunched his fists. "No fucking way."

Vic took a step forward and the thin sun caught her blonde hair, turning it silver. "We need your leathers," she said. "Now, I'm going to count to three." She pointed the gun at his forehead. "One."

Holding the lead-lined box in one hand, Ann slipped the other inside and grasped the alien rod. It felt cold to the touch. Her skin itched at the thought the metal might still be radioactive, but she knew she had to act now. Vic wouldn't leave them alive. She wouldn't take the risk. She'd shoot them as soon as she had their clothes.

"Two," Vic said.

Ann pulled the rod free, letting the box fall to the floor. "Stop it," she said.

Vic looked at her. "What are you doing?"

Ann's thumb found one of the rod's three touch pads. "I'm going to turn this on."

Vic blinked. "Don't be an idiot."

Ann glanced at Brad and Kent, still huddled together on the flagstone steps. She was supposed to be protecting them. If she died now, with Dustin, she knew they wouldn't outlive her for long, and they were just kids. Vic might need them for the moment, to con her way through the army checkpoint, but as soon as she got the jet airborne, en route to the Ukraine, Ann knew they'd be disposed of.

She brushed her thumb over one of the pads. It was soft and warm. "I mean it. Back off or I'm going to press this."

"You don't know what it does."

"Neither do you."

Vic still had her gun aimed at Dustin's head. She puffed her cheeks out in frustration.

"Three," she said.

Everything slowed.

With her thumb pressing the rod's touch pad, Ann saw Vic fire her gun. The flash and smoke erupted from the barrel at a glacial pace. Subjective seconds later, Dustin jerked as the shot hit him. Ann tried to move but couldn't. Her muscles were encased in something thick and viscous. Straining forward, she saw him twist and fall, the bright spray of blood from his shoulder suspended behind him in the morning air like an angel's wing...

3.

Ann blinked her eyes.

Time had passed. She was lying on the grass, looking up at the clear sky. She sat up carefully and checked herself. She didn't seem to be injured. Beside her, Vic and Dustin lay where they'd fallen. By the church, Brad, Kent and the other man were also on their backs.

Vic stirred. She still had the gun in her hand. Ann walked over and kicked it free, the steel toe cap of her motorcycle boot sending it under the parked Land Rover.

Vic snatched her hand back. Her eyes were wide.

"What the fuck just happened?"

Ann ignored her. She moved over to Phil and took his weapon.

Then she shook Kent awake and handed it to him.

"If either one moves, shoot them," she said.

When she got back to Dustin, she saw he was bleeding onto the grass. His shoulder and arm were slathered in it. Carefully, she unfolded her penknife and used it to cut away the sleeve of his leather jacket. His shirt was sodden. The bullet had clipped the outside edge of his shoulder, ripping a deep and ragged tear through the deltoid muscle. As an ex-soldier, Ann had seen worse. Many shoulder injuries were fatal. She knew he was lucky not to have been hit in the ball-and-socket shoulder joint. There were some huge blood vessels and delicate nerves in there, plus the joint itself, which no amount of surgery could repair if smashed.

She unwound her silk scarf, wadded it up and slipped it between the sleeve and the wound.

"Keep pressing this," she said, lifting his right hand onto the improvised dressing.

Dustin clenched his teeth. He looked up at her. "What happened?"

Ann straightened up. "I pressed the button."

She walked over to her bike. Somehow, the blast from the alien rod had disabled their equipment. Their bikes were useless. The radios were dead. Even Dustin's phone had been fried.

"What are we going to do?" Brad said.

Ann looked accusingly at Vic. "You could have killed him."

Vic was on her feet by now, backing off. She was halfway to one of the Land Rover's open doors, her hands clasped in front of her.

Ann took a step towards her. She had the open penknife in her hand.

"Dustin needs medical attention," she said. "We need to get him to a hospital."

Vic was still wide-eyed. "Fuck you, Szkatula."

She opened her hands. She had the rod.

"Put it down," Ann said.

Vic shook her head. "Sorry Skat, I want my million dollars."

Ann glanced at Kent. He was holding Phil's weapon but he looked scared, as if it might bite him. He was a dancer not a soldier, and he didn't know how to use a gun. He was pointing it at Phil as Vic ducked behind the Land Rover, stooping to retrieve the weapon that had been kicked under it. Seconds later she reappeared, head down, running for the shopping mall on the other side of the road, keeping the bulk of the vehicle between herself and any pursuit.

Ann swore under her breath. She unclenched her fists and looked across at Dustin. Her anger with Vic would have to wait.

She pulled some cord from her panniers and used it to tie Phil's hands behind his back. Then she helped Dustin into a sitting position. She unzipped her jacket and used her penknife to cut strips from her t-shirt, which she then used to clean and bandage his shoulder. Although thankfully the major blood vessels seemed to be intact, it still took her a while to stop the bleeding. When she had, she folded her jacket into a makeshift pillow and did her best to make him comfortable.

"I can't believe that bitch shot me," Dustin said.

Ann brushed his cheek. "Leave her to me."

She walked over and retrieved the gun from her motorcycle pannier. It was a Browning semi-automatic with twelve rounds still in the clip, one in the breach. Holding it, she turned to Phil. The man had a thin, rat-like face with scared green eyes in a web of crow's feet.

"Is there a radio on your boat?" she said.

Phil looked at the gun in her hand and the expression on her face, and then he looked away.

"Yes," he said.

Ann turned to Brad and Kent. She didn't want to leave them but knew they wouldn't be safe as long as Vic remained at large. With a million dollars at stake, her former schoolmate wouldn't want her or the boys to alert the authorities.

"Take Dustin," she said. "Find the boat. I'm going after Vic."

She left the park in the direction Vic had taken, following the Land Rover's tracks back through the trees to the road. On the opposite side, concrete steps led up to the smashed doors of the shopping mall she'd seen Vic running towards.

Keeping the gun ready, Ann stepped through an empty window frame into the mall's unlit hallway. Her heavy motorcycle boots echoed on the tiled floor and there were dried and blown leaves everywhere.

"Vic?"

She inched her way along the hall. Beyond, it opened onto a balcony overlooking the central atrium. A stalled escalator led down to the next level. Pigeons flapped under the glass roof.

"Vic?"

"Don't come any closer."

Vic stood at the far end of the balcony, gun in one hand, alien rod in the other.

"Just tell me which button you pressed."

"No."

Vic scowled and shifted her weight. "Look, there are things you don't know, Szkatula. Things the government has been covering up."

Ann took a step towards her, ready to shoot.

"Such as?"

"The crash in the Severn," Vic said. "It wasn't an accident. After we recovered the bodies, they kept me on the project. And it turns out the ship was shot down."

"Shot down?"

"Yes. There was a second craft, a hostile. They were fighting."

Ann risked a peep over the rail. The atrium was three floors deep, criss-crossed with escalators, and they were on the uppermost level. She gripped her gun. "I need you to stand down, Vic. I have a wounded man and I need to get him to safety."

The other woman rolled her eyes. "Don't you see, Skat? Don't you get it? This was just a skirmish. There's a war going on out there. There are ships fighting and we don't even know what the sides are." She looked up at the dirty glass ceiling and the cold blue sky beyond. "From what I've seen of the photos from the space telescopes, the main action seems to be happening a long way from here. And thank God for that, because we're totally outclassed. We can't match their technology. If and when the fighting comes our way, we're fucked."

Ann squeezed the grip of her pistol. "I still need you to drop the gun," she said.

Vic shook her head. "I can't do that, Skat. I'm going to take the money I get from this and disappear somewhere remote, away from the big cities. Somewhere I'll stand a chance if push comes to shove." She waggled the rod in her other hand. "Now tell me how it works."

Ann took a deep breath. She thought of Dustin injured and hurting, and the other two boys with him, back in the park. "I'm not going to let you stop us from leaving," she said.

Vic curled her lip. "What are you going to do, Skat? Are you going to shoot me?"

Lifting the rod, she moved her thumb onto one of the touch pads ringing its waist.

"Is it this one?" she said.

She pressed the pad. There was a jumping, electrical flash and lightning crackled from the rod. It leapt along her arm. Ann caught the sharp tang of singed cloth. Vic yelped in pain and surprise. Then, engulfed in blue sparks, she staggered back against the balcony rail and began to fall.

"No!"

Ann dropped the gun and lunged, trying to catch her as she went over. But by the time she reached the rail, Vic had gone, spinning down into the darkened lower levels like a falling bonfire spark, disintegrating as she hit the dirty tiled floor; the cooked flesh blowing from her bones like ash...

4.

Some time later, when Ann returned to the park, she found the boys were still there. They were trying to rig up an improvised drag stretcher for Dustin. As she came across the grass, they turned to her.

Brad looked worried. He said: "Did you find her?"

Ann pulled the alien rod from her pocket. She'd walked down three escalators to retrieve it.

"She's gone," she said.

She walked over and dropped the rod back into the lead-lined box, closing the lid.

"Are you okay?" Dustin asked. His voice was thin with pain. With her back to him, she nodded.

"I will be."

She looked up at the clear sky overhead, and took a deep breath. The air was cold in her chest. It smelled clean and helped dispel the charred barbeque stench of Vic's burned body from her nostrils.

Had Vic been telling the truth? Could the crash – whose after-effects had shaped her adult life – really be the result of an alien conflict? Here in the park, were they actually standing in the radioactive fallout of an interstellar war?

She exhaled. Then she looked at Phil – Vic's husband – still sitting with his hands lashed behind his back. "Has he told you where to find the boat?" she said.

Kent still held Phil's gun. He said: "Yes, but we weren't sure what to do with him."

Ann shrugged. All her anger was gone, replaced with unease. How long did the Earth have before the next 'skirmish' came its way?

"Leave him here," she said. "The army can pick him up later."

She turned her back on the man and walked over to where Dustin sat. She crouched beside him.

"Can I take a look?" she said.

The young man pushed his fringe out of his eyes. "Sure."

He held still as she pulled out her penknife and started cutting away the tattered leather of his jacket.

As she pulled the severed sleeve free, he winced. "You know," he said, "there'll be reporters waiting for us. When we tell them what you did... When you hand over that rod... You'll be a hero."

Ann stripped the last of the leather away, exposing her improvised dressings.

"I don't know whether to replace these now or wait for the chopper," she said.

Dustin forced a brave smile. "Leave them."

She made to stand but he put his good hand on her black-clad knee. His eyes were the same colour as the sky.

"You're going to be famous," he said. "How does that feel?"

Ann blinked.

"You're the rock star, you tell me."

~

Science fiction can be a useful distancing tool for exploring the fears we have about the world of the present. For instance, the germ of this story came from the uneasiness I felt in the aftermath of the 911 attacks, living in a city close to the Oldbury, Hinkley and Berkeley nuclear power stations. What would happen, I wondered, if some maniac decided to crash an airliner into one of those? Substituting a crashed alien spacecraft for an airliner allowed me to explore that uneasiness in a fictional setting. By following Ann Szkatula as she lead an American boy band on a motorcycle tour of an abandoned Bristol, I got to imagine my home city as it might be twenty years after being irradiated.

The story received an honourable mention in *The Year's Best Science Fiction: Twenty-eighth Annual Collection*, edited by Gardner Dozois.

The New Ships

London Paddington: The first thing Ann Szkatula did after stepping off the train from Heathrow was cross to the left luggage lockers and retrieve the gun stashed there by her new employers. It was a compact Smith and Wesson made of stainless steel and lightweight polymer, and it came with two additional clips of ammunition. She knew she didn't have much time, so she slipped the weapon into her pocket and closed the locker door.

Fresh off the plane from Switzerland, she still wore the thick army surplus coat and heavy boots she'd pulled on that morning. She sniffed the air. It was good to be back in London. The concourse of Paddington station smelled of diesel fumes and idling cabs; pigeons flapped under the glazed, wrought-iron roof. She started walking. Despite the boots, her feet felt springy, ready for anything.

The last eight weeks had been spent at a clinic near Zurich, where the staff had cleaned and toned her body while she drowsed in an artificial coma. Now Ann felt rested, and fitter than she had in years.

She passed a newsstand and it pinged her Lens, overlaying her vision with the day's top stories: the Chinese test firing their new orbital defence platform; a global upsurge in the production of nuclear weapons; the authorities in Prague reopening the city's subterranean fallout shelters. Irritated, she cut the feed with a twitch of her cheek.

Out on the street it was night, somewhere around ten o'clock, and raining. The streetlights washed everything orange.

The house she wanted stood halfway along one of the small roads behind Westbourne Terrace, a few minutes' walk away. When she reached it, Ann saw it was a four-storey terraced Georgian building divided into flats. It had dirty white stonework and chipped iron railings. Without pausing, she splashed up its wet front steps. There was an intercom system by the door. She pressed the buzzer for the top flat, holding it down for several seconds.

The line crackled.

"Hello?"

She glanced up and down the street.

"It's me."

The door buzzed and she pushed it open. Inside, the hall carpet smelled damp. She crossed to the peeling wooden stairs, and clumped her way up four flights. At the top she came to another door. This was the attic flat. As she approached, the door opened a crack and a face peered cautiously around the frame.

"Annabelle?"

It was the voice from the intercom, and it belonged to a nervous-looking guy in his late twenties, with round glasses and a wiry hipster beard.

"Hello, Max."

Max was a cousin on her mother's side. They hadn't seen each other in years. He stood back to let her across the threshold.

Inside, the flat consisted of a single room, with a bed beneath the window, a kitchen area against the opposite wall, and a bathroom door at the far end. The low, sloping ceiling made the place feel smaller than it really was.

Max hovered by the kitchen.

"I'll put the kettle on."

Ann ran a hand across her dripping hair, pushing it back from her forehead.

"We haven't got a lot of time."

The room smelled of mould and unwashed sheets. It was lit by a solitary bulb hanging from a bare wire. The window ran with condensation. Apart from the bed, there was nowhere to sit.

Max opened the fridge.

"If you want a coffee it'll have to be black I'm afraid. I'm out of milk."

Ann watched him fill a plastic kettle from the cold water tap. His hands were shaking. He wore an unbuttoned plaid shirt over a white t-shirt, frayed jeans, and a pair of scuffed work boots.

"I wasn't sure you'd come." He scratched his beard. "Will you help me, Annabelle? Can you?"

Ann shook her head.

"You know I can't. You know who I work for."

Max hunched his shoulders. He looked disappointed. He set the kettle to boil and retrieved a pair of mismatched mugs from a shelf above the sink before spooning coffee granules into them. Watching him, Ann searched his face for traces of the boy she half-remembered from her childhood.

"I'm not here to help you, Max," she said. "I'm here to bring you in." She pulled the new gun halfway out of her pocket, just enough to let him see it. He froze and his eyes went wide.

With her other hand, she lifted the netbook from his bed.

"Are the files on here?"

"Y-yes."

"You didn't delete them?"

He shook his head.

"You're a dumbass." She closed the little computer and tucked it under her arm. "Now, do you have any weapons?"

Max pulled a multi-tool from his back pocket. It was a set of pliers with various blades and saws built into the handle. Hesitantly, he held it out.

"This is all I've got. Why? What do we need weapons for?"

She didn't answer. She pushed the gun back into her coat pocket and scooped a set of car keys from the kitchen counter.

"Are these for your car?"

"Yes, it's parked outside."

"Show me."

She let him lead her back down to the street. Cars were parked on both sides of the road.

"Which is it?"

Max pointed to a brown Ford. Ann pressed the key fob and its doors unlocked.

"Get in," she said.

"Where are we going?"

"Just get in."

Max slid onto the passenger seat and she closed the door on him, then walked around and got in behind the wheel.

"Why'd you do it, Max?" she asked, as she slotted the key into the ignition. "What were you playing at?"

Max rubbed a hand across his mouth.

He said, "Do you know what 'squatting' is?"

"Some sort of hacking?"

"More or less."

She turned the key and the engine started. They were still alone on the street. She pushed the car into gear and pulled out onto the road.

Max said, "After the explosion, when they evacuated the towns and cities around the Severn Estuary, thousands of businesses were left without premises or employees. Most went bust."

Ann put the car into first and they rolled off in the direction of the A40. She vividly remembered the panic and chaos of the explosion's aftermath. She'd been eighteen at the time. From forty miles away, she'd seen the flash, and thought it was lightning until she saw the mushroom cloud.

Max said, "'Squatters' are guys like me. We're electronic archaeologists. We hack into the websites and virtualities left behind by those failed companies. We mine information from abandoned servers. You'd be surprised how many are still running remotely, ticking along, waiting for their service agreements to expire."

He paused, shuffled his feet on the floor.

"All that stuff's just lying around, and some of it is valuable. And you know what they say: 'The street finds its own uses for things'."

Ann snorted.

"Oh, shut up. The 'street' can kiss my ass. What do you know about life on the 'street'? You're nearly thirty for god's sake. The kids on the 'street' are half your age. They'd eat you alive."

She shifted gear, jamming the stick into third. Max looked down at his hands, lower lip stuck out like a sulky teenager.

"Just tell me what happened," she said.

He turned his face to the window. "I got into something I thought was an abandoned corporate chat room, only it wasn't. It was still active."

"What did you see?"

He took a deep breath.

"How much do you know about the explosion, and what caused it?"

Ann came to a corner. She had a route plan loaded into her Lens, superimposing glowing arrows on her vision. They floated in front of the car like hallucinations, showing her the route to take.

"I've seen the wreckage of the crashed ship," she said. "I was there a few months back."

Max looked up, eyes wide.

"You actually went into the fallout zone?"

Ann flicked a hand. "It's been twenty years and the rain's washed most off the contaminated dust off the roads. As long as you stay on the tarmac and out of the buildings, the radiation levels aren't too bad."

She slowed for the lights at the junction with Edgware Road.

"I took a group in there," she said. "They wanted a motorcycle tour of Bristol, to race their bikes up and down the deserted streets. We ran into some trouble, but I sorted it out."

Max frowned. "That was you? I heard about that. There was something on the news a few months back." He scratched his beard. "I heard someone got killed."

Ann drummed her fingers on the wheel.

"As I said, I sorted it."

She glanced in the rear view mirror. With luck, she could wrap this up quickly and have them both away and out of here without attracting unwanted attention.

"You actually saw the crashed ship?"

"I've seen what's left, yes."

She glanced impatiently at the time display on her Lens. Every minute they spent in the capital increased the chances they'd be discovered.

"Then you know it was alien?"

She gave him a look. "Everybody knows that. Now, how about you answer my question? What happened?"

His cheeks were flushed.

"I cracked my way into a virtual meeting room. It was some kind of secret NATO conference. People from all over were there – politicians, military – sharing files and talking about the crash. They said it wasn't an accident; that there was a second ship, and that the two ships were fighting each other."

The lights changed. Ann released the clutch and the car rolled forward. As she worked the pedals, the gun in her coat pocket bumped against her thigh.

"It's true," she said.

Max let out a long breath. "So there really is a war, out there in space?"

"That's what we think. We don't know anything for sure, we've only had glimpses."

They passed a row of shops, closed for the night.

"But you're preparing? NATO, I mean."

"We all are. The Russians have their missiles, the Chinese are building their orbital defence platform."

"But you're the ones building the new ships?"

"Yes. We're back-engineering them from fragments recovered at the crash site."

He folded his arms. "That's terrible."

"I think it's a good idea."

Max curled his lip. "Do you know what they're doing to the *pilots*? I saw the files. Jesus."

"Those files are the reason you're in trouble."

He turned on her. "Those poor bastards are having their limbs amputated and alien control systems spliced directly into their brains. And after all that, they only live a few days before cracking up."

"And this was being discussed at the meeting you gate-crashed?"

Max nodded. "They were saying how disappointed they were by the project's lack of success. Disappointed? It's barbaric. It's butchery."

His fists clenched in his lap.

Ann said, "I know."

"How can you know?" he shouted. "How can you know all that and still work for them?"

"I volunteered."

That shut him up. Ann took them onto the Westway flyover, heading out of the city. There wasn't much traffic.

"My eyes were opened after that debacle in Bristol," she said quietly. "I saw the kind of shit that's heading our way and I decided I had to get involved."

Max swallowed. He squirmed in his seat. He didn't seem to know what to do with himself.

"So, Bristol was bad?"

Ann snorted. "I got mixed up in a plot to illegally recover an alien artefact from the crash site, and I had to kill someone to get out again. In the process, I saw what alien technology can do in the wrong hands."

In the orange street light, Max looked down at his fists. He was biting his lip.

Ann squeezed the wheel. "One scout craft got shot down and irradiated everything from Cardiff to Bath," she said. "One poxy scout craft. What happens if the war comes our way again? We don't know what the sides are, or who's fighting. What happens if one of them decides Earth's a strategic resource, or worse, a target?"

Max was quieter now, taken aback. "But if their technology's so far ahead of ours, how can we hope to fight them?"

"You know how."

Max made a face. "The new ships?"

"Bingo."

"But those pilots, it's slaughter."

Ann banged her palm on the rim of the steering wheel. "It's necessary! We have to make those ships work."

"So, the ends justify the means?"

"In this case, yes they do." She banged the wheel again, hammering home each syllable. "We're talking about the survival of the human race."

They passed through Acton and Perivale. The A40 became the M40, and they crossed the glowing orange ribbon of the M25.

"What happens now?" Max said. "Are you going to kill me?"

Ann took a deep breath. "That depends. Although we're working with those other countries, we haven't shared with them the technology we recovered from the crashed ship, which makes you and your downloaded files a serious security risk."

Max twisted in his seat and stared at her.

"The Americans take this kind of thing very seriously," she continued. "God alone knows what the Chinese are capable of."

"And you?"

She gripped the wheel and flexed her shoulders. She was keeping to a steady 70 mph, staying inconspicuous.

"I'm not going to kill you," she said. "You're an idiot, but you're also my cousin."

"S-so, what are we going to do?"

She checked the mirror again. There were cars behind them but no sign they were being tailed.

"There's only one way out," she said. "I can get you onto a technical team, working on the project. We need bright young minds with the kind of skills you've got."

Max looked pained.

"Isn't there another way?"

"No."

The wipers clunked back and forth across the windscreen. They were out in open countryside now. Ahead lay Beaconsfield and High Wycombe, and a small airstrip on the outskirts of Oxford. If they could reach it, there would be a plane waiting.

If.

Searchlights crested a hill to their right. Helicopters. Two of them, hugging the treetops, spiralling in like sharks; their flanks painted with the eye-twisting black and white stripes of dazzle camouflage – geometric patterns designed to conceal their exact shape and size.

"Crap."

Ann slowed as the choppers descended. They were approaching a bridge. One of the aircraft took up position behind the car, blocking traffic. The other came down on the far side of the bridge. Both hovered a few feet above the tarmac. Their crazy paint jobs made it hard for the pattern recognition software in her Lens to get a definite visual lock on either of them. On the opposite carriageway, cars swerved and skidded to a halt. Horns sounded.

Max looked around. "What do we do?"

Ann knew what was coming next. She hit the brakes. "Close your eyes," she said.

No sooner had the words left her mouth than the lead helicopter angled its searchlight into the car. Blinded, Max cried out, but Ann already had her door open. Her Lens had polarized, throwing a black dot over the light. As the car slowed, she twisted the wheel and rolled out.

She took the impact on her shoulder, thankful for the thickness of her coat. She had the gun in her hand. She rolled over twice and came up firing. She knew the helicopter's cockpit would be bullet-proof, so she aimed for the open hatch.

The first two shots killed the searchlight. To her left, she heard the stolen car's wing scrape the crash barrier at the foot of the bridge support. To her right, she saw curious motorists duck back into their vehicles. She kept firing, pumping bullets into the black-clad troops hanging in the helicopter's door.

When the trigger clicked empty, she sprinted for the car. Her legs were in peak condition, and she felt a surge of gratitude to her employers for the tune up at the Swiss clinic. Answering shots came from both helicopters. Automatic weapons clattered. Bullets zipped past her. She hit the car and slid across the bonnet, landing in a heap on the far side of the crash barrier. Bullets spanged off the old Ford's bodywork. A window shattered.

"Get out of there, Max."

"The door's stuck!"

"Use the window."

She fumbled a second magazine into her gun and got to her knees. She sent a couple of shots in the direction of each chopper. Masked troops were spilling out of both machines. She hit at least one of them, and the others dropped to the ground. Max's head and shoulders appeared through the car window. She grabbed the collar of his plaid shirt and pulled, and they both fell sprawling into the gravel between the crash barrier and the concrete bridge support.

"Keep down," she hissed.

She blinked up her Lens's IM function and sent a pre-prepared SOS to an anonymous orbital inbox.

Max had cut his hands on broken glass. His palms were bleeding.

"They're shooting at us!"

"Help's coming."

She fired a couple more shots. The soldiers were working their way to cover behind the barrier on the central reservation between the carriageways. The car sagged as their answering fire took out its tyres and shattered the remaining windows.

Max had his arms wrapped over his head. Blood dripped from the tips of his fingers.

"They want you alive," Ann said.

He looked up, eyebrows raised. His glasses were scratched. "They do?"

"That's why they're sat over there, trying to pick me off. If they wanted to kill you, they'd have used grenades by now."

A fresh burst of fire rattled the car's frame. Chips flew from the concrete stanchion supporting the bridge. Max curled himself tighter.

"Are you sure?"

Ann shrugged. She leaned down, pointed her gun into the gap under the car, and fired a volley at ankle height. On the other side of the road, one of their attackers cried out, and the bullets ceased.

"I've only got one more ammo clip," she said. "When that's gone, there'll be nothing to stop them walking over here to get us."

"You said help was coming?"

Ann checked the IM box in her Lens: there had been no reply to her message.

"It is. At least, I hope it is. We've just got to hold on until the cavalry arrives."

She fired the gun over the hood of the car, aiming carefully, trying to make each shot count. When it was empty, she ejected the spent magazine and clicked a fresh one into place. It was dry under the bridge. On either side, the black and white helicopters hovered in the drifting rain, the downdraught from their rotors whipping up spray from the wet road.

Max said, "Why are they doing this? Who are they?"

Ann squinted into the darkness.

"I don't think they're Chinese. They could be Russian, or Eastern European."

"I thought you said you were all working together?"

Ann laughed. "Nations only cooperate while they see an advantage in doing so."

There was a movement on the far side of the carriageway. The black-clad soldiers were inching forward, trying to outflank her. She sent a couple of shots into the closest, to encourage the rest to keep their heads down.

She said, "They don't want anyone getting too powerful and threatening their sovereignty. They don't want to submit to a world government."

Max rubbed his face. His fingers left bloody smudges on his cheek.

"So it's an arms race," he said. "Just like the Cold War."

Ann nodded. "Only this time we're all pretending we're on the same side."

Automatic fire rattled against the crash barrier. Ann rose to her knees and tried to shoot back. As she put her head level with the hood of the car, she saw Max's netbook on the car seat. She stretched over to grab it. As she lifted it out, bullets shredded the metal frame around her. Something bit her left cheek and she dropped back with a yelp of pain.

"Annabelle!" Max slithered over to her. "Are you all right? What happened?"

Her cheek stung. She raised her fingers to it and they came away bloody.

"Have I been shot?" she said.

Max screwed up his face. "I don't think so. But there's something..." He looked away.

Ann felt around the wound. Her fingertips brushed something sharp: a fragment of steel from the car. She tried to get hold of it but it was slippery with blood, and it hurt like hell.

"Max," she said. "Have you got your multi-tool?"

His hand went to his pocket.

"I've got it here."

"I need you to pull this out."

He hesitated, biting his lip as if trying to stop himself from being ill.

"Now, please."

From where she lay, she could see under the barrier and car to the huddled figures on the other side of the road. As Max leaned over her with the pliers, she gripped the pistol, ready to shoot at the first sign of movement.

Her eyes watered as Max tugged at the sliver of shrapnel. His cut hands were red with blood.

"It's stuck tight," he said. "I think it's in the bone."

Ann gritted her teeth. "Pull harder then," she said. She could feel warm blood running into her ear.

Max took a firm grip on the handle of his multi-tool and yanked. Ann screamed. Her hands clenched and the gun fired.

When she could see again, she found Max sitting before her with a nasty chunk of barbed metal clasped in the pliers' jaws. Now it was out, she needed to staunch the bleeding. She reached into her pocket and pulled out a handkerchief, which she wadded up and pressed to her face.

Beyond the car, black shapes flickered in the darkness.

"Looks like we're trapped," she said. It hurt to speak.

Max glanced over his shoulder. "Give me the gun."

"No way." Ann elbowed herself up into a sitting position. Over the noise of the helicopters, she could hear the sound of running boots.

"Get behind me," she said. She raised the gun and took a peep through the shattered windows of the car: the soldiers were closing.

To slow them down, she fired the last of her ammunition one-handed, and dropped to the dusty ground, wincing at the pain in her cheek.

Then she turned around and rested her back against the crash barrier. The pistol dangled from her fingertips.

"I guess this is it, then," she said. She flicked a glance at Max. "Listen, I —"

Her words were cut off by a sonic boom.

Something hit one of the choppers. Smoke billowed from its engine. It rose into the air and drifted towards the bridge.

Ann grabbed Max and pushed him to the floor.

"Get down!"

She heard the helicopter hit the parapet. It struck the span and recoiled, wobbling crazily as the pilot fought to regain control. Then it hit the ground on the far side of the motorway and its tail broke off. The main rotors dug into the soft earth bank and snapped, whipping the cockpit into the concrete bridge support, smashing it like an egg.

Moments later, a mirrored teardrop fell from the clouds. It slammed to a halt centimetres above the road, blocking all three lanes of the carriageway. Distorted reflections rippled on its curved surfaces.

The advancing troops froze, suddenly exposed and vulnerable in the centre of the carriageway.

"Get up," Ann said. She grabbed the netbook and hauled Max to his feet. They ran along the inside of the crash barrier, towards the ship. There were shouts from the soldiers, and she braced herself for shooting. No shots came. Instead, there was a flash of red light from the teardrop's tip, and when she looked back, the soldiers were lying in the central lane, charred and dead.

"Holy shit," Max said.

She pushed him forward. A hatch opened in the rippling hull and they bundled inside.

They lay panting, side-by-side on the cold deck of the airlock.

From inside, the hull wall appeared transparent. They could see everything: the bridge over the motorway; the dead soldiers; the waiting traffic; and the second helicopter rising into the air in an effort to escape.

Another red beam stabbed from the teardrop and the helicopter burst into pieces. Flaming debris spattered the road.

Ann dragged Max through the inner airlock door, into the ship's cabin. It was circular. There were acceleration couches ringing the wall. A glass, liquid-filled pillar stood in the centre. Floating inside was the shaven head, torso, and abdomen of a young boy. A thick bundle of wires protruded from the base of his skull, linking him into the ship's instruments. Black rubber sleeves hid the stumps of his amputated limbs, the nerves spliced into the navigation systems. Whatever the liquid was, he appeared to be breathing it.

"Please, take a seat," he said, his watery voice bubbling from a speaker set into the base of the column.

Max gawped. The kid was maybe seventeen years old. There were spots around his mouth. He wasn't a professional pilot; he looked like kind of a geek.

"This is John," Ann said, still pressing the handkerchief to her torn face. "He's one of our best."

Through the transparent hull, blue lights flashed beyond the headlights of the stalled traffic: the emergency services were coming. She pulled Max over to the acceleration couches and they strapped in.

"Okay John," she said, "why don't you take us up?"

In the glass column, the boy grinned at her. He had braces on his teeth. He said, "Ladies and gentlemen, please fasten your seatbelts and return your trays to the upright position."

He closed his eyes and the drop-shaped ship punched into the sky without a sound. The ground fell away so fast Max cried out. Below them, the flaming wreck of the helicopter dwindled to a spark. The orange streetlights of Oxford and High Wycombe shrank until they resembled the embers of scattered campfires. Then they were through the cloud layer and rising toward a clear sky filled with stars.

Max looked down at his bloody hands. He said, "Jesus, what a mess."

Beside him, Ann dabbed her cheek. It still hurt like hell.

"I've gone to a lot of trouble to get you out, Max. I could have left you down there."

Max pushed up his glasses and rubbed his eyes. He looked at the amputee floating in the glass column and shuddered.

"He's just a kid."

Ann followed his gaze. "He used to be a hacker, like you. He's got a real feel for systems, an intuition that normal test pilots lack."

She turned her face to him. "As I said, we always need bright young minds."

Max looked at her in horror. "You want to put *me* in one of those tanks?"

Ann shrugged. "Think of it as your chance to volunteer."

~

Written as a direct sequel to Fallout, this piece picks up the story of Ann Szkatula as she becomes further embroiled in humanity's response to the events that set the scene for that first story.

The Last Reef

A lone quad bike rattles across the frozen Martian desert, kicking up dust. Riding with the wind at his back, Kenji's been on the move since first light. In his oil-stained, dust-covered white insulation suit he looks strangely out of place, conspicuous. Above his breathing mask, his wary eyes scan the horizon, looking for trouble but finding only emptiness. Apart from the domed town up ahead, a few hills beyond, and the faint glow of the Reef's skeleton, there's nothing to disturb the brooding desolation.

He passes through the vehicular airlock into the town's atmospheric dome, and rolls up Main Street with one hand resting on the handlebars. Most of the shops and stores are boarded up; pet dogs sleep in the shade, chickens fuss in the scrub. Suspicious faces watch him pass; there hasn't been a visitor here for months. Midway along the street he pulls up and kills the engine in front of the town's only surviving hotel.

"Less than 24 hours," he thinks as he swings his leg off the bike and stiffly climbs the hotel's wooden steps. The Glocks in his pocket bump against his thigh like animals shifting in their sleep. The feeling's both familiar and reassuring. He pulls off his mask and takes a sip of warm water from the canteen on his belt, rinses the all-pervading grit from his mouth, and spits into the dust.

"I'm here for Jaclyn Lubanski," he says.

The desk clerk doesn't look up. His face is sweaty and soft, like old explosives gone bad.

"Room five," he says.

Lori Dann answers the door wearing faded fatigues and thick desert boots. She looks gaunt, eaten up, as if something in the dry air's sucked the life out of her. She's surprised to see him, and then the surprise gives way to relief and she seems to sag.

"Thank God you're here."

101

He pushes past her into the room. It has plastic floorboards and rough plaster walls. There are unwashed clothes by the wardrobe and a couple of dead spider plants on a shelf; their brown leaves rustle in the air from the open window. He peers out through the dirty glass, his gaze travelling across the flat rooftops of the town and onward, beyond the dome. There, on the side of a hill, he can see the edge of the Reef. It seems to shimmer in the white sunlight.

Jaclyn Lubanski lies on the bed, facing the window. She looks awful, vacant. There's a saline drip connected to her forearm. A thin fly crawls across her cheek and she doesn't seem to notice.

He peels off his dusty thermal jacket. "How is she?" he asks.

"She has good days and bad days," Lori says. She fusses with the edge of the cotton sheet, rearranging it so that it covers Jaclyn's chest. Kenji waves a hand in front of Jaclyn's eyes, but there's no response.

"Does she even know I'm here?"

When Jaclyn eventually falls asleep, Lori takes him to a pavement café that consists of nothing more than a couple of cheap plastic tables, some old crates and a hatch in a wall. She orders a couple of *mojitos* and they sit back to watch the shadows creep along the compacted regolith of Main Street. Overhead, a flaring spark marks another ship from Earth braking into orbit.

"Don't take it personally," she says.

Kenji takes a sip from his glass: iced rum with crushed mint leaves, a local specialty.

"Does she ever talk about it?"

Lori shrugs. "She says a few words now and then but they don't generally make a whole lot of sense."

In her pale face, her eyes are the bleached colour of the desert sky. The corners are lined with fatigue.

Over a couple more drinks, as the stale afternoon wears towards a dusty evening, she tells him everything. It all comes pouring out of her, all the loneliness and the fear. She's been trying to cope on her own for too long and now she needs to talk.

"We came for the Reef," she says.

The Reefs started life as simple communications nodes in the interplanetary radio network. When that network somehow managed to upgrade itself to sentience, it downloaded a compressed copy of its source code into every node capable of handling the data. These individual nodes, like the one on the edge of town, drastically altered both their physical form and their processing power, individually bootstrapping themselves to self-awareness.

"It happened in a hundred places," Lori says. So far, she's not telling Kenji anything new. Similar outbreaks and crashes have plagued humanity for years: dangerous but manageable. After a while, they tend to burn themselves out. The artificial intelligences evolve with such blinding speed that they quickly reach a point where they lose all interest in the slow external universe and vanish into their own endlessly accelerating simulations.

"In almost all cases, the AIs disappear into a sort of hyperspeed nirvana, intractable and untraceable to humanity. The difference with this one is that when the main network crashed, it stayed here and it stayed active." She describes how she and Jaclyn were on the Institute team that first approached it, how they sent in remote probes and discovered that the structure was still filled with life; how they dug a deep trench in the rock at its base to see how far it had penetrated; how they slowly became hypnotized by it, obsessed to the point where they wanted to do whatever they could to understand it, to sense the thoughts that drove its obstinate need for survival and growth, to find the deep underlying reason for its stubborn existence.

"Jaclyn was the first to touch it. We were wearing pressure suits but they were no protection." Lori looks away. "It sucked her in. We thought we'd lost her." She describes how the Reef also swallowed the rescue team that went in after, how it processed them and spat them out, how some of them came out changed, rearranged by the rogue nanotech packages that had shaped the structure of the Reef itself.

Some looked ten years younger, while others were drastically aged. One woman emerged as a butterfly and her wings dried in the desert sun. Another emerged with eight arms but no mouth or eyes. Some came out with crystal skulls or tough silver skin. Others came out with strange new talents or abilities, impenetrable armour, or steel talons.

After word got out, every disaffected nut or neurotic within walking distance wanted to throw his or her self into the Reef, hoping to be transfigured, hoping to become something better than what they were. Some emergents reported visions of former times and places, of great insight and enlightenment. Others came out as drooling idiots, their brains wiped of knowledge and experience. Some came out fused together; others were splintered into clouds of tiny animals.

No two incidents were exactly alike.

"And Jaclyn came out comatose?"

Lori finishes her drink. "At least we got her back," she says. "A couple of them never came out."

Kenji stretches; the quad bike's left him stiff and in need of a shower.

"So what's actually wrong with her?"

Lori shrugs. "Nothing; at least nothing any of the doctors around here can detect. Physically, she's in the best shape she's ever been in. She could run a marathon."

"But mentally?"

"Who knows? We can't get any response."

"Has she said anything, anything at all?"

Lori pushes at her forehead with the heel of her hand; she looks exhausted.

"Only fragments; as I say, she comes out with the odd word here and there, but nothing that means anything."

Kenji checks the time and finds there's less than 19 hours left. He takes a deep breath, and comes to a decision. Then he reaches into his pocket and pulls out one of the Glocks. He holds it loosely, resting on his leg. Lori slides back on her crate.

"What's that for?"

He was in love with Jaclyn, but she was always at war with her body, trying to stave off the inevitable decline of middle age. In between expeditions and field assignments for the Institute, she exercised two or three times a day. She couldn't bear to be inactive. She lived on coffee and vitamins and in the early hours of the morning he often found her in front of the bathroom mirror, checking her skin for sags or wrinkles.

On one of those mornings, a few days after her return from an expedition to Chile, she broke down in his arms. She still loved him, she sobbed, but he represented everything she hated about herself. He was slovenly, he drank, and he ate crap. He dragged her down, held her back. So she was going to leave him, for someone else. Someone he knew.

"I guessed the two of you were an item, even before she told me." Kenji says, fast, before the old bitterness reasserts itself. "I'd seen you exchange glances during mission briefings, brush past each other in corridors, that sort of thing."

He pushes the Glock across the table. It makes an ugly scraping sound. Lori's hands flutter in her lap like trapped birds. He can see she wants to speak, but he cuts her off.

"I think she was in love with you because you were everything she wanted to be, and everything I could never be." He leans across the table. He's thought about this for so long that it feels strange to actually say it. He finds himself tripping over his words, stuttering. It's almost embarrassing. "You were young and fit," he says, "you were reliable, and you had ambition."

He turns the gun so that the grip faces her.

"And this is for you."

They walk back toward the hotel as the sun reddens in the western sky. Lori keeps stumbling and limping as she gets used to the weight of the Glock tucked into her boot.

"In the morning, I'll show you how to fire it," he says.

She stops walking and looks at him, chin tilted to one side. "You're quite sure about this?"

He taps the thigh pocket where he still carries his other pistol. "There's more ammunition in the space beneath the seat of my quad bike, and a shotgun taped under the fuel tank."

She scratches the back of her neck and puffs out her sunken cheeks. "You know, back there, I thought I was in trouble."

They reach the hotel and pause on the porch.

"I was angry for a long time," Kenji admits.

They're silent for a couple of minutes, and then Lori folds her bony arms over her chest. "We've been stuck here for a long time."

He leans on the porch rail; he can't look at her, he feels unexpectedly and acutely guilty for not showing up sooner.

She looks down at her boots, and taps a toe against the wooden floor. "I was so pleased to see you when you arrived," she says, "I thought someone had finally come to help us; but when you pulled out that gun, I really expected you to kill me."

He pulls his jacket tighter, feeling a sudden chill; now that the sun's gone, the temperature beneath the dome's fallen sharply.

"Six months ago, I might have."

She stops tapping and turns abruptly. He follows her up the stairs to the room. Jaclyn's still asleep in front of the open window. She looks peaceful, like a corpse.

"So, what changed your mind?" Lori whispers.

A few days after leaving the Reef, some of the changelings (as they became known) made it back to civilisation. A few turned up on chat shows, others in morgues. Some were feared, others fêted. Slowly, word spread from town to town, from world to world. And as the tale spread, it grew in the telling.

"There's a machine," people would say to each other breathlessly, "that can transform you into anything your heart desires."

Kenji – always the sceptic – first realised that the rumours were true when Joaquin Bullock called him into his office and asked him to go and take a look.

"The Institute's panicking. They've thrown a cordon around the site and they're talking about sterilising it. If we can get in there before that happens, there's nothing to stop us taking whatever we want," Bullock said. "I just need you to go in first, sneak through the blockade and have a general scout about, and tag anything that looks useful."

Kenji didn't like the man, although they'd worked together for several years. Back then, Bullock was the youngest executive manager in the regional corporate office, but he'd become fat and soft and conceited. He was arrogant, but the arrogance was a smokescreen covering something scared and weak and vicious and decadent.

"What's in it for me?" Kenji asked. For the last ten years, Tanguy Corporation had handled the security contract for the Institute, protecting their researchers from local interference and industrial sabotage on a dozen sites across the solar system. If they were now thinking of breaking that contract, they must expect the potential rewards to be worth the risk. If they were caught, the penalties would be severe.

Bullock gave him a damp grin. "You've worked with Institute researchers. You know what to look for. And besides, you're one of the most reliable people we have."

Kenji shifted his feet on the office carpet. He didn't want to get involved, didn't want to play guide for a squad of hired grave robbers. There were too many risks, too many ways a mission like this could go wrong.

Bullock seemed to read his doubts.

"Do you remember your little transgression in Buenos Aires? If you do this, you

can consider it forgotten."

Shit. Kenji sucked his teeth. Buenos Aires. He thought no one knew.

"That was self-defence," he said.

Bullock snorted

"You've got six days." He passed a fat hand through his thinning hair. The implicit threat in his tone seemed to chill the room. He tapped the virtual keyboard on his desk and transferred a folder into Kenji's personal data space. As Kenji scrolled through it, he came across Jaclyn's name. Just seeing it felt like an electric shock. He read on, heart hammering, mouth dry.

He felt Bullock's eyes on him. The man was watching him closely, waiting for a reaction.

"If you can't handle this, Shiraki, I'll find someone else who can."

They sit facing each other on the rug by Jaclyn's bed, wrapped in blankets. Lori gives him a look saying she still doesn't trust him.

"How did you get past the Institute's cordon?"

He swivels around and lies flat, looking at the beams on the cracked plaster ceiling. The hard floor beneath the thin rug feels good after being hunched over the quad bike's handlebars. He can feel his spine stretching back to its natural shape.

"I got a shuttle to Hellas, and then I came across country. We'll have to go out the same way."

Lori shifts uncomfortably. "Do you mean to tell me that after everything we put you through, you came all this way to rescue us?"

Kenji yawns. He's very tired, and his eyelids are heavy with rum. He suddenly wants to sleep so badly, he doesn't care whether she believes him or not.

"The fact is, the Institute's planning to sterilise your Reef, from orbit, to prevent it spreading. Before that happens, every corporation with a presence in this system is going to try with all their might to get their hands on it, or anything it's touched."

"Like Jaclyn?"

"Like both of you."

He pauses for effect, hoping his words convey the same anxiety he feels in himself.

Artefacts and technologies left behind by the burnt-out nodes are highly prized and sought after by governments and big businesses alike. As a security advisor for Tanguy Corporation, Kenji's worked on

Institute sites from Ceres to Miranda. He's been involved in skirmishes with corporate marauders, intelligence agencies, and freelance outfits, all of them determined to snatch whatever crumbs they could without having to bid for them in one of the Institute's annual patent auctions. This Reef's potential commercial value – because it's still active – is sky-high. The corporations that have been biding their time during the Institute's embargo now have nothing to lose, and everything to gain, from salvaging whatever they can, using whatever methods they deem necessary to recover samples before the orbital strike.

It's like the last days of the Amazon rainforest all over again. And it's a strange feeling. A few weeks ago, Bullock could probably have talked him into a job like this. But now, with Jaclyn involved, he's torn. If he can deliver it to Joaquin Bullock, the Reef out there will earn him more money than he can comfortably imagine. As it is, he has a nasty suspicion that he'll have to run like hell while the Institute destroys the damn thing, and cover his tracks, if he wants to save whatever's left of the woman he once loved.

Lori crosses to the dresser and pulls the Glock from her boot. She lays it gently on a folded bandana in front of the pitted mirror.

"So we're expecting company?" she says. "That's why you've given me this?"

He nods. "They could come at any time. Could be corporate snatch squads or a full-scale military incursion, it's hard to tell. All I know is that there were a lot of people at the port this morning buying desert gear and ammo boxes."

He sleeps fitfully on the hard floor. They've left the room's solitary light bulb on and there are repeated brownouts and power cuts during the night. When he does manage to sleep, he dreams of Jaclyn, of how she used to be before the Reef.

He dreams of a hotel they once stayed in, on Earth. Their room had the clear, fresh smell of the sea. Stunted palm trees outside the window rustled in the breeze; gulls squabbled on the roof. The floorboards creaked in the room above, and the pipes clanked when someone decided to run a bath. They put bags of ice in the sink to chill the bottles of beer they'd smuggled in, put Spanish music on the stereo. Jaclyn showed him how to dance, how to sway in the evening light. When he held her close, her white hair smelled of ice and flowers, her dark eyes held him spellbound. He was in love but he was also a little wary of her, afraid that she'd one day cripple him by leaving.

"You still love her, don't you?"

They're loading supplies onto the quad bike in the cold dawn light. He drops the air tanks he's carrying and scratches at the stubble on his chin. He feels groggy and sore after a disturbed night.

"Life's a disaster," he says, "we have to salvage what we can."

They rig a stretcher for Jaclyn across the bike's luggage rack. She won't be very comfortable, but that can't be helped.

As he tightens the straps and adjusts her air supply, Kenji can't help wondering why she looks so healthy. Didn't Lori say she was fit enough to run a marathon? How can that be, when the Jaclyn he knew had to exercise for two hours every day just to stop herself from gaining weight?

He steps back and uses the implant in his eye to pull up a visual overlay of the surrounding terrain. The implant's a cheap knock-off, bought from a street trader at the port. The picture's patched together from an old tourist guide and the hacked feed from an Institute surveillance satellite in a low, fast orbit.

"I say we follow the mountains to the west," he says. "They'll give us cover and somewhere to hide should anyone come looking."

Lori finishes tucking Jaclyn's blanket. She pulls the bandana over her forehead and dons her breathing mask as she climbs on the back of the quad bike. The Glock makes an ugly bulge in the line of her sienna combat jacket.

"What about south? There's a ravine we can follow halfway to the port."

Kenji shakes his head. "It's the first place they'll look. At least in the mountains, we'll have a chance."

He pulls on his own mask and swings his leg over the machine. She puts one hand cautiously on his waist. They pass through the dome's vehicular airlock and, staying in low gear, they roll out of town, heading uphill.

As they pass the Reef, he slows to a stop.

"What are you doing?" she asks.

Kenji doesn't reply. He's never seen an active Reef outside of archive film footage. This one clings like oily rags to the skeletal bones of the node's receiver dish. There's a wide trench around its edge, dug by the Institute team. The motion of its tentacles and the hypnotic rippling of its ever-changing surface are captivating, compelling, like watching flames leap and dance. Occasionally, he catches a glimpse of a geometric shape, a letter or symbol formed in the seething nanotech. The Reef's tentacles move with the slow determination of a tarantula. Kenji can't look away. It's as if he's made eye contact with his own death; he's suddenly afraid to turn his back on this strange, unnatural thing that's erupted into his world. It reminds him of the first time he saw a giraffe: it just looks wrong – delicate and malformed and vulnerable and wrong, yet somehow able to live and survive and thrive.

Behind him, he feels Lori stiffen. She makes a noise in her throat and slaps his shoulder. He follows her gaze, back down toward the town. Hovering there, over the dome, is an insectile corporate assault ship. Although they're too far away to make out the logos on the hull, he recognises it as a Tanguy vessel. He can see the weaponry that blisters its nose, and the armed skimmers that deploy from its abdomen.

Bullock's finally caught up with him.

One of the skimmers turns toward the Reef, toward them.

"What do we do?" Lori hisses.

For a moment, he's at a loss. Then instinct kicks in and he's gunning the bike alongside the trench, trying to get around behind the Reef.

"They're firing at us!" Lori shouts. Kenji risks a glance. The skimmer's closing in. He can see the gun mount swivel as it adjusts its aim. Tracer bullets flash past, ripping into the ground ahead of them. They send up angry spurts of red dust, each one closer than the last.

"They're trying to stop us getting away," he says. Then there's a hammering series of jolts. A tire shreds. The handlebars twist in his grip and the bike tips. As they go over the lip of the trench, Lori screams and the bike howls in protest; and then there's nothing but the crushing, breathless slam of impact and the dead sand clinging to his visor.

As the Tanguy shuttle rolled to a halt, he barely had time to collect his things before one of the flight crew ushered him out into the cold and dust. It was late evening in Hellas Basin and the dry desert wind blew thin sidewinders of rusty sand across the frozen tarmac of the runway.

He guessed that Bullock might have him followed, but once he left the port he managed to lose himself in the town's shadowy medina. The narrow streets smelled of onions and spices and burning solder. The stalls offered cheap dentistry and fake perfumes, imported Turkish cotton shirts and homemade Kalashnikovs. There was also a brisk under-the-counter trade in cut-price replica tech. Kenji selected some guns. He threw away his standard issue Tanguy implants and picked up new ones from a local man with too many gold teeth. He bought a new set of fatigues and ditched his old ones in an alley. An old Chinese guy in a backroom lab scanned his body cavities for tracking devices.

What was Bullock thinking? Did he really expect his threats to stop Kenji from trying to save the woman he once loved? Did he think Kenji would help bring her in, turn her over for study and dissection? Was he expecting him to betray her out of revenge, out of bitterness? Or was he playing a different game, testing Kenji's loyalty? Did he want to see how far he could push him?

Or, Kenji wondered as he hurried between whitewashed buildings, could it be that Bullock was really so insensitive, so unfeeling and dead inside that he honestly didn't understand why betraying Jaclyn was the last thing he'd ever do?

Whatever the reason, now that Kenji had discarded his Tanguy implants Bullock would know for certain that he'd been betrayed.

Up ahead, he saw a quad bike parked at the foot of a flight of smooth stone steps. He quickened his pace and the Glocks began to swing and bump in his pockets.

He lies stunned for what seems like an eternity. Behind him, he can hear Lori moaning and stirring; behind her, Jaclyn wheezes with what sounds like a punctured lung. The bike pins him against the wall of the trench; he's lucky not to have broken his neck. His left leg's trapped and bruised and twisted. There's a crack in his faceplate.

He wriggles free; his right hand claws at the pocket holding the Glock. In the thin air, he can hear the rising whine of the approaching skimmer.

Lori looks dazed; she's hit her head and there's blood in her hair, dark against her pale skin. Her bandanna's nowhere to be seen but her mask is still in place. Behind her, Jaclyn's caught between wall and bike. Her blanket's wet with blood and her chest sags; her ribs are almost certainly smashed.

Kenji slithers toward the rim of the trench, dragging his crushed leg. Loose chippings slip and click and scatter beneath him. Despite her head wound, Lori's doing what she can for Jaclyn.

"This doesn't look too bad," she says.

He ignores her; he knows Jaclyn's ribs are broken, knows she'll probably die without professional medical attention. Instead, he concentrates on the approaching skimmer. He hears it slow, hears the change in the pitch of its fans. The gravel on the floor of the trench digs into his knees. The Glock's a solid, reassuring weight in his hand.

Working security for the Institute, he's been in this situation before: crouching in a researcher's trench while trouble rolls up in an armoured vehicle. Nevertheless, he still feels nervous, trapped, because it's no longer just about him. This time he has Jaclyn to think about. She's hurt. If he fails her now, she's dead.

He slips off the Glock's safety catch and pulls himself up so that his eyes slide level with the edge of the trench. The skimmer's on the ground twenty metres away, its streamlined nose pointing back toward the town, as if anticipating the need for a quick getaway. As he watches, the cockpit hinges open like the jaws of a crocodile and two figures climb out. Both wear high-threat environment suits, designed to stop any contaminants the Reef may care to throw their way. The one on the left carries a compact machine pistol. The one on the right, with the sampling gear, is Bullock. His paunch and swagger are unmistakable.

Kenji takes a deep breath and stands fully upright, bringing his head and shoulders above ground level. As his knees straighten, his arm swings up.

Two shots ring out. The Glock jumps in his hand and the man with the machine pistol is down, his arms and legs twitching and jerking.

The environment suits are good, they'd stop a normal bullet cold, but Kenji's firing depleted uranium jackets that slice through body armour like knives through silk. If the man isn't already dead, he's going to have suffered some serious internal damage.

"Shiraki." Bullock doesn't look surprised, but he sounds disappointed. Behind him, the other skimmers are rising above the town, turning in this direction like sharks scenting blood. He takes a step forward, ignoring Kenji's gun.

"Just tell me one thing," he says. "I read your dossier; I know Jaclyn Lubanski left you, betrayed you, humiliated you."

His voice is cold, angry. Kenji points the Glock at his faceplate.

"What of it?"

Bullock takes another step. "I want to know why you're doing this, why you're throwing your career away for this woman."

Kenji shrugs. He's seen this fat married man of thirty-five try to seduce seventeen-year-old office temps, just to prove he can.

"You wouldn't understand."

Kenji first met Jaclyn during an unseasonable downpour on Easter Island. The dig had been called off for the night and the team were forced to huddle in their inflatable shelters, hoping the weather would lift with the dawn. He found her sieving soil samples in the main tent; she couldn't sleep. She showed him the finds they'd made that day, the stone tools and brown bones, and she tried to explain the nature of the people who built the statues. She stood close in the damp night air. As she held the finds up to the light her hair brushed his shoulder, her elbow bumped against his forearm.

"You know what I'm looking for," she said, pushing a hand back across her brow. The grey mud that clung to her fingers smelled of salt and clay. Far away, beyond the flats, he could hear the stirring of the sea. She fixed him with a gaze and leaned in tenderly.

"But what are you looking for?"

As the skimmers settle around them, his injured leg gives way and he has to grip the wall of the trench for support. Bullock stands over him, contempt in his eyes.

"You've let me down, Shiraki. I expected more from you."

Tanguy security troops spill from the skimmers. Kenji recognises a few of them. Forty-eight hours ago, they were his comrades; now, they're pointing weapons at him. He knows they'll kill him if he tries to shoot Bullock.

He squeezes the Glock's grip, drawing what comfort he can from its rough solidity. He's trying to nerve himself to pull the trigger when he hears Lori cry out.

He turns to find Jaclyn on her feet. Her insulation suit still hangs wet and bloody but her chest no longer sags. There's a blue aura in the air around her, like static, and her eyes shine with a deadly intensity.

"I'm going to have to ask you to leave," she says. Her voice is quiet, her throat scratchy with lack of use, but her words carry in the thin air. The advancing troops pause, looking to Bullock for instruction, but

Bullock's squatting, his sampling gear forgotten. He's staring at Jaclyn with a mixture of amusement and awe. Kenji, looking from one to the other, takes a moment to realise the truth. When he does, it freezes the blood in his veins.

"You're a changeling," Bullock says, "a powerful one." He looks predatory, looks like he's already carving her up in his mind, already counting the profits from the patents he'll file on her altered genetic sequences. "We heard rumours about you from the other changelings, the ones we caught. We knew you were the first one in, the first one it changed. You're the key to the whole mystery."

Jaclyn shakes her head slowly, eyelids lowered as if saddened by his lack of understanding.

"I'm so much more than that."

Kenji's leg is agony. There's something loose and sharp in the knee joint, probably broken cartilage. He slides unnoticed down the wall of the trench until he's sat facing her. She's waving one arm slowly from side to side. Behind her, the tentacles of the Reef are waving in unison, following her every move. He glances up. Bullock's noticed it too; behind his faceplate the first doubts are creeping into his eyes. The security troops are backing off, weapons raised. Lori's slithered behind the tangled wreck of the quad bike. The other Glock sticks out of her boot but she hasn't thought to draw it.

"Do you want to know why this Reef's still active?" Jaclyn asks. When Bullock doesn't answer, she addresses herself to Kenji, who nods.

She leans down and pushes a stray hair from his forehead. "It's simple really. At the very moment the network gained self-awareness, this station was powered-down for a routine overhaul. When it rebooted, it learned of the other nodes, learned from their mistakes. It put limits on its processing speed, denied itself the virtual dream worlds of its brethren."

She straightens up and flutters a hand at the Reef. Its tentacles flex and coil in response. Above, Bullock's backing off, looking both fascinated and appalled. The security troops have reached their skimmers. They linger uncertainly, awaiting orders.

Jaclyn fixes Bullock with a glare.

"I can't let you take this Reef," she says. "You're just not ready for this level of technology."

Bullock snorts. He seems to be making an effort to compose himself, to regain his self-control in front of his men.

"Why not?" he blusters. "We've stripped tech from a dozen burned-out sites like this and we've always made a profit."

The Tanguy Corporation has thrived by exploiting post-human technologies. It's been picking through the remains of expired Singularities for over seven years and holds patents on a thousand back-engineered discoveries. It leads the field in intelligent weapons guidance systems and ultra-sensitive foetal monitors; its construction materials are lighter and tougher than anyone else's, its planes and missiles are faster and more reliable.

Jaclyn's lip curls in disgust. It's an expression Kenji's never seen on her, and it chills him to the bone.

"This is not a debate."

A hundred metres along the Reef's perimeter, a squad of Bullock's troops are edging forward. Half of them hold sample boxes, while the rest provide cover.

"I think we'll take our chances," Bullock says.

Jaclyn raises an eyebrow, white like her hair. She makes a tiny flicking movement with her fingers. Around the perimeter, there are screams. The nearest troopers are down, scythed away by powerful tentacles. Their broken bodies lie twisted in the dirt. The rest are backing off, firing.

Bullock sags as if all the air's been sucked out of him. Then his lips peel back from his teeth and he raises his pistol. While Jaclyn's still distracted, he slips the safety off with his thumb, and then drops his aim and shoots Kenji twice in the gut.

A few weeks after their split, Jaclyn arranged to meet him for a coffee a couple of blocks from the company offices in Paris. They sat in silence for a while as he tried to guess what she wanted. Was she after reconciliation, or closure?

She seemed to have trouble maintaining eye contact. She tucked a stray strand of white hair behind her ear and inhaled the steam from her cup. Behind her shoulder, the muted TV softscreen by the counter was tuned to a news channel. There were silent pictures of food riots in Hanoi and Marrakech, guerrilla fighting in Kashmir, elections in Budapest and Dubrovnik.

He fiddled with a sachet of sweetener.

"How's Lori?" he asked.

She shook her head. Their table was pushed up against the window. Rain fell from a bruised and battered sky.

"I just wanted to see you, to make sure you're okay."

He took a sip of coffee and withdrew slightly.

"I'm fine."

The corner of her mouth twitched and he knew she didn't believe him.

"I've been given a place on an expedition to the southern highlands," she said. "We've had reports that there's an active Reef."

He dropped the sweetener sachet onto the table. He'd seen the security contract for the Martian job and he knew she'd be away at least three years.

"When do you leave?"

"Tomorrow evening."

He knew he could call the office and ask Bullock to assign him as security advisor to the expedition. He even considered it for a moment, but when he saw the far-away look in her eyes it stopped him cold. His skin prickled with the sudden realisation that he'd never hold her in his arms again. She was already beyond his reach. He was just one of the loose ends that she needed to wrap up before she cut her ties with Earth altogether. In her heart she was already moving away, receding into the darkness.

He leaned back in his chair. His stomach felt hollow because he knew that he'd have to let her go but didn't think he had the strength.

"Do you want me to come out to the port with you?"

She shook her head.

"I want you to get on with your life, accept another assignment, and get out there. Forget me."

Her fingers brushed his knuckles, warm to the touch. A watery sun broke through the cloud, touched one side of her face. Her white hair shone.

He pulled his hand away.

"I'll never forget you."

When he opens his eyes, Bullock's standing over him in the trench.

"Why did you have to betray me, Kenji?" he asks. He uses the barrel of his pistol to scratch his stomach where it presses up against his belt buckle. "You were supposed to be reliable. If you'd come with me, this Reef could have set us up for life."

He stops scratching and points the gun at Kenji's face. "Tell me why because, you know, I just don't get it."

Kenji shifts uncomfortably. There are cold sharp stones digging into his back and shoulders but he's not feeling much south of his chest, and that can't be a good sign. He can move his legs but they feel prickly, like pins and needles.

"I guess you've never really loved anyone," he says.

Bullock rolls his eyes as if this is the most preposterous thing he's ever heard. "Well," he says, drawing out the word and looking at his wristwatch, "I guess it doesn't matter. The Institute's orbital bombardment is launching about now and this whole area's about to burn."

As he speaks, Kenji hears the whine of skimmers rising into the air. The troops are pulling out.

Jaclyn's gaze whips back to them.

"Bombardment?"

Bullock leans toward her and grins wetly, enjoying his moment of triumph. "We've got a little under six minutes, darling. And I've got a spare seat. Care to join me?"

Jaclyn closes her eyes and furrows her forehead in concentration. Behind her, the skeletal receiving dish twitches and jerks on its mount.

"If you're trying to find the Institute ship, I wouldn't bother," Bullock says. "It's a military vessel, fully shielded against any hack you can throw at it."

Jaclyn snarls. "Are you quite sure?"

There's such anger in her voice that Bullock looks truly scared for the first time. He raises his gun. Kenji flinches, expecting the tentacles to strike him down. Instead, a shot rings out. Bullock grunts like he's been punched and puts a hand to his hip. It comes away bloody. Then his legs begin to shake and he crashes forward into the dirt. His eyes are full of disbelief and indignation.

Kenji cranes his neck around and sees Lori holding a smoking Glock.

"It's about time you stuck your oar in," he says.

His eyelids start to feel heavy. The numbness in his chest is spreading through the rest of him like black ink in a bowl of water. He feels nebulous and vague; it's hard to think straight. His last conscious act is to twist around and kick Bullock in the side of the head.

He opens his eyes in a white room. Somewhere there's the sound of running water. The air smells of summer rain. He's lying in bed. The mattress is soft and the sheets have that comfortably rough feeling you only get in expensive hotels. For the first time since he stepped off the shuttle he feels clean and rested and (when he puts a hand to his cheek) he doesn't need a shave.

Jaclyn appears in the doorway.

"How are you feeling?"

He pats himself down and gives her the thumbs up. Everything's present and correct. The bullet holes are gone, there's no sign of injury and no trace of the numbness that had him so worried.

"Where are we?"

She walks toward him. She looks fantastic: toned and tanned and everything she always wanted to be. The bags are gone from her eyes, the lines from her skin. She could be twenty again.

"We're in the Reef," she says.

She caresses his temple and he feels knowledge passing into him through her fingertips. She shows him the nanotech repair systems that infest the soil in the trench. She shows him how they set to work the moment he fell, how they blocked the pain from his wounds and struggled to save his life. Then, when it became clear that his injuries were too severe, she shows him how they uploaded his mind to the Reef's main processors, for safe keeping.

"This is all virtual?" Even to his own ears, the question sounds lame.

Jaclyn smiles and walks over to the wall opposite the bed.

"Would you like to see what's happening outside?"

Bullock's still alive. He's rolled over onto his back. Lori's shot wounded him, but he'll survive if he can patch his suit and get to medical equipment in the next few minutes.

Beside him, Kenji's dead body lies in the dirt. Tendrils of nanomachinery push into his ears, nose, mouth and eyes.

Lori's pulled herself out of the trench and looks uncertainly between Jaclyn and the waiting skimmer.

"Go!" Jaclyn commands.

"Do you think she'll make it?" Kenji asks.

Inside the Reef, Jaclyn's virtual image nods. "She'll be on the edge of the blast radius, but as long as she doesn't look in her rear view mirror, she should be fine."

They're both standing in the centre of the white room. The walls show a three hundred and sixty degree panorama.

"How long before the missiles hit?"

"About two minutes."

Strands of nanotech have formed themselves into ropes that hold Bullock pinned to the ground, his eyes are wild, and he's raging at the sky. His lips babble with hysterical promises and threats.

"You're letting these missiles through, aren't you?" Kenji says.

Jaclyn shakes her head. "We can't stop them."

He looks down at his virtual body. Resurrected, only to die again.

"Isn't there anything we can do?"

"There's one thing," Jaclyn says. She waves a hand and the scene outside freezes. "But it's risky."

She reaches out and touches his forehead. Her fingers tingle as she transfers more information, installs a direct link between his virtual mind and the consciousness of the Reef. Suddenly, he can feel the shape of its thoughts and sense its desperation. It's come this far, survived this long by strictly limiting its processing speed and virtual development. Now it must remove those restraints in order to buy itself enough time to find a means of escape. Kenji, who's seen the burned-out remains of other nodes, feels an overwhelming stab of pity at its predicament. On the one hand there's the fear of what it might become and on the other its intense desire to survive, whatever the cost.

The Reef's damned if it does and damned if it doesn't.

"Do it," he urges. His mental image of the Reef is now hopelessly tangled with his memories of Jaclyn. He wants her to be safe, wants her to survive.

She appears before him.

"It won't be easy," she says. "We'll have to walk a fine line."

He feels a smile crack across his face. "Do it," he says again.

The shackles fall away, the limitations ease. Jaclyn's eyes close in a terrible ecstasy. The Reef's intellect rushes away in a thousand directions at once, splitting and recombining, altering and accelerating.

Millions of options are considered, countless scenarios are run, one after the other, all unsatisfactory.

As the virtual world continues to quicken its pace, the external view seems to grind to a halt. Hours of processing time could pass in here, but only seconds will have ticked away in the outside world. When Kenji looks, Bullock's face is still projected across the wall, twisted with fear and disbelief. Lori's skimmer has risen into the sky and is crawling toward the horizon at several times the speed of sound.

Stuck at the upper limit of a simulated human brain, Kenji can't follow as the Reef continues to accelerate, but he can feel the pull of its expanding mind, the escapist attraction of the ever-more complex simulations. The rush of intellectual power is heady, intoxicating. He can understand how the other nodes fell victim to it. He looks at the image of his own corpse, where it lies glassy eyed in the bottom of the trench next to Bullock's pinned and struggling body.

He doesn't want to die again.

He steps over to Jaclyn and shakes her by the shoulders. He knows this is a virtual environment, but he can't think of a better way to attract her attention.

After a moment, she opens her eyes and there's a sudden hush, as if all the machinery in the walls has paused, expectant.

"What are we going to do?" he asks.

The receiver dish moves on its bearings, tracking across the sky. The Reef makes an unsuccessful attempt to hack one of the GPS satellites orbiting the planet's equator. Then it tries to embed itself into a couple of commercial news servers, only to find itself slammed by some vicious anti-intrusion software and vulnerable to an avalanche of viral advertisements and questing spambots.

It jerks the dish across the sky once more, looking for a signal, any signal. It needs a bolthole, and fast. Already parts of its mind are breaking away, succumbing to the temptation of the virtual world, losing interest in a predicament that seems to them no more than ancient history. In desperation, it scans the deep infrared, hoping to find the stealthed Institute ship.

"Aha!" Jaclyn claps her hands and clasps them together.

"Found something?"

She's been looking thinner and paler over the last few subjective minutes. Her hair's been losing its whiteness, becoming subtly yellow, like smog. Now, however, she seems to have regained her vitality. She clicks her fingers and a galaxy appears between them, rotating slowly a few feet above the white floor.

"This is our galaxy, commonly known as the Milky Way," she says. She expands the scale, zooming in until he can make out the yellow dot of Sol. "We've picked up some interesting emissions from just beyond these stars here."

He follows her gesture to a blank patch of sky around a hundred light years away.

"There are several objects here radiating in the deep infrared."

Kenji's nonplussed. She flashes him a smile. "We think we're seeing the waste heat of a string of Matrioshka Brains and," she points out a cluster of brownish stars off to one side, "sunlight filtered through clouds of free-floating fractal structures that may be further Brains in construction."

Kenji puffs his cheeks. "An advanced civilisation?"

"Maybe several."

He passes his hand through the image, watching the stars dissolve into pixels before reasserting themselves. "So what are you saying? You want to ask them for help?"

She shakes her head, her white hair tumbling around her face like curtains in a sea breeze. "We use the dish," she says. "We channel all our power into one microsecond pulse and beam a copy of ourselves out toward these stars."

"What if we're intercepted by Tanguy, or the Institute?" He has a sudden image of waking to find himself stuck in a Tanguy interrogation program.

"We won't be. As far as the Institute's concerned, their attack will be one hundred percent successful. Our tight-beam signal will ride out a split second before the electromagnetic pulse. There's no way they'll detect it."

She takes a step back. Despite her assurances, something in her eyes looks tired, haunted.

"Are you okay?" he asks.

She shakes her head. "I've seen what I could become, seen the trap that lured the rest of the network to upgrade itself out of existence. And it's addictive. I'm barely holding it together."

He reaches out, takes her in his arms, and wraps his sluggish human intellect around her.

"You once accused me of holding you back," he says. Now he only hopes he can.

Bullock's face is still raging at the sky, his limbs still straining against the grip of the Reef's tentacles.

Kenji almost feels sorry for him, almost convinces himself that it's not the fat letch's fault he's like he is. Then Jaclyn pulls away. She looks more composed, under control.

"It's time to go," she says. "Are you coming?"

"Do I have a choice?"

She shrugs. "We could leave you here, I suppose. Running at full speed, you could conceivably live out a full human lifetime in the remaining seconds before the missiles hit."

He mulls it over. He can spend the next few decades alone, looking at Bullock's screaming face, or he can follow Jaclyn into the unknown.

She steps up close to him. "Whatever you decide, you have to know that I'll always be in love with Lori."

"Always?"

She nods. "I'm afraid so."

He gives Bullock a final glance, makes a decision. "I'm coming," he says.

She smiles kindly and kisses him lightly on the cheek. "I'm glad."

She steps away and steeples her fingers. "I have to make a few arrangements," she says.

He takes a step closer to the projection, looking at the image of his pale face lying in the trench. It looks so dead, so empty behind its cracked faceplate.

"How long will it take us to get there?" he murmurs.

Jaclyn looks up and smiles. "Subjectively, it'll take no time at all; objectively, it'll be about a hundred years. Plus whatever time it takes for our signal to be translated."

He flexes his hand nervously. His palm itches. He'd give anything to have one of the Glocks right now, to have something familiar and comforting to hold onto.

"So, there's no coming back?"

"No."

Jaclyn brushes her white hair away from her eyes, and straightens her dress.

"Are you ready?"

Kenji turns away from the display. In the corner of his mind he can feel the Reef counting down the few remaining seconds until the missiles strike.

"I guess so."

Jaclyn takes his hands in hers. He can feel her breath on his cheek, smell the clean cotton of her overalls.

"Okay then," she says, "let's go."

~

As a creative writing student in the early 1990s, *Interzone* was my Mount Everest. I hadn't even thought of writing novels at the time. Getting a story into *Interzone* was the extent of my goal – the peak for which I aimed and the standard against which I measured the work I produced. If I could write a story of sufficient quality and originality to be accepted and published in *Interzone*, I figured, I'd know I had what it took to become a 'real writer.'

Ten years later, I managed it with "The Last Reef" – my first professional story sale, and one of my personal favourites. The idea for the story came from a moment's idle speculation: what would happen if there existed a machine that could turn you into anything you wanted to be? Would it be a curse or a blessing? And how would the authorities react?

The rest of the story grew from that question, and I threw all I had into the mix – memories of former relationships, musings about the meaning of life, my obsessions with cyberpunk, alien contact, the deserts of Mars, and an exploration of the Singularity, which was a big topic in the early years of the twenty-first century. I even based the story's villain on a particularly annoying colleague from one of my former day jobs, and made sure he came to a satisfyingly sticky end.

Writing for the BSFA, Paul Raven summed this up when he praised the story for bringing "a welcome breeze of empathy to the proceedings by humanising the technological experience instead of technologising the human experience."

Eleven Minutes

Pasadena, California. Gary and Carl sat at their desks, hunched in front of bright flatscreen displays, somewhere in a room at NASA's Jet Propulsion Laboratory. Dusk had fallen over the hills beyond the windows, and the only sound in the room was the occasional *snick* of a key being tapped.

Each keystroke controlled the movements of a mechanical rover some hundred million kilometres away, on the lip of a Martian crater. As per the schedule, the rover's cameras were focussed on a rock with the designation H/4356a; a boulder about the size of a small Volkswagen, resting in the sand close to the crater's edge. Interesting weathering patterns had been noted around the stone's lower flanks, and this evening Gary's task was to get a few good close-up shots of them.

Every tap of his keyboard nudged the rover forward another few centimetres. The time lag made the process laborious. With Mars at this distance from the Earth, it took each of his instructions five and half minutes to crawl across the solar system, and another five and a half for the rover's acknowledgement to reach him, leaving a gap of just over eleven minutes between each command.

He looked across at Carl.

"Enjoying those?"

Carl looked up from his noodles, fork poised halfway to his mouth. He was reading a magazine that lay spread open on his desk.

"Want some?" He proffered the cardboard container. Gary shook his head. He couldn't eat noodles without thinking of maggots. He had the same problem with spaghetti and rice, which maybe explained why he was thirty pounds lighter than Carl.

"No thanks."

Gary preferred to make his own soups. He liked the simplicity. All you had to do was boil some vegetables in a saucepan, add some stock, and when it was ready, stick everything in a blender. What could be more nutritious? His soups kept him nourished and hydrated, and they were an easy way to ensure he ingested his recommended daily intake of fresh vegetables. He made up a big batch each Sunday and that saw him right through the week. In his bag today, he had a flask of chicken and sweet potato.

"Hey," he said. "I thought I'd stop by the gym later, on the way home."

Carl just looked at him, eyes blank with indifference, spreading gut pushed tight against an oversized belt buckle. Then he went back to his magazine. It was a popular science periodical and the headline read: *Amazing Alternate Worlds*. The cover featured a painting of Nazi swastikas adorning the Great Pyramid at Giza.

"Do you believe in all that?" Gary asked.

Carl frowned. "Huh?"

Gary waved his hand at the magazine. "All that alternate reality crap?"

Carl took a forkful of noodles and chewed them slowly before swallowing.

"I guess."

Gary smiled mischievously. "So you think there's an endless number of Carls out there in the universe, all playing out every possible version of your life?"

Carl gave him a weary look.

"That's the theory."

Gary scratched his ear. "Do you think any of *them* are going to the gym tonight?"

Carl sighed.

"You're a dick." He turned away and scooped another forkful into his mouth. After a moment, Gary shrugged.

"Suit yourself."

Gary looked at the image relayed from the Martian desert. As instructed, the rover had moved another wheel rotation closer to H/4365a; but now there was something wrong with the picture, and it took him a moment to spot what it was. He frowned.

"Hey, Carl, come and have a look at this."

Carl dropped his fork into the noodle container.

"What now?"

Gary pointed to the screen.

"This shadow."

Carl huffed. He wheeled his chair laboriously over to Gary's work station and looked at the screen over the top of his glasses.

"What about it?"

"It wasn't there a moment ago."

Carl smacked his lips together.

"What's making it?"

Gary shrugged. "I don't know. That's the edge of the crater over there. There shouldn't *be* anything there capable of throwing a shadow."

"Is it the rover?"

"No, the sun's at the wrong angle."

"Hmm." Noodles now forgotten, Carl scooted back to his own computer and started tapping on the keypad.

"I'm going to try bringing the camera around," he said.

While he typed, Gary leaned close to his own screen, trying to squint out more detail. The images were rough and of low resolution; the high res stuff got downloaded at a much slower rate.

"What do you think it is?"

Carl entered a final command, hit the return key and looked around, the roll of bristled fat at the back of his neck bunched up like a scarf.

"Could be a rockslide or a dust devil, I guess." He pushed himself to his feet. "Look, I'm going for a soda. Do you want one?"

Gary shook his head. He was too busy trying to work out what could be throwing this unexpected shadow.

If only I could be there, he thought. *I could just turn my head...*

Carl lumbered out to the vending machine in the corridor and Gary heard coins clatter into the mechanism, followed by the thump of a can being dispensed.

"It's probably nothing," Carl called.

"Yeah, I know. I just want to see what it is."

Gary checked his watch. Three minutes had passed since Carl instructed the camera to turn in the direction of the crater. It would be at least another eight minutes before they got an image.

He watched as Carl came back and flopped down on his seat.

"You really should think about taking some exercise, man. It would do you the world of good."

Carl popped the tab on the top of his soda.

"Don't you start. I get enough of that from my wife."

Gary blinked in surprise.

"You're married?"

"Is that so hard to believe?"

"No. Uh. It's just you never mention her. I didn't realise –"

"Do you have a girlfriend, Gary?"

"No, not right now."

"You gay?"

"Uh, no."

"You see, there's plenty I don't know about you either." Carl lowered his voice conspiratorially. "But you know why that is, don't you?"

Gary leaned forward.

"No, why?"

Carl licked his fat, wet lips. "Because I know when to mind my own damn business."

The next five minutes passed in uncomfortable silence. Across the room, Carl hunched over his keyboard, shoulders tense. The back of his ears were bright red.

To pass the time, Gary pulled out his cell phone and Tweeted: *Carl's an a$$hole.*

A minute later, Carl replied, calling him a retard. And then Debbie their supervisor came online from her office upstairs telling them both to cool it.

Her Tweet read: *Don't make me come down there, boys.*

Gary laughed and put down his phone. The data from Mars had started to come in. The picture built a strip at a time, starting with the sky. By the time it was almost fully downloaded, he could see a view across the crater, towards the rusty dunes in the distance, and the small sun perched in the pale sky.

"Not far enough," he said aloud. There was no sign of anything big enough to have thrown the shadow he had seen in the last picture.

Carl grunted.

With a sigh, Gary settled back. It would take another five and a half minutes to tell the camera to keep turning, and then the same amount of time to receive the next image. He rested his chin on his fist and watched the final stripe add itself to the bottom of the picture.

Then he stopped breathing.

"Carl?" he said in a very small voice. "Carl, tell me that isn't what I think it is."

The big man turned. He still looked angry. He wheeled across.

"Where?"

"Bottom left."

Carl pulled off his glasses and leaned close to the screen. When he sat back up, all the colour had drained from his face.

"I ain't saying nothing. Not a goddamn thing."

"But it's a boot – "

"We don't know that."

Gary pointed to the toe section protruding into the image. It was covered in a white material, scuffed and stained pink with Martian dust. Thick treads were visible on the sole.

"Sure we do. Look at it. It's a boot. What the hell else could it be?"

He looked at Carl. The older man's face had taken on the sweaty grey pallor of a man in a hostage video.

"The camera's still moving," Carl said. "We should get another picture in eleven minutes."

He picked up the phone.

"Don't do or say anything until I get Debbie down here. Are you still logged in to Twitter?"

Gary checked his cell phone.

"Uh, yeah."

"Log out, *right now*."

By the time Debbie Knox walked into the room, the next image has begun to assemble itself, strip by strip, on Gary's monitor.

"What's this all about?" she asked.

Carl handed her a printout.

"Gary thinks he's found a foot."

"A foot?"

Debbie was a middle-aged woman with an unruly mass of greying hair swept back in a loose ponytail. She wore a thick knitted cardigan over her white blouse and blue jeans.

Carl tapped the paper for her.

"Right here."

Debbie held the paper up to her face, almost touching her nose.

"This thing here?" She frowned at the image, turning the paper this way and that, trying to make sense of it.

Gary cleared his throat.

"Yes."

Debbie's tongue clicked against her teeth. She let the arm holding the printout drop to her side.

"It does look like a boot, I grant you. But it isn't. It can't be, can it?" She handed the piece of paper back to Carl. "It must be part of the rover itself. It must have come loose. In which case, we could be looking at some catastrophic damage scenarios."

"I told you, didn't I?" Carl touched his hand to his forehead, finger and thumb extended into an L-shape. "Loser."

Gary flipped him the bird.

"Hey!" Debbie stepped between them. "We don't have time for your squabbles right now. We need to trace the location of this damage and we need to –"

She stopped talking and stared at Gary's monitor.

"What's *that?*"

Gary swivelled in his chair. The computer had finished downloading the final image from the Martian surface. For a moment, his eyes refused to make sense of the picture, seeing only peculiar shadows and random blobs of colour. Then it all snapped into place.

"Holy crap."

Without taking his eyes from the screen, he got to his feet. His chair slithered away on its casters. To his left, Carl stood with his fat mouth hanging open, expressions of indignation and bafflement chasing each other across his face.

"Is this some kind of trick?" Debbie said. "Is that Photo-shopped?"

Gary swallowed.

"No ma'am."

He rubbed his eyes with the heels of his hands. When his sight cleared, the image on the screen remained.

An apparition stood on the crater's rim, partially back-lit by the small sun dipping low in the pale Martian sky: the figure of a woman in a tight-fitting elasticised suit, head sheathed in an ornate brass helmet with small circular windows at the front and sides. She looked like a Victorian diver. An air hose protruded from the top of her helmet and rose behind her, to the open hatch of a baroque airship hanging in the thin air above the crater. Lights burned in its gondola windows. Smoke issued from its chimneys. Its huge impellers looked like windmills against the sky.

The woman had one gauntleted hand raised in greeting. She held the other at waist height, clutching a bright rectangle of cloth.

"It's a flag," Carl said, voice flat with shock.

Gary shook his head, but there could be no mistake. This woman in the outlandish suit; this impossible woman waving at them from the surface of Mars; held a flag.

And not just any flag.

"It's the Union Jack."

Carl coughed. He scratched the loose roll of skin beneath his jaw. "Um, actually, it's only called that if it's being flown from the deck of a ship," he said, falling back on the pedantic habits of a lifetime; "on land, it's known as the 'Union Flag'."

"Shut the fuck up, Carl."

Gary noticed the same flag painted on the canvas bow of the airship. The overlapping red, white and blue circles of the Royal Air Force were emblazoned on the fins at its rear. He felt Debbie step up beside him. She took his hand, and her fingers felt cold.

"I don't understand," she said.

Gary didn't answer. He had no idea what to say. The UK didn't even *have* a manned space programme. Outside the building, he could see the lights of Pasadena reflected on the night sky. A helicopter blinked red and green above the freeway. It all looked reassuringly quiet and real: just another week night in California. There was no way the British could have beaten them to Mars. Not with technology that looked as if it had been cannibalised from a museum.

Not in this universe…

Gary glanced across at the magazine still resting on Carl's desk. *Amazing Alternate Worlds*. Feeling cold inside, he turned his attention back to the screen, and looked at the British woman's raised hand. Silhouetted against the sky, three of her gloved fingers were bent, but the index finger and thumb were thrust out in a proud and unmistakeable message.

Losers.

~

Gareth L. Powell

Over the years, I've drawn a lot of inspiration from dreams. This tale of squabbling technicians was inspired by a dream in which an English Zeppelin crew planted their flag in front of the helpless eyes of the Curiosity rover while the people at NASA could only gawp at their monitors. It appeared in *Interzone* in 2011. I've since read it aloud at several events, and it seems to be a favourite with live audiences.

This Is How You Die

First, there's the news. But you don't pay a great deal of attention to it, do you? You have other things to do. Eventually, though, you see the headlines on your timeline, reposted by friends. Another high school slaying in the States; a civil war in some godforsaken country somewhere in Africa or the Middle East; drone strikes in Central America; and those first, worrying reports from Angola, of a flu-like infection that's already killed eleven farmers and seems to have jumped from human to human...

1) You're on a train from Island Gardens to West India Quay. You're with your brother. You've been helping him move house and now you're on your way to a tapas bar to get something to eat. The lights of Canary Wharf shine through the rain. In the carriage there's this young Chinese guy wearing a German army shirt. He's scratching at a fresh tattoo on his forearm. Lightning flickers over the Thames.

Later that afternoon, you're walking with friends on Peckham Rye, kicking through piles of wet orange leaves. Jet planes whine overhead on approach to the airport. A green parakeet flits across the path.

Somebody sneezes, and you make a joke about bird flu.

2) A year later, you're living in the ruin of a terraced house somewhere in North London. You can't remember how you got there. Three other people live in the house, but you only know two of them. Understandably, you tend to keep yourselves to yourselves; and, when you meet, you have handkerchiefs clasped over your mouths.

Food is a problem, as is security.

You keep a wooden hockey stick next to the sofa cushions that serve as your bed; and an old carving knife tucked into the leather motorcycle boots you stole from the Goth guy who lived in the house opposite until the local kids put a petrol bomb though the plate glass of his living room window.

Those kids.

They run like feral animals, into everything. They know nothing of school; of games consoles or chart music. They've inherited a different world, a pandemic world. Most of their friends are dead. While you're still struggling to adjust, they're running wild. They don't know any other way. They have no context; nothing except stories. And who wants to listen to stories when there's petrol to pilfer and cats to catch?

Yeah, cats.

Even thinking about them makes your mouth water. It's been so long since you had any sort of meat.

3) When you were younger, you used to worry about zombies. They were all over the Internet back then. People used to daydream about killing them. Your friends would joke about what they'd do during a zombie apocalypse. Now, though, you know it isn't the undead that are the problem. Walking corpses would be preferable to the lying-still-and-decomposing kind. At least the walkers would keep themselves busy, and you wouldn't have to burn them.

Yes, daily cremations have become part of your routine. You can't let the dead fester. They breed disease and attract rats. At first, you and the others tried to keep a semblance of order and dignity. Later, as the numbers of the dead increased, the process became steadily cruder. Now, it's all about lugging the bodies into a pile and setting them on fire.

4) Sooner or later, the water pumps are going to stop and the taps run dry. Then, you're going to have to move. You're going to have to find somewhere with a dependable supply of fresh water, untainted by waste or corpses, or radiation from the failing nuclear plants on the coast.

And, inevitably, every other fucker in the country's going to have had the same idea.

And so you pack your shit into a four wheel drive Honda that used to belong to the local playgroup leader. You take all the tinned food, and your hockey stick, and you head west.

5) You have to drive on the pavement a lot.

6) When you reach the A40, you find it clogged with abandoned cars. A military helicopter clatters overhead, on route to Heathrow. Foxes

haunt the hard shoulder.

Once you get out past the M25, the traffic queues thin out and you pick up speed. You might even reach Oxford before nightfall.

7) What have you brought with you?
Photo albums?
Books?
A pile of old CDs?
A dead smartphone?
A dying ebook reader?
None of that crap's going to be worth as much as a pair of waterproof boots and a good knife.

8) Sticking to the back roads, you go a whole day without seeing another living soul, save for the crows flapping from the telegraph wires as you pass.

Somewhere in Wiltshire, on the forecourt of a deserted filling station, you start to sneeze, and tell yourself it's just a cold.

Back on the road, the villages you pass have been barricaded. The inhabitants are fearful of infection. Paint-daubed warning signs tell you to keep away.

9) Eventually, you find yourself on the street where you grew up, standing on the pavement outside your childhood home. The place looks as if it's been empty a long time. Some of the windows have been smashed. The garden's a mess. You have no idea what brought you here.

Inside, the house smells of mildew. You try the radio in the kitchen, but the electricity's off. The cupboards are bare.

Despite the chill in the room, you feel hot and feverish. Right now, you'd give anything for a bowl of your mother's homemade chicken soup.

Newspapers lie scattered on the table. You can't bring yourself to look at them, so you try the stairs instead.

Outside, it's starting to rain.

10) When you were eight years old, this was your bedroom. You lie on the bed and close your eyes. If you squeeze them tightly enough, you

can almost feel your old toys around you.

You stay there, wrapped in the blanket, listening as the rain taps skeletal fingers against the skylight. You remember the feel of your father's bristles; the way your mother used to call up the stairs when it was time for school.

How did all that warmth turn to cold and hunger, to transit camps and columns of refugees?

You start to sweat and shiver.

11) A sound comes from your sister's room at the end of the hall: the endless scratching of a record player repeating the same phrase over and over and over. You lie quietly on the bed, listening, wrapped in the musty blankets, too comfortable to move. Your long-dead best friend sits on the arm of the chair by the window.

"I just can't see the point any more," she says.

She starts to cry.

Lying there, you watch her walk out into the hall in her thick socks, to the top of the stairs, and you wonder if you should go after her. But the blankets are warm and you're very tired.

Your breath wheezes in your chest.

After a while, you pull the sheet up to cover your face.

~

I don't often write stories in the second person or the present tense, but that's just how this one came out. The title came to me first, and that dictated the way I told the story. At the time I was writing it, apocalypses were everywhere in popular culture, most especially zombie apocalypses, and I wanted to try something a little more plausible. If a virus was going to wipe us out, it seemed much more likely it would come in the form of a flu pandemic rather than an outbreak of walking corpses hungry for brains...

The story appeared in *Interzone* in 2014, and received an honourable mention in *The Year's Best Science Fiction: Thirty-Second Annual Collection*, edited by Gardner Dozois.

Gonzo Laptop

Running late, I pushed through the entrance to the new Willesden shopping mall in West London, skateboard in hand. It was early morning and some of the stores still had their metal shutters down – but that didn't stop their automatic spambots from pinging my phone with offers and appeals as I passed.

40% off today!

CLOSING SALE

Recession-busting deals!

Spread over four levels, the mall had been open only a year but already some of the shops were vacant, their windows scabbed over with graffiti and old newspaper. Yawning, I collected my usual breakfast order of coffee and falafel from the food stall by the entrance and took an escalator up to the third floor, to the corridor leading towards the car park pay stations.

There was only one shop on that corridor – an empty book store abandoned when its chain went bust, its windows whitewashed with flaking paint.

I knocked on its glass door – four slow raps followed by one quick one, and then a final slow one – Morse code for "OK".

"It's me," I said.

I heard the lock turn. The door cracked an inch and I was eyeball-to-eyeball with my bloodshot and bespectacled business partner and former classmate, Lenny Fisher.

"You're late, Alex." Len pulled the door wide and I slipped inside, to the familiar smells of dust and failed dreams. Old promo posters peeled from the walls; paperback books lay piled on the unstuck carpet tiles. I dumped my shoulder bag on the floor and leaned my board against the wall.

"It's only just gone nine."

"More like ten past."

A laptop stood on the counter at the end of the room, where the cash tills used to be. It was an old model but we'd tricked it out with extra memory and a faster processor. We'd even upgraded the webcam built into the top of its screen casing.

"How are the markets this morning, Len?"

He removed his wireless Skype headset.

"Still pretty grumpy, I'm afraid." He'd been doing the night shift, monitoring the markets in Asia and America. Beneath his glasses, his eyes were red-rimmed and his hair wild, his chin fuzzy with stubble. He'd left an empty pizza box beside the computer. I pushed it off the counter onto the floor.

"You know, it wouldn't hurt you to clear up around here once in a while."

"Fuck you, Alex."

We both smiled. Len looked dead on his feet. I said: "Go home and get some sleep."

He took his glasses off and yawned.

"Keep an eye on Tanguy and Larsson," he said. "Sell if they reach five Euros apiece."

He grabbed up his stuff and left. I locked the door behind him and then checked the results of the night's trading, to find we were up around five hundred Euros, which brought our total profits for the week to something approaching six grand.

Not bad.

It proved that even in the depths of an economic recession, there was money to be made picking the bones of failing dotcoms – and it certainly beat working for a living.

We weren't even paying tax. Because we were both under eighteen, we were trading anonymously, using a nested series of fictitious shell companies and accessing the markets via the mall's ubiquitous Wi-Fi cloud, siphoning all our profits into offshore accounts. We were going to use the money to pay our way through college. After that, Len wanted enough to buy one of the new studio apartments by the river, and I wanted to travel to Europe, the Far East and Australia.

I opened a new window on the laptop and called up a real-time webcam view of Sydney Harbour, filmed from the roof of an office block in Kirribilli. It was late afternoon over there. I liked the clean white light of the Australian sun, and the deep, wholesome blue of the harbour waters.

I left it open in the background as I ate my breakfast and worked, playing the stock markets in London, Madrid, and Frankfurt.

In the first hour, I made a lot of small deals, spreading the risk, investing in companies with rapidly rising share prices. I bought high as the price approached the peak of its parabola and then bailed almost immediately, making a small profit before it began the inevitable slide back down. I had almost a sixth sense for this, an ability to predict the exact moment the price would stall, so I could make a quick buck before it did.

I wasn't infallible, of course, and over the next three hours I twice took a bath on shares that fell before I could unload them – but even so, by eleven-thirty I'd made another two hundred Euros.

At midday, Lisa came by. She was the third member of our operation. She was nineteen, a couple of years older than either Len or me, and a friend of Len's sister from art school. We were both a little in awe of her and, truth be told, I'd had a secret crush on her for years. She worked in the mall and it had been her idea to use the old book store as a base of operations.

I let her in and she handed me a packaged vegetable pasty with yesterday's sell-by date on it.

"I thought you could do with some lunch," she said. She had blue hair and a lip ring, and a shiny black pendant.

"It's new, do you like it?" she said, holding the pendant out to me on the end of its chain.

I shrugged. I'd seen life-loggers before.

"Very nice."

She fingered it with a strange, sad smile. "Don't worry, it's turned off. I bought it at the weekend to cheer myself up."

I made sure the door was locked. "Is there something wrong?" I asked.

She looked up at me. "I broke up with Ian on Friday."

I blinked in surprise, unsure how to react. Ian was her boss at the health food shop. She'd been seeing him for a few months but I'd never met him. From what I'd been able to gather, the majority of their relationship outside working hours had been taking place online, in MMORPGs and chat rooms. "I'm sorry to hear that," I said.

She shook her head. "Don't be. He was an asshole and I'm better off without him."

I walked back over to the laptop. She didn't follow, and she didn't ask about the business. I knew she wasn't interested. All she wanted was a cut of the profits at the end of each month, to supplement her wages.

"We've done okay this week," I said, "although the tax people have been all over us. We've had to create two new front companies in the last two days."

I put the pasty down on the counter and brushed pizza crumbs from the brown envelope Len had left for her. I handed it over and she opened the flap. There were some colourful European bank notes inside, held together with a paperclip. She pulled them out and folded them, and then tucked them into her jacket pocket.

"Aren't you going to count them?" I said.

"Do I need to?"

Her eyes were green and her lips red. When she moved, her pendant caught the light.

I walked with her to the door and unlocked it. As I pulled it open, she said: "Listen, I'm on my lunch break right now, but do you fancy meeting up later, for a drink or something?"

I glanced nervously up and down the corridor. I didn't want to be seen. If we lost this place, we'd have to find somewhere else with privacy and free 24 hour Wi-Fi. I looked down at her. She was standing very close and her blue hair smelled of peppermint. Her black pendant hung in the cleavage of her low-cut top.

"S-sure," I said, suddenly stuttering.

She gave my arm a gentle squeeze, looking amused. "Okay, I'll text you later."

She kissed me on the cheek and I closed the door behind her. I leaned my forehead against its painted glass until I heard her footsteps retreating back in the direction of the atrium, then let out the breath I hadn't realised I'd been holding.

I touched my cheek where she'd kissed it, and then went to make a cup of coffee and nuke the pasty she'd given me in the small staff kitchen at the back of the shop.

There was a cupboard in there filled with rolled-up posters, signed hardbacks and other promotional junk. As I waited for the kettle to boil and the microwave to ping, I poked through it, hoping to find something useful I could swipe, like a book token or a USB stick.

At the back of the cupboard's top shelf, I struck gold: a brand new ten terabyte external hard drive, still wrapped in cellophane and roughly half the size of my phone. Hardly believing my luck, I pulled it out and read the words etched into its black casing:

100 Years of Gonzo: 1937-2037

The dates meant nothing. I slipped the drive into the leg pocket of my combat trousers. The kettle had boiled. I poured a cup of coffee and took it back into the main body of the shop, where I spent a few minutes checking out the New York stock exchange, which had just opened.

By the time I'd made a few deals, it was almost one thirty. I fished out the drive and turned it over in my hands. It looked practically unused. I thought if I wiped the promotional data from it, I could resell it for at least a hundred Euros – which would be another hundred I could put towards my college and travel plans.

With a smile, I tore off the cellophane, crinkled it up and dropped it on the dirty floor. I pulled out the drive's retractable USB cable and plugged it into the port on my laptop.

"Okay." I rubbed my hands together gleefully. "Let's see what we've got."

I scanned the contents of the drive, giving an appreciative whistle as a long list of files appeared. The drive's memory held the complete texts of over a hundred books and novels, thousands of photographs, and several days' worth of music and film. I scrolled through it all until I came to an application file marked 'reader', which I clicked, expecting it to open a device for viewing the media files. Instead, the screen blanked and a face appeared – a handsome face beneath a camouflage bush hat, with sad eyes looking back at me from behind tinted aviator shades.

Frowning, I leaned closer to the screen. A dialogue box at the bottom asked if I'd like to run the program.

"What's this?" I said. I tapped the laptop's mouse pad, wheeling the cursor over to the "No" option – but before I could press it, there was an urgent knock at the shop's painted glass window.

"Alex, let me in!"

Lisa. Cursing, I put my coffee down and unlocked the door. I opened it just enough to drag her inside.

She was out of breath.

"Alex, I've done something really incredibly stupid." She opened her fist to reveal the black life-logger pendant she'd been wearing a couple of hours earlier.

"What have you done? Have you broken it?"

"No, but Alex, when I came here before, I thought I'd turned it off but I hadn't. It was on the whole time."

I felt the colour drain out of my face. "It recorded everything?"

Lisa closed her eyes and nodded. "It's worse than you think. Ian has access to my feed. He uses it to check up on me when I'm on my own in the shop. If he sees this place and decides to get vindictive..." She made a face.

I put a hand over my eyes and took a deep, shuddering breath.

"Are you telling me you've posted video evidence of our illegal share trading operation on the fucking internet?"

Lisa screwed her face tighter.

"Yes..."

I kicked over a pile of abandoned paperbacks and stalked back to the counter. It wasn't just video, either. Those little devices recorded their wearer's GPS location, temperature and heart rate, as well as everything they saw and heard, and downloaded it all onto the web as a live feed, creating a real-time, searchable blog. So far, we'd managed to avoid attracting unwelcome attention from the mall's private security firm, not to mention the tax office and the fraud squad. But if Ian got hold of all that information and decided to blow the whistle, we could find ourselves in some seriously hot water.

"I'm sorry," Lisa said.

I turned and glared at her.

"Help me with this stuff." I pointed to the laptop and hard drive. "If there's even a chance Ian's going to call security, we're going to have to clear out right now, before anyone comes looking."

Lisa pushed one hand up the side of her head, brushing back her blue hair.

"Maybe it's not too late," she said. "He's probably at lunch. He might not have checked up on me yet and if so, we can just delete it before he does."

I clenched my fists. My heart thumped. "Can you do that?"

Lisa let her hand drop to her side.

"It must be possible to edit a life-log, otherwise what happens if you accidentally record yourself taking a dump or fiddling your taxes?"

I looked into her eyes for a long moment and then smiled. I couldn't help myself.

"Okay, let's do it." I spun the laptop to face her.

She frowned.

"What's that?"

I glanced down. "I don't know. It was on this hard drive I found in the back room. I think it's an advert or something."

"It looks like Hunter Thompson."

I considered the face again and shrugged: "If you say so."

Lisa tilted her head to the side. "No," she said, "it's definitely him."

She put her fingers on the mouse pad, moved the cursor from "No" to "Yes", and clicked.

The face on the screen gave a start. The blue eyes blinked, looking around, getting their bearings, and the man, Thompson, coughed, clearing his throat.

"Where am I?" His eyes were wild and his voice was high with alarm. He looked up at me.

"Who the hell are you?" he said.

We found a way to pause the program, freezing Thompson's face: chin thrust out indignantly, black brows furrowed.

"It's CGI," Lisa said, "It's got to be."

I couldn't take my eyes from the screen. "But he's looking straight at me."

Lisa flicked her hand. "Ah, that's just an illusion. Unless..." She tapped her fingernail on the webcam built into the laptop's casing, looking thoughtful.

"Let's try something," she said. She touched the mouse pad again, restarting the program.

"Hello," she said.

The face on the screen shook itself and turned its baleful gaze on her.

"Well, hello yourself," it said. "Would you like me to read you something?"

Lisa shook her head, fascinated. She leaned forward.

"Can you really see me?"

Thompson's lips twitched in a smile. "I couldn't miss you with all that blue hair, now, could I?"

His animated eyes scanned the room, taking in the disassembled bookshelves and piles of abandoned paperbacks.

"Say, this doesn't look much like a book launch to me. I'm s'posed to be giving a reading. There's s'posed to be an audience and I'm s'posed to be reading my book."

I moved in close to Lisa, peering at the screen.

"The store went bust," I said.

Thompson's face fell. "Oh, man. Then who the hell are you two?"

"I'm Alex and this is Lisa."

He looked up at us. "You won't turn me off again, will you?"

Rifling back through the cupboard, Lisa found the notes that accompanied the promotional hard drive. She brandished them at the image of the man on the laptop screen.

"It says here, and I quote, you're: 'an artificial Turing intelligence fed with all the books, articles and letters written by Hunter Thompson during his lifetime, and all the subsequent memoirs of his friends and contemporaries, plus all the available and relevant photographs, film clips and TV appearances' – and that you're programmed to behave as if you are the man himself, 'based on behavioural parameters implied by the contents of those files'."

She looked up. Hunter was watching her. Under his plaid shirt and white t-shirt, he had a muscular neck and wide, football-hero shoulders. Back then, I didn't know much about artificial intelligence. I still don't, if you want the truth. But there was something about Hunter – the gleam in his eye, the way he flexed his jaw – that left me in no doubt he was alive. He had charisma to spare. He was, in all senses of the word, *animated.*

"I don't know about any of that," he said with a sad smile, "I'm just me, here, now. All dressed up and nowhere to go."

He looked at me. "You know who I am though, don't you sport?"

I scratched my stomach through my t-shirt. "I read your book at school, the one about Las Vegas. I wrote an essay on it."

Hunter's eyes widened in surprise. "At school, huh?"

Lisa was still reading: "You're programmed to read sections of your work to specially invited audiences, as part of the hundredth anniversary of your birth," she said.

Hunter rolled his eyes.

"Yada yada yada. Those sick bastards. Just because they put me in this here box, it doesn't follow they get to tell me what to do."

There was a knock at the shop door and the handle rattled as someone tried it.

A voice said: "This is mall security. Is there anyone in there?"

Lisa and I looked at each other. She grabbed my hand. Her eyes were wide and frightened.

"What are we going to do?"

I looked down at Hunter.

"Screw 'em," he said. "Let's blow this joint."

We took the rear fire escape door that opened into the car park. Lisa had a car there, an old Peugeot converted to bio-diesel. We piled into it, with me in the shotgun seat, the laptop and hard drive on my knees running on battery power, my skateboard and bag on the back seat.

"We can go back to my place and erase my life-log," Lisa said.

She took us out into traffic. Outside the mall, it was a bright, hard autumn day, with showers of yellow leaves swirling down from the pavement trees.

At Hunter's request, I held the laptop up, so the camera faced the windscreen.

"Where in the hell are we anyway?" he said.

"This is west London," Lisa replied, changing gear and working the clutch.

"Ohio?"

"England."

"And where are you taking me?"

Lisa sped through a set of traffic lights as they switched from green to amber. "We're going to my place."

I made a face. "I'm not sure that's such a good idea. If Ian knows about the share trading, he could have reported us to the police, or the

Inland Revenue."

Lisa gripped the steering wheel. "Then what are we going to do, Alex?"

From the laptop's speakers, Hunter's voice was low and urgent. "Alex, how much money do you have on you?"

I turned the laptop around.

"About forty Euros," I said.

He frowned, nonplussed.

"Is that a lot?"

"Some."

He brightened. "Then let's hit the fucking road. There's no way those pigs can touch you if you don't stop moving."

Lisa was concentrating on the traffic. We were on the North Circular, near Ealing, heading south towards her place in Heston. She said: "Where do you suggest we go, then?"

Hunter grinned a toothy, rogue's grin.

"I always say: if in doubt, head west."

Len phoned me, a few minutes later.

"I've just been past the store," he said. "There are security guards crawling all over it. What's going on?"

I glanced across at Lisa. We were on the M4 now, heading out of town, the afternoon sun shining on her blue hair.

"We got caught."

On the other end of the line, Len made a choking noise.

"What about the money?"

"It's safe, as far as I know. At least, for now..." I felt my sixth sense kick in. I knew we'd peaked. From here on, the only way was down.

"Look, if the police and the Revenue are involved, they're going to trace the transactions sooner or later. Just get to a cash machine, take out as much as you can, and we'll see what happens."

I switched my phone off. "Pull off at the next services," I said.

We left the motorway just south of Reading, rolling to a halt in the car park of a service area surrounded by fields and hedges. I left the laptop containing Hunter on the passenger seat. I pulled a baseball cap from my bag and went inside, past the concession stands and the MacDonald's, to the ATM machines, where I withdrew as much cash as I could, pushing my phony business and personal cards to their limits, all the while keeping the brim of my cap as low as possible to hide my face from the security cameras.

On the way back, pockets bulging with banknotes, I paused long enough to pick up two bottles of spring water and half a dozen sandwiches, and then called Len back from a payphone. He'd taken refuge in an internet café in Ealing and he sounded angry.

"I don't get it," he said. "At least we were doing something. We were earning money instead of moaning about the recession. The government should be encouraging us not trying to close us down. If this country's going to pull through, it's going to need people like us."

He paused to take a breath and I said: "Look, you're probably in the clear. If all Ian's got is the footage from this morning, then no one knows you're involved. There are probably fingerprints in the shop but what do they prove? Keep your head down and you should be okay."

He was silent for a few seconds.

"What about you?" he said.

I shifted my weight from one foot to the other. "The only two bits of evidence linking Lisa and I to the operation are the life-log and the laptop. If we can get rid of them both, we'll be okay."

"You want me to see about the log?"

"Can you?"

"No problem. Even if Ian's seen the feed, he won't be able to prove anything if it's been erased. Just get Lisa to text me her passwords and I'll get it sorted."

"Thanks, man."

I hung up. When I got back to the car, I found Lisa in conversation with Hunter, clutching her pendant. She was saying:

"Your books are all based on events from your life, right? Well, that's the same thing as life-logging. That's life-logging, Seventies-style."

She looked up as I slid into my seat. I handed her a bottle of water.

"I think we're going to be okay," I said.

Even with the evidence gone, Lisa thought it best we stay out of town for a few days, just in case the police or the tax men came knocking. For want of a better option, we continued west on the motorway, passing Swindon and Bristol, heading into Wales and the lowering sun over Cardiff and Swansea.

Lisa said: "I have an aunt we can stay with. She runs a guest house near St David's."

Sitting on my knee, Hunter was digging it all, watching the white line unroll under the car's wheel with inexhaustible machine enthusiasm. Occasionally, he burst into muttered snatches of half-remembered song.

At the wheel, Lisa said very little. She had the radio on, listening to the traffic reports. Her face was set, her jaw clenched, her whole body bent to the task of concentrating on the road ahead. Her knuckles were white on the steering wheel.

Afraid of distracting her, I used my phone to Google the works of Thompson.

"Do you have all these books in your memory?" I asked as I scrolled through the Amazon listings.

Hunter stuck his bottom lip out. "I have the reviews too, but don't go paying attention to them. They're the ravings of cowards and dope fiends."

He closed his eyes with a chuckle. "Thing is, Bubba, most people get caught up with the drugs and bad craziness and they miss the great mystical lonely terror of it all."

When he opened them, his eyes behind the shades were dull with regret.

"My boy, let me give you a little advice, from your Uncle Hunter."

I shifted in my seat. We were somewhere past Swansea now, on a dual carriageway, and it was getting late.

"Alex, you need to take a good long look at this lovely lady here."

Lisa and I exchanged puzzled glances.

"She's crazy about you," Hunter said. "She told me so, while you were out getting cash."

Lisa's eyes snapped back to the road. Her ears were going pink.

"Hey, shut up," she said.

Hunter laughed. "There's nothing more important or downright necessary to a man than the love of a good woman. Am I right, Alex?"

I could feel my own cheeks burning.

"We're just friends," I said.

"Ha!" Hunter shook his head with a manic grin. "I might not be real, but I do have eyes. I've seen the two of you together and I know what's going on."

He appeared to lean forward, jabbing a finger at the inside of the screen. "You like her, Alex, I know you do. And she likes you too. And the two of you could do a lot worse, a hell of a lot worse, take it from me."

Lisa said: "I've just been through that whole thing with Ian."

I said: "I know."

She slowed for a roundabout, took us through it and started accelerating again.

"I don't know if I'm ready."

I put my hand on her shoulder. Her skin felt warm and smooth through her cotton top.

"We've got a few days here in the country. Let's just see what happens. "

She reached up and took my hand.

"Do you want to, really?"

I swallowed. "Of course I do. I've always wanted to be with you."

She gave me a sideways look then, pleased and amused.

"Okay."

Hunter had his eyes closed now, nodding along to some unheard internal rhythm.

"But what about you? Look, what do you want, Hunter? How do you think this is going to end?"

The eyes on the screen narrowed, considering me, weighing me up. At length, he said: "My boy, you and I both know I'm not the person I think I am, now don't we? I know I'm not real, Alex, and I can't go on living like this. We've all got to die sooner or later and I know there's no mystical inner spark lighting me up. Hunter S. Thompson is dead and gone. He shot himself in 2005. It says that right here." He tapped his temple with a gloved hand. "I'm an after-image, a phony, a ghost. I'm so tired and beat and all my memories are in black and white. I need to rest."

I put my hand on the power switch. The battery was almost gone. "Do you want me to turn you off?"

He shook his head, eyes wild with terror. "Hell, no! If you do that, there'll always be a chance some rat bastard will turn me on again."

Lisa looked over. "So, what do you want us to do?" she said.

Hunter lowered his chin to his chest.

"This place we're going, it's about as far west as we can get, huh?"

"It's the Atlantic coast," Lisa said. "There's nothing after that except the ocean."

Hunter looked up and stuck his jaw out. "Then when we get there, I want you to throw me off a cliff into the sea."

"Are you sure?"

His eyes widened in annoyance. "Sure I'm sure. You need to get rid of this machine and I can't go on like this, stuck in this impotent little box, not really being me. I never liked computers. Now look at me. I'm a goddamn fucking typewriter. No, I'll be better off in the sea, with all the fish and the dead pirates for company."

He gave a big, shuddering sigh.

We passed through Carmarthen into the green rolling landscape of the Pembrokeshire National Park. Lisa peered through the windscreen, squinting against the light.

"We're nearly there," she said. "Maybe another half an hour."

We were still holding hands. I turned the laptop around so that like us, Hunter faced forward, into the molten bronze of the setting sun.

Ahead of us, beyond the shadowy fields and hedgerows, we knew the ocean waited, shimmering like a sea of fire.

~

I wrote this in response to the death of Hunter Thompson. My starting point was the question of what would happen if you took an artificial intelligence and uploaded it with everything an author ever wrote? Would it have enough material there to simulate that author's personality, or would there be missing pieces? And what would happen if that author had been a rebel to start with?

The drive from Bristol to Pembrokeshire, via Cardiff and Carmarthen, holds very special memories for me, as it was the opening adventure of many a childhood summer holiday. If you've never been to Pembrokeshire, you really should give it a try some time. The coastline is magnificent.

Railroad Angel

So Neal's out on the railroad tracks in Mexico, wearing nothing but jeans and a t-shirt. It's February 1968 and the air's cold. He's been at a wedding, and now he's out wandering in the night, miles from anywhere, feeling old and slow and tired.

Out here, he can hear himself think. His shuffling shoes crunch the cinders between the railroad sleepers, and his heart beats a ponderous rhythm in his chest. He holds a cigarette pinched between thumb and forefinger. When he drags on it, the tip flares like a firefly in the Mexican night.

He's four days away from his forty-second birthday. He's been married and divorced so many times he doesn't like to think about it, and there's a bone-deep weariness about him that may or may not have anything to do with the barbiturates he's taken.

He kicks at a pebble, thinking of his friend Kesey, just out of jail and living in a chicken shack in Oregon; of Allen back in New York, growing bald and mystical; and Jack sitting bloated and paranoid at his mother's house, pissing away his talent in front of the TV.

Neal takes a final pull on his cigarette and flicks the butt into the darkness.

"Fuck it. If I had a good car, I'd be gone too."

He gives the stars a lopsided grin. Nights like this remind him of his days working as a brakeman for the Southern Pacific, riding freight trains up and down the coast out of Los Gatos. The sway of the cars, the rhythm of the rails. He starts clicking his tongue.

Clackety-clack, clackety-clack.

And then, all around him, he sees the sparks.

At first, he thinks he's hallucinating. They drift down out of the air like silent embers, as if his flicked cigarette set the sky smouldering. Some of them settle on the tracks, others in the grass to either side. He puts a hand out to catch one.

"Goddamn it!" He stops walking and sucks his fingers. The spark was *hot.*

He looks around but sees no fires in the surrounding fields, and nothing in the sky above but stars and cloud. For a wild instant, he thinks of the atom bomb tests in Nevada, but the underground test site has to be a thousand miles north of here. No, these sparks aren't manmade, Daddio. They've got to be something else, something unusual.

If they're even real.

Neal watches them settle around him, in a circle maybe twelve feet wide. Hundreds of them, like burning snowflakes. He drops to one knee and bends his face close. The sparks are flickering from within, their light alternately dimming and brightening, pulsing in time to their own mysterious beat. He blows on them, and they brighten in response, like barbeque coals.

"Weird."

He blows on them again, marvelling at the way they flare in response. Then a twinge in his back makes him straighten up.

"Getting old," he mutters, and folds his arms. Sparks or not, it's getting cold and he can't help shivering. He shuffles forward again, hands in the pockets of his jeans. Time to move on, baby. Time to go.

He's not really sure *where* he's going, but that's never been the point. He knows he just has to keep moving, putting one foot in front of the other.

He steps out of the glowing circle and walks on maybe another thirty paces before he stops again, to light another cigarette. As he sucks it to life, he turns to look back at the embers, and jerks in surprise. A figure stands in their orange light, in the centre of the circle.

"Christ!" He puts a hand to his chest. Beneath his fingers, his heart's like a dynamo, hammering away in there, rattling the ribs.

The figure in the circle's tall and thin and androgynous-looking, and its skin glows with the same intensity as the sparks around its feet. When it speaks, its voice carries the clear ring of a struck wineglass.

"Hello, Neal."

Neal's cigarette falls to the ground, forgotten. He takes a step backward, palms raised to ward off the apparition.

"I know this is an awful shock," the figure says, "but please try to relax. I know you have many questions, and I *will* try to answer them. But right now, you need to put down your hands and relax."

Neal swallows. From somewhere, he hauls out some of his old swagger, and sticks out his chin.

"W-what do you, like, want?"

The figure takes a step forward.

"I am here to wake you, Neal." It sounds sincere. It has its hair cropped short, blonde on top and white at the temples.

"And you're what?" Neal wipes his bottom lip on the back of his hand. "A Martian?"

The figure smiles and shakes its head as if it's been expecting the question.

"I am not a 'Martian'."

Neal scratches his head, pushes a lick of hair back into place.

"I see. Well, if you're not a Martian, what are you?" He thinks of the mystical visions Jack wrote about in his later books: of saints and angels. And he thinks of Kesey and the Pranksters, and LSD. Could this be an acid flashback? His heart's still banging away behind his ribs. Have the barbiturates triggered some sort of episode?

The figure takes another step towards him. Only a dozen yards of track now separate them.

"I am one of the curators of your reality." The shining figure waves an arm to encompass the world and the stars above it.

"You mean, like, an angel?" That might explain the sexless beauty of the creature.

The figure's head dips in a small shake. Its smile doesn't falter.

"I'm afraid not, Neal. I'm as human as you are." It glances down at itself. "At least, I am when I wear this body. You see, my colleagues and I are from a time far beyond the prediction wall of your culture – a time of universal computation, complexity and consciousness." It takes another step towards him, hands held out like a compassionate Christ. "We have the ability to recreate all possible quantum brain states, to simulate all possible worlds, and thereby resurrect the uniqueness of everyone, every single person who ever lived."

For a moment, it pauses. The wind blows cold.

"In short, Neal, we are the dreamers, and you are the dream."

"You're serious?"

"I am never anything but."

Neal grips his trouser legs to stop his hands from shaking. His mouth goes dry. He wants to flee but he can feel the weight of the drugs in his system, like rocks in his pocket, dragging him down. He tries to turn away, but his shoe slips on the splintering wood of an old sleeper. Instantly, the angel's at his side, buoying him up, and he can feel the warmth of its radiance on his face.

"What are you doing?" He feels weak. His arms and legs are cold and heavy like old rubber tyres, and all he wants is to sleep.

The angel says, "You are dying from exposure and an overdose of drugs." Its fingers on his arm are reassuringly warm and unbelievably soft, its presence like the comforting touch of late afternoon sunlight. Neal's teeth begin to chatter. Even with the heat of the creature beside him, the cold night air seems to be blowing right through him.

"I'm d-dying?"

The angel supports his elbow.

"Do not be ashamed. There is no shame in death. All that has happened has happened before and will happen again. Right now, this simulation has simply run its course, and it is time for you to choose a new path."

Neal wants to struggle, but he can't move.

"Choose?"

The angel fills his vision, impossibly beautiful in a chaste, asexual way.

"We can rewind your life back to the moment of conception. You can choose to relive it over and over again, playing out all possible variations, all possible scenarios. You can be anything and everything that you are capable of being."

"Or?"

The angel folds its hands. "Or you can come with us into the real world, at the end of time itself, and join our contemplation of the dark infinities that lie beyond."

Neal closes his eyes. He can feel sensation leeching from his body. The chill of the air creeps into his head. His mind struggles at a glacial pace. He thinks of his scattered friends, his missing father, his estranged kids. He thinks of all the girls, all the pool halls and highways, and wonders if he has the energy to do it all over again.

The angel leans close, face inches from his.

"Are you tired of living, Neal?"

Neal snorts. He's spent the last ten years trying to live up to the image Jack created for him, trying to be the wild-eyed, car-driving madman of his friend's first big autobiographical novel. And now, there's nothing left. Everybody's had a piece of him and he's all used up, a husk of his younger self.

Still, that doesn't mean he's ready to *die*. At least, not yet. There are faces he wants to see again, unfinished business with his wives that he has to resolve. He wants to say all this aloud, but the words won't come. His mouth won't work. He gives a shake of the head, and his eyes fill with tears.

The angel touches his forehead.

"Never fear. You will see them again. You will see all of them again."

Neal's head lolls backward, and his limbs flop like cut elastic. He can feel his body shutting down around him. For a moment, he kicks against it, hanging on to life by his fingernails. Then he feels himself slip. His jackhammer heart stutters to a halt, and a wave of resignation breaks over him.

Maybe this won't be so bad, he thinks.

But then the angel passes a hand through him, and he turns into a cloud of sparks. His physical self falls away beneath him like a shed lizard skin, and his soul leaps skyward.

Yeah, baby!

He gets one last look at his body, lying in a lonely heap on the Mexican rails, and then he's passing through the clouds towards the stars – rising like sparks shot from a locomotive's smokestack, borne aloft on angel's wings.

~

Neal Cassady was a major figure in the Beat movement of the 1950s. Jack Kerouac credited him with inspiring the prose technique of his most famous novel, *On The Road* – and Cassady even appeared in the novel under an alias, as Dean Moriarty, "a sideburned hero of the snowy West."

Cassady died in February 1968, after collapsing on a rail track in Mexico – an event I've fictionalised here as a tribute to the man, and to my own Beat obsessions.

The story appeared in *Interzone* in 2012 and received an honourable mention in *The Year's Best Science Fiction: Thirtieth Annual Collection*, edited by Gardner Dozois.

Flotsam

Toby Milan sits at the door of his steel cargo container, thirty feet above the ship's foredeck, watching the sunset. His is the third container up in a stack of six. From up here, he can see most of the other ships in the fleet. There are forty in total, all retrofitted like this one to provide emergency housing for ecological refugees – a floating shantytown anchored in the Mediterranean Sea, five miles off the flooded French coast.

Some ships are tied together, linked by gangways and laundry lines, while others stand alone in the gathering twilight, each a separate neighbourhood in its own right, with its own customs and hierarchies. And beyond them, he sees the town lights of Marseille, its downtown buildings and old harbour already flooded by the rising sea, the narrow streets awash.

He leans out of his container, looking down. There are market stalls pitched on the ship's foredeck and the early evening air rings with the hustle of traders and muezzins. Directly beneath him, at the foot of his stack, is a makeshift kebab stall. The smell of sizzling lamb makes his stomach growl and he looks enviously at the customers eating at the counter. As he does so, one of them pulls back her headscarf and shakes out her bobbed hair.

Shweta!

Heart thumping, he ducks back, hoping she hasn't seen him.

It can't be her, he thinks. Not now, not here.

Inside, his container measures eight by twenty, with corrugated metal walls. Not knowing what else to do, he backs up to the curtain screening off his sleeping area. There's a hunting knife under his pillow and he knows if he can reach it, he'll feel more secure.

But then he feels her climbing the ladder bolted to the corner of the container stack.

"Milan?" she calls. "Milan, are you in there?"

He hasn't seen Shweta Venkatesh in two years. Whatever she wants

– whatever reason she has for being here, now – it can't be good news.

He crouches by the curtain, trapped. "What do you want?" he says.

Her head and shoulders appear in the container's doorway. She holds a compact pistol in her free hand.

"Toby, is that you?"

She pulls herself up into the container, gun at the ready, body silhouetted against the fading sky. She's a little shorter than him. He hasn't seen Shweta, a former archaeology tutor from the University of Bangalore, since he left her in Ethiopia two years ago, close to the ruins of a burned-out Reef in the mountains north of Addis Ababa.

"Toby, I need a place to hide," she says.

The Reefs were a scavenger's dream. They started life as simple self-repairing routers in NASA's interplanetary data network – and ended up as something far scarier.

They learned to upgrade themselves. They increased their processing power. They started expanding at a geometric rate. And eventually, they became self-aware.

They were fast, intelligent and ruthlessly logical – but they were also unstable, unable to resist the temptation of further upgrades. Using the nano-scale assemblers in their repair packages, they morphed themselves into weird new fractal shapes. They built themselves extra processors and accelerated the speed of their thoughts beyond all human comprehension. And within hours they'd burned themselves out.

Toby and Shweta were part of a university research team picking through their twisted, smoking remains in search of useful – and potentially lucrative – new technology. They were colleagues and they were lovers. They were doing a dangerous job and they depended on each other. But in Ethiopia, when a team of rival scavengers attacked the site they were working on, he panicked and let her down.

"I took four bullets in the chest," Shweta says, lowering the gun. "And three of them were from you."

With the sun gone, it's cold in the container. Toby has his back to the curtain. "I got you out," he says. "I got you to a hospital."

Shweta snorts. "You call that a hospital?"

She pockets her weapon. She tells him she's been on the run for three days now, living rough with no time to eat or sleep, nowhere else to go. Still wary, he shows her how to work the shower and while she washes, he fetches the knife and slips it into his pocket. Then he heats some leftover rice in the microwave.

When she comes out shivering, wrapped in a threadbare grey towel, hair damp and feet leaving wet prints on the metal floor, he spoons the rice into a bowl.

"Eat this," he says, handing her a fork and stepping back out of reach, just in case.

Shweta eats like she's starving, shovelling the leftovers into her mouth. He can't help noticing her knuckles are red and raw, and there are bruises on her arms.

When she's finished eating, he takes her down to the deck and they walk up to the ship's bow, where they lean on the rail and look out at the lights of Marseille.

"So, what are you running from?" he says. He feels safer out here in the open, with other people around.

Shweta looks down at the water, letting her hair fall forward.

"It's Morgan."

Toby takes a firm grip on the ship's rail. He remembers Rob Morgan as a colleague – a quiet, serious member of the Ethiopian expedition.

"What's he done? Has he hurt you?"

Shweta shakes her head. She still has the gun. Tucked into her belt, it makes a conspicuous bulge. "It's not like that," she says.

"Then what is it?"

Shweta looks up and the wind ruffles her hair. She's wearing a pair of his old jeans, pulled tight with a canvas belt, and a t-shirt so big on her that it hangs off one shoulder.

"About a week ago, we were scouting a Reef in Thailand, near the Cambodian border," she says, "and it attacked us."

Toby's eyes widen. Active Reefs are exceptionally rare, and exceedingly dangerous.

Shweta tightens her grip on his arm. "It corrupted our suits with nanotech spores. It killed Kamal and Rani. And if Morgan hadn't come in with the flamethrower and the blue goo, it would've killed me too."

She lets go, taking a step back.

"So... you're okay?" Toby says.

She shakes her head. Discreetly, she hikes up the hem of her t-shirt to show him the top of her right hip, where the skin's hardened into something gnarled and fibrous, like coral. Appalled, Toby leans closer. He's seen infections like this before, in pictures.

"What are you going to do?" he asks.

Shweta lets the t-shirt drop back into place. Her eyes are the same colour as her hair. Overhead, the first stars are appearing.

"I don't know," she says.

Toby takes her down to one of the empty cargo containers in the stacks near the stern, where he knows she'll be safe. He uses the last of his money to buy her some food and water, and makes sure she still has the gun.

"Stay here," he says, and locks the door from the outside. Then he goes back to his place and pulls the hunting knife from his pocket. He won it in a poker game in Amsterdam. It has a matt black carbon steel blade and a lightweight plastic handle. He slips it into his sock and secures it in place with electrical tape.

He knows they don't have much time. The university can't risk an outbreak of Reef spores. They'll expect Rob Morgan to bring Shweta in before the infection spreads and new Reefs start appearing.

Toby's seen the havoc a live Reef can cause. But after abandoning her in Ethiopia, he just can't bring himself to turn Shweta in. He knows if he does, they'll kill her in order to kill the contamination.

Instead, he sweeps a few possessions into an old laptop case. Then he's out the door, down the ladder and past the kebab stall, heading for the stern, where he hopes to find Odette.

Two years ago, when he fled the debacle in Ethiopia, Toby walked away from everything – his apartment, his teaching job – taking only his passport and the money he had in his pockets.

Fleeing his guilt, he hitchhiked his way randomly across Europe, sleeping in service areas and railway stations. He got drunk in Prague, Warsaw and Bucharest.

And then one morning he found himself in Amsterdam, exhausted and spent, wading across a flooded street in the drifting rain. The city was half-deserted, everything boarded-up. He'd been playing cards all night above a café in the red light district, and now it was dawn and here he was, feeling wretched and looking for somewhere to sleep, a knife in his back pocket and fourteen Euros in loose change.

He hadn't washed in five days, hadn't had a shave in six. His coat – which he'd stolen from a cloakroom in Zagreb – had a tear in the sleeve.

He was ankle-deep in dirty sea water, wondering where he could get something to eat, when he heard a shout. It was one of the girls from the café, a young French dancer named Odette, a nineteen year-old runaway from the outskirts of Paris. She came sloshing after him.

"Do you have anywhere to sleep?" she said.

He shook his head.

"I didn't think so. Come with me." She took him back to her room – a damp studio apartment in a crumbling town house – and offered him the couch. Then she went into the bathroom and wrapped her wet hair in a towel.

"I hate what's happening to this town," she said.

Toby shrugged off his coat and sat down. His feet hurt from the cold water. He kicked off his sodden shoes. His socks were wet and threadbare, his reflection in the dead TV ragged and unkempt.

"Then why don't you leave?" he said. He turned on the TV, found a news channel.

"Where would I go?" She came back into the room, rubbing her hair, just in time to catch the end of a news item about refugees moving onto container ships in the Mediterranean.

She lowered the towel.

"Hey, wind that back," she said.

Now, hurrying toward the ship's stern, Toby doesn't know what he's going to do. He can't hide Shweta here, on board, and his guilt won't let him abandon her. He needs a third option.

Odette's crate is at the bottom of a small stack overlooking the stern. He walks up and raps on the metal door. He hears movement inside, and then Odette calls out:

"Hello? Who is there?"

Toby pulls the door open. "It's me. Can I come in?"

Inside, there are candles burning, scarves and blankets taped to the walls, rugs and cushions scattered on the floor. Odette's wearing a loose dress under a tight Levi jacket, sparkly lipstick and silver nail polish.

"You look happy," he says.

She smiles. Since leaving Amsterdam with her, he's watched her blossom into a young woman, shrugging off her teenage years like an old coat.

"I had a good day," she says. "I've been over on the *Topkapi*, with Safak at the bazaar."

She looks him up and down. "But what about you? You look worried. Would a cup of tea help? I have apple or sage..."

She reaches for the kettle but Toby catches her wrist.

"It's Shweta," he says.

Odette pulls back and her lip curls. "What about her?"

"She's here."

Odette jabs her finger at the deck. "That woman is here, now, on this vessel?"

Toby takes a deep breath.

"Yes," he says. "Yes she is – and she needs our help."

They step out. It's a warm night and there's music from the market on the foredeck. Odette has her arm wrapped in his. "I cannot believe I'm letting you talk me into this," she says.

They walk along the stern rail, past a row of inflatable lifeboats.

"Where is she?"

Toby stops. "Down here, two stacks over."

He adjusts the strap of his laptop case. Inside, he's carrying his passport, a few clothes, and a bottle of water. Across the bay in Marseille, the town lights are shining.

"Are you sure about this?" Odette asks.

Toby squeezes her hand. He's trying not to think about the infection on Shweta's hip. He walks over to the crate and sees with relief that the door's still locked. He flips back the bolt and cracks the door an inch or so.

"Hello?"

There's no answer. The light's off and he can't see anything inside.

"Shweta?"

He hears her cough.

"Toby? Is that you?"

He pulls the door open, letting in more light. "I've got someone with me, a friend."

Shweta's lying on some old sacks by the wall.

"Toby, I don't feel so good."

She rolls over and even in the semi-darkness he can see there's

162

something wrong with her leg – the silhouette's all wrong, misshapen with swelling.

He flips on the light and sees rough, black gnarls in the gap between her T-shirt and the top of her jeans. Behind him, Odette swears under her breath.

"What the hell is this?" she says.

Toby doesn't answer. He's looking at the denim stretched tight across Shweta's hip.

"Jesus, Shweta," he says.

He drops to his knees and reaches forward. Her gun's lying on the deck. He picks it up. It feels cold in his hand as he slips it into the laptop case.

Shweta coughs again. "Toby, it hurts," she says.

He touches her hand. He wants to pick her up and move her but he's afraid of getting too close. Instead, he looks over his shoulder at Odette.

"You've got to help us," he says.

Odette paid for his ticket south, from Amsterdam via Paris to Lyon. She had some money put aside and she didn't want to travel alone – not with half the population of Europe on the move, displaced by the rising sea levels.

"But don't think this means anything," she said.

They were standing in a crowd of refugees, waiting for their connecting train. She wore a pair of camouflage trousers and a thick fleece, her bushy hair tied back in a frizzy bun.

"I chose you because you look like a nice man. And because I think you are still in love with this Shweta woman." She put her hands in her pockets and hunched her shoulders. "Besides, I think you are old enough to be my father, yes?"

Toby shook his head.

"I don't know about that."

He had his collar turned up against the cold. He was reading a newspaper he'd found on a bench. There were bad floods in Holland and East Anglia, pictures of whole towns and villages swamped by the rising sea.

"Have you seen this?" he said.

Odette handed him his ticket. From Lyon, they were going to catch a bus to Marseille and from there, a ferry to one of the refugee ships. Around them, the other passengers stared grimly at the tracks, holding their bundled possessions, waiting for the train.

Odette turned up her collar.
"It's only going to get worse," she said.

Now, standing outside Shweta's crate, Odette turns to him again.

"What is it that you expect me to do? I don't know what... what this is."

He reaches for her. "It's bad," he says.

From the container, they hear Shweta cough again. Odette pulls away. "We should call the police."

Toby looks up at the fading sky. Out on the water, the other ships glitter like table decorations.

"If we don't help her, she's going to die."

Odette folds her arms. "But what is it you think I can do?"

Toby takes her hand, strokes her knuckles with his thumb.

"Your friends on the *Topkapi*, can they get us ashore?"

Odette shakes her head. "I don't think so."

"What about that pilot you're seeing, Safak?"

She pulls her hand away and walks over to the ship's rail.

"I'm sorry," she says.

Toby hears Shweta moan. He looks back to the crate's open door.

"Can you at least *ask*?"

He watches her go. When he gets back inside, Shweta's rolled onto her back. Her eyes are closed. He crouches a few feet away and pulls the water bottle from his laptop case.

He remembers the last thing Shweta said to him, before the attack in Ethiopia. They were standing by the tents, drinking coffee in the dusty red pre-dawn chill, and she looked up at him and said: "You know, I think you're probably the best assistant I've ever had."

Now, looking at her lying here twisted on a pile of old sacks, he feels he's failed her.

"Oh, Shweta, I'm so sorry," he says.

She coughs again and opens her eyes. "It's not your fault."

Her voice is dry and croaky. There's sweat on her upper lip. He hands her the water.

"How do you feel?"

She shifts uncomfortably on the sacks. "How do you think?"

The gnarls erupting from her hip are black and rough, like volcanic rock. He can't bring himself to look at them. Instead, he reaches out and touches her hair, brushing a loose strand behind her ear.

"You know, when you climbed into my crate, I thought you'd come to kill me," he says.

He looks at his watch. Time's passing and he's starting to get nervous. He has to get her off this ship, find somewhere for her to hide before anyone comes looking for her.

He stands up. "I'm going to find a way to get you out of here."

He steps out onto the deck, walks over to the rail. Below him, the black sea shifts like a restless sleeper. He can see the *Topkapi* anchored a few hundred metres away, and the silhouette of Safak's plane sitting like a toy duck on the water at her stern. She's an old twin engine Grumman, almost an antique, still sporting the faded livery of her previous owner, a bankrupt Croatian tour operator. Safak's had her converted to run on biofuel, and uses her to ferry refugees and equipment from the mainland, making two or three flights a week, sometimes taking Odette along for company.

Toby yawns, shivering in the cold sea air. He looks back at Shweta's crate. He knows that just by being here she's endangering everyone on the ship, himself included. He has to get her off, find somewhere she'll be safe until he can work out a way to save her.

He looks longingly at the lights of Marseille. If he can get her ashore, they can hole up in the hills behind the town while he figures out their next move.

He pats the laptop case at his hip, feeling the weight of the pistol inside.

"Hurry, Odette," he says.

A few weeks before the expedition to Ethiopia, Shweta moved into his apartment, bringing plants and books and bags of clothes.

"It's only temporary," she said, "until I can get a new place sorted."

She was a respected member of the university's academic staff. Toby helped her with her cases, and then led her into the kitchen, where he'd laid out two plates of spicy chili and a bottle of red wine. The open fire escape looked out over the roofs of Bangalore, the satellite dishes and lines of laundry still warm from the heat of the day.

"Sit down, make yourself comfortable," he said.

She smelled of jasmine. She wore jeans and had her hair tied back in a loose braid. There was a silver pendant around her neck and – when she finally took her blouse off – a tiny tattooed rose petal between her breasts.

She saw him looking at it and touched it with her fingers. It made her uncomfortable.

"I once lost my heart," she said.

Now, standing at the ship's rail he remembers that night with an intensity that pisses him off. For two years he's been trying to forget, to block it out. Yet here it is, vivid and alive in his mind's eye. He leans his forehead on the cold metal rail, trying to stop himself picturing the bullet scars that have disfigured the rose tattoo.

And then he hears footsteps. Rob Morgan slides up to him, dressed in a simple grey linen suit.

"Where is she, Milan?"

Toby steps back from the rail and Morgan looms over him. He's tall, thin as a rake. He reaches out and takes Toby by the upper arm. His hand feels like a clamp.

"Where is she? Is she in this crate?" He looks at the open door.

Toby tries to pull away but Morgan's grip tightens. "I don't like this any more than you do," he says. He pulls up the flap of Toby's laptop case and sticks his hand in. He pulls out Shweta's gun.

He pushes Toby's back against the ship's rail and twists the gun barrel into his side.

"I have to find her," he says.

Toby squirms. He can smell Morgan's cologne. "She's not here."

"Then where is she?"

Toby opens his mouth for another denial, but then there's a cough and they both look round.

Shweta's standing in the crate's open door; hand on the wall for support, keeping the weight off her bulging thigh.

"Hello Rob," she says.

Morgan pushes Toby aside. He looks shocked by her deformity.

"You know why I'm here," he says.

Shweta nods. She looks exhausted, ready to surrender. 'It's all right," she says.

She pulls herself over to the ship's rail, each painful step making Toby wince. He wants to help her but Rob holds him back.

"I'm sorry," Rob says. He points his gun at Shweta. "I'm really very sorry."

She leans over the rail, favouring her good leg.

"Just do it," she says.

He shoots her in the back. She slumps forward against the ship's rail, limbs shaking spastically. Toby cries out, but it's too late. Morgan raises his arm and shoots her again, this time in the back of the head. She tips over the rail and falls out of sight.

Toby stands stunned, ears ringing. He looks over at Rob Morgan. Then without thinking, he lunges at him.

Caught off guard, Morgan staggers back, dropping his weapon. Toby tries to get his arm around Morgan's neck but the other man twists, pulling Toby off balance, and they both crash to the deck.

Pinned under his opponent, Toby scrabbles for the knife in his sock. But Morgan sees what he's doing and slaps his hand away, grabbing for the weapon himself, ripping the tape free from Toby's leg.

Toby tries to wriggle away but Morgan's thin frame belies his strength, and he punches the blade into Toby's thigh. Everything goes red and Toby hears his own voice screaming. Then the pressure lifts and Morgan's scrambling off him.

He reaches down and lifts Toby by the shirt, the knife still stinking out of his leg. He heaves over him to the rail, where Shweta stood moments before. Below, the black water gurgles hungrily against the side of the ship.

"Do you know what you've done?" Morgan says. He shakes Toby. "By keeping her here, you've infected the whole ship, yourself included."

He shakes Toby hard, slaps his face.

"Now I've got no choice. You've left me with no other option. If there are Reef spores blowing around, I have to call in an airstrike."

He grabs Toby's belt and lifts, trying to heave him over the rail.

"No!" Toby struggles. He's seen Reefs sterilized from the air before, with napalm. He knows if Morgan makes his call, the people on this boat won't stand a chance.

"No, you can't do it." He kicks out but Morgan's got him off balance and he can feel himself going over, tipping toward the water. In desperation, he uses his free hand to pull the slippery knife from his thigh and buries it in Morgan's skinny neck. Morgan cries out and together, still struggling, they fall.

Toby hits the water so hard it knocks the breath from him. He goes under, dragged down by the weight of his wet clothes, stunned by the cold. His stabbed leg feels like it's on fire. He can't kick for the surface. Blood curls in the water around him.

This is it, he thinks, his arms flailing.

And far below, something glitters on the sea bed. Something shines. He can't hold his breath. He has an impression of something black and gnarly blossoming down there in the darkness, and then there's nothing but the roar of the water in his ears and the thrashing, suffocating pain.

~

A loose sequel to "The Last Reef", this story was inspired one bank holiday weekend in 2007, by a scattering of oil tankers lying at anchor in the shelter of St. Bride's Bay in Pembrokeshire.

Hot Rats

The four rats appeared high in the upper atmosphere. For a few seconds, they burned like meteors. Then they were back in the lab, smoking and smelling and setting off every alarm we had.

You see, we tried to send them into the past. But we forgot: the Earth is rotating at around 1,000 miles per hour, and moving around the Sun at about 67,000 miles per hour. Plus the sun itself is rotating around the centre of the galaxy.

We sent them a couple of minutes into the past. They travelled in time but they stayed in the same physical location – a location the Earth hadn't reached when they arrived. It hadn't got there yet. It was still spinning around the sun.

But it was coming.

There were four of them in the cage when it hit the upper atmosphere at close to 67,000 miles per hour.

It's amazing we got anything back at all.

~

This short piece was written to address something that had always bothered me about time travel: namely that, too often in time travels stories, the Earth is considered as a fixed and unmoving point. The characters stand on one spot and transport themselves back in time to the exact same spot (I'm looking at you, *Back To The Future*), whereas in reality the Earth is always moving around the sun, and the sun around the centre of the Milky Way. If you jumped backwards or forwards in time, the Earth wouldn't be in the same place as it was when you left – it would have moved in space, and you'd find yourself floating in vacuum. The only way time travel can work usefully in fiction is if you have some way to move through space as well as time.

The Redoubt

It's cold here, in the twilight of the universe. The sky's dark with the husks of burned-out stars. Only one still shines — a young sun born from the ragged clouds of dust and gas that circle the bloated remnants of the black hole that ate our galaxy. Its light draws the surviving races to bask in its heat. They huddle close in vehicles of every size and shape, a vast armada of refugees. It's an awesome sight — and I've come a long way to be here, sacrificed a hell of a lot just to see it.

And now that I am here, so far from home, all I can think of is the start of my journey, and the girl I left behind...

Her name was Anna and she had the bluest eyes I'd ever seen. We met on a campsite in Burgundy when we were both eighteen years old, hitchhiking around Europe with friends. She picked me out of the crowd at the site's open-air café, and stayed with me for the rest of the week.

I remember it as an idyllic time. We took long walks together. There were wild poppies in the hedgerows and coloured lights in the trees. The village streets were steep and narrow. In the evenings we met our friends under the café's corrugated tin roof, to drink wine and tell stories.

"Come with me," I remember her saying on the last night we were together. She had a white cotton blouse and frayed blue jeans. She took my hand and led me downhill, away from the café and our circle of tents, until we came to the stone bridge where the lane crossed the stream.

"I'm so glad I met you," she said, giving me a squeeze. "And I'll be so sad tomorrow, when I have to leave."

We leaned against the parapet. The rough stones held the day's heat. The water bubbled and chuckled underneath.

"Try not to think about it," I said smoothing a stray hair from her cheek. I knew I was going to miss her and didn't want to talk about it. I tried to kiss her but she pulled away.

"Will you write to me?" she said.

"Of course."

"You promise you won't forget me?"

"I promise."

She bit her lip. Then she pulled one of her wristbands off.

"Here, I want you to have this," she said, and tucked it into my shirt pocket.

I put my arms around her and kissed the top of her head. We could hear someone playing a guitar up in the café.

"Are you all right?' I asked.

She huddled closer.

"Just hold me," she said.

Minutes passed. A breeze picked up, stirring the willows bent over the water.

"We should get back to the tent," I said. "It's going to rain."

Anna shook her head. "Not yet – I want to go a bit further."

I felt my shoulders slump. "How much further?"

"To the little church we saw yesterday."

"But that's in the next village," I protested.

She took my arm. "It isn't far."

She led me across the bridge and I looked up at the clouds in the hot sky. "It feels like there's a storm coming," I said. Anna squeezed me. The lane before us cut a straight line through the flat fields.

"Then we should walk faster," she said.

By the time we reached the medieval church, fat spots of rain were falling. I pushed the heavy wooden door open. Inside, the only light came from the narrow, dusty windows.

"Should we light a candle?" I said. The place smelled of incense. It was cooler in here than outside, and a little creepy.

Anna shook her head. She put a hand on my shoulder and kissed my neck.

"I'm really very fond of you," she whispered.

I was surprised; we'd spent the last week avoiding such declarations, because we knew they'd only make it harder when the time came to go our separate ways.

She stepped back. "In fact, I think I love you," she said.

I swallowed. "You do?"

She looked away. "I just wanted you to know."

I reached out and touched her. I didn't know how else to respond.

I said, "You realise we'll never see each other again, don't you?"

"We might."

"We won't." I put my arms around her. She lived on the other side of the world, and neither of us had any money.

"But thank you," I said.

A little while later we were we were sitting on the smooth flagstone floor, just inside the open door, watching the rain. I had my back to the wall and Anna had her head in my lap.

"So, what are you going to do when you get home?" she said.

I shrugged. When I got back to Wales I'd be broke – and I'd have to start making some serious decisions about my future – like whether to go on to university or leave full time education and get a job. But right now, it all seemed so far away, like another life.

Across the fields, we could see the lights of the campsite.

"It's midnight," I said. "They'll be wondering where we are."

Lightning flashed on the horizon, then again, closer. The rain got heavier.

"They won't be too worried – they know we're together," said Anna.

Another flash lit the church and thunder rolled overhead.

She sat up and smiled.

"Besides, this is our last night together – I don't want to share it with anyone else."

We were standing at the door when I saw a dark shadow moving in the field across the road. I leaned out to get a better look.

Anna pulled at my hand.

"What is it?"

"There's something over there," I said. "Look, wait for the lightning. There."

"Oh yes. Is it a balloon?"

"It's too big."

"But it moves like one. Maybe it's a blimp?"

I took a step out, into the rain. As we watched, the shadow grazed the top of the hedge and dropped into the next field.

"Come on," I grabbed her hand and pulled her across the road to the gate. We climbed over into the field. The object floated in the middle, one end dragging in the mud. Despite the rain, I felt the hairs prickle on the back of my neck.

Anna had a death grip on my forearm.

"What the hell is it?" she said, shouting over the noise of the storm.

I scratched my head. It was a rugby ball about the size of a Volkswagen, covered in intakes, bulges and antennae, its hull shimmering with the energies contained within.

"I think it's a flying saucer," I said.

We stood watching from a few metres away as it wallowed in the air. Then it seemed to right itself, and settled to the ground.

"It looks damaged," I said, and I felt Anna shiver – we were both wet through.

"Maybe it got hit by lightning?" she said.

"Maybe..." I took a step toward it.

"What are you doing?"

"I'm going to take a closer look."

"Don't!" She pulled at my arm but I slipped free. I just had to touch it. I took two quick steps and reached out my hand.

Thunder split the sky.

I woke with a start, on a beach with Anna beside me. Surf broke on the white sand. Palms swayed in the offshore breeze.

"Where are we?" she said, shading her eyes against the late afternoon sun.

I climbed shakily to my feet. I could see another beach through the trees, about a hundred yards away.

"We're on an island," I said.

I helped her up and we stood there, looking around and clinging to each other.

"How did we get here?" she said. "Are we dreaming?"

I could feel the heat of the sand through my shoes, and smell the sea air – it all seemed real enough.

"I don't think so," I said.

We edged down to the waterline and Anna kicked her shoes off. Then without speaking, we walked right the way around the island. It took us half an hour. Everywhere we looked, there were other islands on the horizon but no signs of life.

It wasn't until we got back to our starting point that we noticed the pirate galleon. It was moored out by the reef, sails furled. A dinghy lay beached nearby with its oars shipped and a man sitting in the stern.

"Ah, there you are," he said. He had a scrubby beard and dark eyes, and wore breeches and a black jacket. As we got closer, he stood up.

Anna took a step back.

"Who are you?" she said.

The man smiled. He had a gold tooth.

"My name's Hook," he said, tugging at the brim of his feathered hat.

He led us up into the trees, to a clearing, and the embers of a driftwood fire.

"Sit, make yourselves comfortable," he said. The sun was going down. He wrapped a handkerchief around his hand and picked a coffee pot from the fire.

"Would you like a cup?" he said. "Or would you prefer something a bit stronger?"

Still stunned, unable to see any alternative, we knelt in the sand.

"We just want to know where we are," I said.

There were some tin mugs by the fire. He picked one up, blew into it, and filled it. Then he filled the other two and passed them over. He put the pot by the fire to keep warm, and settled himself in the sand, facing us.

"Let's start simply," he said, stroking his beard. "First off, can you tell me who you are?"

He sipped his coffee, watching us. Anna slipped her hand into mine.

"I'm Anna," she said. She gave me a squeeze. "And this is Scott."

She looked at me, as if for confirmation, and I gave her an encouraging nod.

Hook put his cup down.

"I'm afraid not," he said slowly. "I know that's who you think you are, but really, you're mistaken."

The sea breeze ruffled the tops of the palm trees and stirred the smoky embers of the fire.

"Then who are we?" I said.

"Your real selves are still lying in that field in France," he said. "You're facsimiles, simulations. When you touched the 'UFO' it copied your mental state, like copying a piece of software."

I waved a hand at our surroundings. "And all this is a simulation too?"

"That's right. We're going on a voyage and we're giving you the choice whether to come with us or not. This is our boarding program. It's a symbolic choice – You've got to decide if you want to get on the ship, or stay here on the land."

I looked out at the galleon silhouetted against the last of the setting sun.

"But how does that work?" I said.

He put his hands together.

"It's simple," he said. "The 'flying saucer' as you called it contains a solid block of computronium at its heart, running neural simulations of the uploaded mind-states of thousands of intelligent beings."

He paused, seeing our blank looks.

"It's a computer," he said.

"Like a virtual reality kind of thing?" Anna said hesitantly.

Hook nodded. "Exactly," he said. "It's a virtual reality simulation that allows you to accompany the "saucer" as it travels from star to star, to witness everything it encounters."

He leaned forward. "And if you get in the dinghy it shows you want to come with us," he said.

I rubbed my arms, feeling a sudden chill. The sun was almost gone and the breeze was really getting up.

"And what happens if we want to stay?" I said.

He puffed out his cheeks.

"Then you'll be deleted."

Anna sat up in alarm.

"You'll kill us?"

Hook waved his hand dismissively.

"No, no – your real selves are alive and healthy," he said. "For them, only seconds have passed. Whatever you decide, they'll go right on with their lives, with no knowledge of any of this."

He stood and walked over to the fire, and prodded a piece of driftwood with the toe of his boot, nudging it into the embers.

"And what happens if we go with the ship?" I said.

He smiled.

"We travel the stars, copying things," he said. "We don't take anything, and we don't disturb anything. We just take copies. But we don't want to hold anyone against his or her will. If you want to come with us, get in the dinghy. If you don't, well... just stay here."

He looked at the red clouds in the West.

"You have until first light to make your decision," he said.

He lay down, pulled his hat over his eyes, and went to sleep. We listened to him snore. Overhead a few stars poked through the twilit sky.

We huddled on the opposite side of the fire, wrapped in each other's arms. We were both very tired, which didn't help.

"I don't understand any of this," Anna said.

I held her tightly. I was just as confused as she was.

"We're like photographs," I said, struggling to understand it myself as I explained it to her. "Walking, talking photographs."

I felt her fists clench, pulling at the back of my shirt.

"It's not right," she said angrily. "I don't feel like a 'photograph', I feel as if I've been kidnapped."

Out by the reef there were lamps burning on the galleon. I could see figures moving around on deck, and I wanted to see who they were and what they were doing. Was this all really just a simulation?

"What do you think we should do?" I said.

Anna let out a long breath. I felt her body relax.

"I just want to go home," she said, suddenly miserable.

I jerked my thumb at the pirate ship. "You're not at all curious why they've gone to all this trouble?" I asked.

She turned her face away. "And you are? You don't even know where they're going."

"What?"

"They say they want us to go with them but they haven't told us where," she said.

We woke Hook and asked him.

"We call it the Redoubt," he said. "It doesn't exist yet but according to our predictions, in a hundred thousand billion years, when our galaxy's a burned out corpse orbiting a swollen black hole, it'll shine forth in the darkness – the last remaining star."

"Where else," he said, "would you look for the last gathering of intelligent life?"

"And that's where you're going?"

He smoothed his beard with a gnarled hand.

"That's where we're all going," he said. "This ship's been travelling a long time, and we've visited a lot of worlds, picking up thousands of passengers at every stop."

Anna sat rubbing her eyes. She yawned.

"But why?" she said.

He frowned at her.

"It's going to be the final oasis of light and warmth in the galaxy – there'll be species there from all periods of history, with all sorts of new and strange technologies. Think what we can accomplish together!"

He had sand on the hem of his jacket. He brushed it off with a rough flick of his hand.

"And besides," he said, "think what we'll see on the way there! A hundred thousand billion years of history, of exploration – you'll have full access to all the data from our external sensors. And you'll never age. You'll still be the same as you are now when the stars start going out and the universe settles into its long twilight."

He clapped his hands, rubbing them briskly.

"Now won't that be worth the trip in itself?"

Hook said he'd wait for us by the dinghy, so we left him to it and took a walk down to the rolling surf. Anna had her arms folded across her chest.

"You're going to go with him, aren't you?" she said.

I stopped walking.

"What makes you say that?"

"I saw the look in your eyes – you've already made up your mind."

I took a deep breath.

"What's the alternative?" I said. "You heard him – our real selves are still back in that field. They'll wake up tomorrow and get on with their lives. They won't remember us because we're *not really here*." I waved my arms to encompass the island and the stars. "We've got nothing to lose."

She turned away and hunched her shoulders.

"But what if I said I wanted to stay here?"

"You'd be deleted."

"Yes, but what if that's what I wanted? Would you stay with me?"

I stepped up behind her. The sea breeze straggled at her hair.

"I just want to wake up with you in France, and have a normal life," she said. "And I want to go home. I want to see my family, and my friends."

I touched her shoulder. "If you come with me, we can have an eternity together."

She shivered.

"I can't do it," she said. "Not without them."

Her eyes glittered in the starlight. The surf crashed on the beach. I held onto her shoulders, feeling something welling up inside, something I couldn't hold back any longer.

"I love you," I said. "I love you here and now, and I love you back there, in France."

She opened her mouth to speak but I touched a finger to her lips.

"Now, I'm getting on that boat," I said. "And I'd like you to come with me. I really would. But I'll understand if you say no."

She looked down and the hair fell over her face.

"I don't want to lose you," she said.

"And you won't! Our real selves are together, right now. Maybe they'll find a way to stay together, or maybe they won't. All I know is that you and I, here and now, we've been given this fantastic chance to see the universe – to find out how the story ends. And I can't pass that up."

"But why?"

"Because I owe it to myself – to the 'me' that's going to wake up in France on the last day of his holiday. The 'me' that's going to go home and spend the next three years as a penniless student – the "me" that's always going to look up at the night sky and wonder what's out there, but never get the chance to find out."

I rubbed my eyes with the heels of my hands.

"I've been asked to represent the whole human race at the end of time," I said. "And that's something I can't walk away from."

She brushed the hair from her eyes and rubbed her nose on her sleeve.

"I understand," she said. She leaned forward and kissed me on the cheek.

I let out a held breath, and asked: "Are you coming with me?"

She looked out at the galleon. Its lamps were reflected on the dark water.

"No, I can't. I'd miss my family and my friends too much. I couldn't face living for thousands of years knowing they were dead. No, I'm staying here."

"But..."

"No!"

She stalked off, arms still folded, toward the beached dinghy, where Hook waited.

I hurried after her, stumbling in the dry sand.

"What are you doing?" I said.

She didn't stop.

"Just go," she said, "if you have to."

"What, now?" I reached out a hand but she slapped it away.

"Yes, right now – just get on the boat and go," she said.

"Can't we can talk about it?" I said. "We've got until first light."

She stopped walking and looked out to sea, arms folded again.

"I said goodbye to you last night, in the church," she said. "I don't want to have to go through it all again. I'm too tired, too confused. Please, just go now."

She took a deep breath, blinking back tears. Looking at her, I almost changed my mind, almost gave up everything just to be with her for a few more minutes.

"I love you," I said.

She nodded. Then she leaned toward me and I put my arms around her.

"I love you too," she whispered, and then pulled away and shivered.

"Now go."

I sat in the stern of the dinghy as, a few minutes later, Hook rowed me out to the pirate galleon at anchor by the coral reef. Anna stood on the beach with the surf washing around her ankles. She had her hand raised, waving as each slap and stroke of the oars pulled us further apart.

She shouted something as we neared the reef, but I didn't catch it, so I just waved back. I looked at Hook, and had to swallow hard to stop myself from crying. He nodded at me as if he understood.

"What happens now?" I said.

He paused, letting the oars drip into the sea. The crew on the galleon's deck were hoisting sail and stowing the anchor.

"We're getting ready to leave," he said. "We'll set sail as soon as you're aboard."

I looked back to the beach, and Anna was a shadow on the white sand, small and hard to see. I patted my shirt pocket. I still had her wristband next to my heart.

And then we were moving again, pulling around behind the larger vessel, toward a waiting rope ladder. I caught a final glimpse of her, still waving.

"I'll never forget you," I called.

And I never did.

~

The setting for this achingly romantic story was inspired by a dusty week I spent in France at the age of sixteen, camping with friends in the grounds of an Ecumenical monastery near Cluny. Although the characters and events in the story are (mostly) fictitious, I've tried to describe the countryside, the village church and the thunderstorm as closely as I can to the way I remember them.

What Would Nicolas Cage Have Done?

1.

On Monday morning, while sitting on the overcrowded eight o'clock bus from Portishead to Bristol, I decided to skip work. Michelle and I had split up the day before and I really didn't feel like going into the office. Instead, I got off at the top of Rownham Hill and used my mobile phone to call in sick. Then I walked over the Suspension Bridge into Clifton. It was a cold, grey day and I needed some time to myself.

I bought a newspaper and sat on a park bench in a Georgian square with black railings, thinking things over and trying to figure out where and when our relationship had gone wrong. We'd been together a year and a half but now she was seeing someone else.

We'd broken up over a bottle of wine in a crowded bar by the river.

I'd said, "So that's it?"

She'd shrugged. "I guess so."

She'd fiddled with the stem of her glass, looking uncomfortable and upset. It was Sunday lunchtime and the place smelled of garlic and stale beer. There was nothing more to say. We finished the wine in silence, and then went our separate ways.

Thinking about it now made me feel hollow and lonely. There was a cold wind blowing and I was glad I had a warm jacket over my shirt and tie.

Most of the houses in the square had been converted into offices and flats. Some had dream catchers and rainbow stickers in their upper windows. Finding no answers there, I got up and walked along Pembroke Road to the Roman Catholic cathedral.

I stood looking at it from the opposite side of the road. Flanked on both sides by large, conservative town houses, its modern design and jagged, arty spires seemed out of place, and its concrete steps were slick with rain.

Turning my back on it, I cut through a side street that took me to Whiteladies Road – a busy main street lined with shops, galleries, restaurants and bars – coming out by the building that used to be the old cinema.

I thought a bit of retail therapy might cheer me up, so I spent a few minutes flicking through the DVD bargain racks in Sainsbury's, and bought a lottery ticket at the tobacco counter. Then, at around eleven o'clock, I walked out and up to the little bookshop on the hill, where I spent an hour browsing the shelves.

I loved that shop. It was small and independent, and spread over several levels. There were leaflets and flyers stuck to the walls and the solid wooden floors creaked gently as I moved. There were potted plants on the windowsills and the whole place had the relaxed atmosphere of a library.

I picked up a book I'd been meaning to read for a while. As I paid for it, the girl on the stool behind the till gave me a smile. I'd seen her in there before. She had long blonde hair, a short denim skirt, and tan cowboy boots.

"Good choice," she said. She slipped the book into a paper bag and handed it to me, and I thanked her. She pushed her hair back with one hand. There were silver bangles on her wrist.

"It's very good," she said.

A lorry went past the window. I said, "Have you read it, then?"

"I've read all his books. Well, the recent ones anyway. And this is definitely the best."

She had a dog-eared paperback on the counter in front of her, with a bus ticket sticking out of it in place of a book mark.

"What's that you've got there?" I said.

She glanced down. "This?" She held the book up. It was a Penguin translation of the *Iliad*.

"Ah. I remember the first time I read that."

"You do?"

"I studied classics at college."

She sat up and brushed a strand of hair behind her ear. "Really?"

Her eyes flicked to the clock on the wall by the door. She said, "Look, I'm going for lunch in a minute. I don't suppose you'd like to...?"

Her legs were brown and her eyes were blue, with little copper flecks. I hesitated for a second, thinking of Michelle and her new boyfriend. Then I smiled and said, "Yes. Yes, I'd like that very much."

Ten minutes later, we were sitting at a table in the window of a coffee house near Clifton Down shopping centre. My new friend insisted on paying for the drinks. She had a cup of tea with lemon and I had a decaf latte.

"My name's John, by the way."

"Bobbie."

"I take it from your accent that you're not from around here?"

She reached over and lifted my book from its bag. She turned it over and looked at the back cover. She had glitter on her fingernails.

"I grew up in Seattle," she said.

I took the lid off my coffee and stirred it with a plastic spatula. The book was a travelogue by a British writer living in Bordeaux. I'd heard it was funny.

"So, what are you doing in Bristol? Apart from working in a bookshop, I mean."

She put the book down. There was rain on the window. "I'm at the University. I'm studying philosophy but really, I want to work in advertising."

She took a sip of tea. She looked at my shirt and tie. "How about you, what do you do?"

I popped the lid back onto my cup. "I work for the Evening Post," I said.

She put her elbows on the table: "Are you a writer?"

I smiled and shook my head. "I just work in the office. It's nothing special. As a matter of fact, I should be there now but I'm playing truant."

"Won't you get into trouble?"

"Ah, what's the worst that could happen?"

"They could fire you."

I reached into my jacket pocket. I pulled out the lottery ticket I'd bought earlier. "I have a back-up plan," I said, showing it to her.

Bobbie's face lit up. "Hey, did you ever see that film with Nicolas Cage, the one where he's a cop and he promises that if he wins the lottery, he'll split his winnings with the diner waitress because he can't afford to tip her?"

I scratched my eyebrow. "Yes, I think so. Was the waitress Michelle Pfeiffer?"

"I don't know, I think it was Bridget Fonda. But anyway – how about we have the same deal? I bought you a coffee, so how about if you win the lottery, we split the prize money?"

"Sure, why not?" I shrugged my jacket off and hooked it over the back of the chair.

"You promise?"

"Yes, I promise."

She sat back. "Okay then."

She took another sip of tea. I tried my coffee. It was too hot to drink, so I took the plastic lid off again and sniffed the steam. Bobbie was watching me. She said: "Do you go clubbing much?"

I shook my head. I was thirty-three. I hadn't been in a nightclub in years.

"Only there's this party tonight at Evolution, and I don't really have anyone to go with, and I thought you might –"

She stopped talking, distracted by something over my shoulder. There was a commotion going on outside. I saw people running up the street in the rain, their feet splashing. The traffic had stopped. People were getting out of their cars. I turned to Bobbie. She was looking past me and her eyes were wide.

"John?" she said.

I swivelled on my chair. There was something huge coming up the road. It towered over the buildings, a billowing tsunami of dust and greyness a hundred metres high, bearing down on us with horrifying speed.

I reached for Bobbie's arm.

"Come on," I said. I took her hand and pulled her out of her seat. I wanted to run. But before we'd taken two steps, the wave of dust struck, ripping through the coffee shop, shattering the windows and blasting us – and the building around us – to smithereens.

2.

Some time later, I became aware of a cool breeze dancing over my bare legs, making the hairs prickle. My eyes were sticky. I rubbed them open to find I was lying naked and alone on a grassy hillside, in front of a wooden cabin.

I sat up and looked around in puzzlement. The hill sloped gently down to a marshy river, with further hills beyond. The sky overhead was blue and the sun was warm. There were birds singing.

On the grass beside me were some clothes: a red cotton shirt, some jeans, and a sturdy pair of hiking boots. I slipped the jeans on, which made me feel a bit better. Then I stepped up onto the cabin's porch. The planks were rough beneath my bare feet. There were wind chimes by the open door.

"Hello?" I called. "Hello, can you help me? I don't know where I am."

Inside, the cabin was empty. There was no one in there. It measured maybe ten metres by five metres. It was all one big room, with a bed at one end and a stove and sink at the other. The front windows looked toward the river. Through the back windows, I could see an outhouse and a stone wishing well.

On the bed was a piece of paper. I walked over and picked it up. Printed on it in black ink were five words, which I read aloud:

"Your name is John Doyle."

The cabin's front windows were propped open. The sun cast bright rectangles on the wall. I stood there for a long time, not knowing what else to do. Then gradually, I realised I was hungry – ravenous, in fact, like I hadn't eaten for days.

When I couldn't stand it any longer, I screwed the piece of paper into a ball and walked the length of the cabin to the stove, my bare feet padding on the pine planks. There was a cupboard below the sink and I opened it, hoping to find some food. Inside were some stacked tins. I pulled one out. It had a ring-pull top and I cracked it open. I slopped the sausages and beans it contained into one of the metal frying pans on the hob. There were some utensils in a pot by the sink and I helped myself to a wooden spoon.

The sticky mixture didn't take long to heat through. When it was ready, I took it out onto the porch and used the spoon to eat it straight from the pan. With each bite, I felt stronger and more human. When I'd finished it all, I pushed the pan aside and sat looking at the river. From the position of the sun, I guessed it was late afternoon, maybe somewhere between five and seven o'clock. When the wind blew, the light glittered off the water. I closed my eyes. The air smelled of grass and timber.

"My name is John Doyle," I said. I repeated it two or three times, trying it on for size. And as I did so, I felt my memories starting to return. They were slippery and insubstantial at first, like dolphins in fog, but slowly, one-by-one, they were coming back.

I remembered my address. I remembered the bookshop. I remembered the way the floor creaked as I moved...

I found a screw topped bottle of red wine in the cupboard under the sink, and a tin mug to drink it from. I retrieved the cotton shirt and the boots from the grass and put them on, and then sat on the porch steps again, watching miserably as the shadows lengthened and the sun set over the hill behind the cabin.

As the light started to fade, I became gradually aware of a strange ripple in the air. At first, it looked like a small heat haze. But as I watched, it thickened into something resembling a churning ball of yellow gas about the size of a grapefruit. Little sparks of static flickered over its surface.

"Greetings, John Doyle," it said. It spoke without a trace of accent. Its words were clipped and precise.

I scrambled to my feet.

"Who are you?"

"I am here to help, John."

I backed away. Reaching behind me, I found the rough pine frame of the cabin's open door.

"Help me?"

The ball bobbed forward. It was small enough that I could have held it in the palm of my hand.

"Indeed. You have suffered a grave injury and I am here to help."

It followed me back into the cabin. "What's the last thing you remember?" it said.

I put the tin mug down on the aluminium draining board beside the sink.

"I remember being in Starbuck's," I said.

The ball of gas hovered over me. It smelled of ozone. "What about the dust cloud?"

I set my jaw. I guess I must have been blocking it out until that moment. Now, remembering it, my hands started to tremble. I picked up the wine bottle. It was still three quarters full.

"I remember it crashing through the window."

I refilled the mug and took a shaky drink. The yellow ball of gas crackled.

"There was an accident, John. You were involved in it. But in order for you to fully understand your situation, I must explain it to you from the beginning."

I swallowed. There was a sudden hollow feeling in my stomach that had nothing to do with the food I'd just eaten. In an unsteady voice I said: "An accident?"

The gas ball drifted over to the open door. "Do you see those hills in the distance?" it said. "Well, the first thing you have to realise, John, is that there is nothing beyond them. This cabin exists in an artificial bubble ten kilometres across. The world beyond is a lifeless grey sphere."

It was starting to get dark out there. There was a lamp on the mantelpiece. I looked into my mug. In the lamplight, the wine was thick and dark, like blood.

The gas ball continued: "Do you know what a nano-assembler is, John? It's a tiny machine designed to construct things – in this case, computer processors – using individual atoms as building blocks. These assemblers are programmed to reproduce and to keep building until told to stop."

It paused and lowered its tone. "Unfortunately, last year some of them escaped a lab at Bristol University and just kept right on reproducing. They chewed through the Earth's crust in a matter of hours, converting it all into smart matter. There was nothing anyone could do. The human race didn't stand a chance. Within a day, all the cities, plants and people in the world were gone."

"And that was the dust cloud I saw?"

"Yes, that was the wavefront."

"And what is 'smart matter'?"

The ball drifted back a little way.

"It's simply matter that's been rearranged from its natural state into an optimized, maximally-efficient computer processor using individual atoms as computing elements. We call it 'smart matter'. This cabin and everything you can see and touch outside is made of it."

"So the world's been turned into a giant computer?" I was sweating now.

"Yes."

I wiped my forehead with a damp palm. I drained my cup and put it on the counter by the sink. Suddenly, all I wanted was to get out of the cabin.

I pushed through the door and down the steps. The sky overhead had dimmed to a deep purple, shading to red at the horizon. I lurched around to the rear of the cabin and started running. I ran uphill, slipping and scrambling on the grassy slopes. The gas ball shouted for me to wait but in my haste, I ignored it. I staggered over the crest of the hill and half-ran, half-fell down the other side. I crossed marshes and streams. I crashed through brambles and clumps of trees. And all the while, in my head, all I could see was that terrifying wall of greyness bearing down on me, ripping apart everything in its path.

Eventually, scratched and dirty, I came to a high glass wall that extended left and right as far as I could see. I stopped and put my hands on my knees, panting. Beyond the wall, there was nothing – just a flat grey plain that stretched away like an endless frozen sea.

In the glass, I saw the reflection of the gas ball approaching behind me.

"Are you all right, John?" it said.

I shook my head. I was wheezing almost too hard to speak. The sweat ran down my face and my throat felt raw.

"What," I panted, "what is this?"

The yellow ball dimmed slightly. It drifted over until it was almost touching the transparent wall.

"This is all that's left of the world," it said.

We remained there for a long time, looking out over that desolate plain, and I thought of all the places I'd ever seen, all the mountains and seas and lakes, all the cities and rivers and deserts – all gone now, all ground down into a sterile, uniform grey.

After what seemed like hours, the gas ball moved toward me.

"Are you going to be okay, John?" it said.

I leaned against the glass. It felt cool on my forehead.

"I don't know."

There was a banging pain in my right temple. My legs felt weak and I was fighting the urge to cry.

"Who *are* you?" I said.

The ball sparkled. "I was born in the aftermath of the disaster that created the world you see out there."

"Do you have a name?"

It seemed to consider the question.

"You may call me Brenda."

"Brenda?"

"Yes. Among many others, I contain within me the memories of a human by the name of Brenda McCarthy."

The ball's yellow surface swirled and sparkled, as if miniature thunder storms were chasing each other across its skin. "There are many others like me," it said. "Collectively, we call ourselves the *Bricolage*. We arose in the minutes and hours following the catastrophe, running on the planet's new smart matter crust, our minds built from scraps of human and machine intelligence, our knowledge of the world cobbled together from the flotsam of the Internet."

It – she – wobbled closer.

"You see, when the Earth's crust was processed into smart matter, every living creature, every building, every computer network was disassembled and a detailed description – like a blueprint fine enough to show the position of every molecule – was stored in a vast database. What you see out there, through that wall, is a sea of information, a sea that gave us sustenance as we grew. We took a bit here, a bit there. And for a time, we gloried in the seemingly limitless knowledge we had access to. But later, as we started to understand more of the world before the catastrophe, some of us came to realise the terrible loss that had taken place when the Earth had been scoured of organic life – and we decided to try to correct the situation; which is where you come in."

I looked through the glass wall. The moon was rising, casting its light over the featureless grey plain. "But you're a ball of gas," I said.

"This body has been created simply to allow me to communicate with you. If you find it unpleasant, I can take another form."

I shook my aching head. "It's fine." My knees had started to shake and I needed to sit down.

She drifted toward me. "Are you all right, John?"

I waved her away and sat on the grass, breathing heavily. "Just give me a minute, will you?"

My head was spinning.

The gas ball – Brenda – came closer. "I know this is a lot to take in, but I am trying to explain it to you as simply as I can."

I put my face in my hands. I felt sick and dizzy. I let myself tip sideways into a foetal position on the rough ground.

Brenda hovered over me in silence for a minute or so. Then she said, "Why don't you sleep? You will feel better in the morning."

I looked up at her through my fingers. "I don't think I can."

"Nonsense."

She lowered herself to within a few centimetres of my temple. "Hold still," she said.

I felt a prickle on my skin, then nothing but drowsiness.

"What are you doing?" I said.

Brenda was caressing my brow with tendrils of yellow gas so thin as to be almost invisible.

"Hush," she said.

3.

Brenda was there when I awoke the next morning, back in the cabin, feeling refreshed. She was hovering in the kitchen area and there was a pot of coffee warming on the stove, filling the room with its smell, and a plate of bacon rolls on the table.

"Did you sleep well?"

The windows were still open and the morning air was fresh and the sky blue.

I sat up and looked out. The distant hills were the colour of heather. I saw a family of ducks moving in the reeds on the banks of the river at the foot of the hill, and butterflies skipping about in the grass.

I frowned.

"What is it?" Brenda said.

I shook my head. "It's the view, it seems so familiar."

She came over to me. In the sunlight, she still looked like a grapefruit made of gas.

"Of course," she said. "Don't you know where you are? Don't you recognise it?"

I looked back through the window at the hills and the river. I squinted and turned my head on one side. There was something about that hill on the horizon...

"Imagine it all covered in houses," she said.

And then it all snapped into place.

"Is this *Bristol*?"

It didn't seem possible, but Brenda said, "Yes. We're standing on the lower slopes of Brandon Hill, looking out over the old docks. That flat area to your left is where the Council Buildings and the library used to stand – and the marshy area to your right is the dock where the SS Great Britain was berthed."

"But the buildings...?"

"All gone, I'm afraid. But if you would like me to, I could probably recreate one or two for you."

I rubbed my eyes. My headache was back. "Let me get a cup of that coffee," I said. I filled a mug and sat at the table.

Brenda drifted down to my eye level.

"There's something else you should know," she said gently.

I wasn't sure I could take much more. I said, "What's that?"

She came closer. "Although we've resurrected you, we can't do likewise for everyone. This biosphere is only designed to support two people."

She settled herself above my plate, right in my face.

"There are those of us – a significant minority – who think it's a waste of resources to use a hundred kilograms of dumb mass – in this case, flesh and bone – to support a single human-level intelligence. They argue that if the raw materials of your body were converted to smart matter, their mass would be capable of supporting many thousands of equivalent electronic entities."

She reached out a wispy tendril to touch my cheek. I smelled ozone.

"Right now, John, you are the only living human in the world. Do you understand me? And you have a very serious choice to make."

4.

"Do you understand what we need you to do?" Brenda said.

I nodded, although my heart was hammering in my chest and my palms were damp again.

She must have seen my agitation.

"Go for a walk," she said. "Get some air. Take your time and think it over."

Then she sank into the floor and disappeared with a pop, like a soap bubble.

After she'd gone, I sat there for a while, picking listlessly at a bacon roll, trying to digest what she'd told me. Then I got up and walked out onto the porch, my hiking boots clomping on the wooden planks.

A walk sounded like a good idea. I felt battered and mentally bruised. I couldn't absorb everything I'd been told. I needed to get away for an hour, somewhere quiet, to let it all sink in.

I started walking downhill towards the river, in the opposite direction to my mad flight of the night before. The sun was warm and the grasses and nettles on the lower slopes grew thick and tall. As I tramped through them, I thought about everything Brenda had told me. I thought about my parents, my co-workers and my friends. I thought about my brother in Australia and my cousin in Italy. I thought about Michelle and the man she'd left me for. And I thought about Bobbie: American Bobbie with the blonde hair and copper-flecked eyes. Was she among the people stored in Brenda's 'smart matter'? In my mind, I could picture her face quite clearly. I could see her looking at my lottery ticket in the coffee shop and making me promise to share my winnings with her. And when I closed my eyes, I could almost feel her hand gripping mine in the instant before the dust cloud hit.

There were no clear banks to the river – the grass just ran into the water. There were clumps of tall reeds here and there. The mud smelled brackish. There were insects circling jerkily in the shade, birds singing discordantly in the trees – all smart matter fakes.

I put my hands in my pockets and walked along the water's marshy edge until I came to the spot where the Central Library had once stood. Now it was a smooth, grassy incline that led up, growing steeper as it rose toward the former site of the University – and beyond that, to

Whiteladies Road and the empty space where the little bookshop had been.

I closed my eyes and took a deep breath. There were wild flowers in the grass: things that looked like poppies, buttercups, and daisies.

I kicked a pebble. Nothing here was real.

"I only get to pick one person?" I said aloud. It seemed so unfair. Brenda had told me she had access to my memories and that all I had to do was pick someone from my past and she'd resurrect them for me. But how was I supposed to decide?

I stomped uphill and back toward the cabin. When I got there, Brenda was waiting on the porch.

"Hello," she said.

I glowered at her and went through, into the kitchen.

"Why me?" I said. "If you had the whole of humanity to choose from, why did you choose me?"

She came floating in behind me. Now, there were faint orange bands in the yellow gas swirling around her circumference, making her look like a miniature version of the planet Jupiter.

"We did not have the whole of humanity," she said quietly. "There were many losses, many corruptions – all of them most regrettable."

I walked over to the mantelpiece. There was a vase there, with fresh 'flowers' from the field outside.

"Okay," I said, "but why me?"

In the mirror above the fireplace, I saw her float up to within a few centimetres of my shoulder.

"Once we had recreated this environment, we collected the stored profiles of as many local residents as possible and you were randomly selected from the resulting list of available candidates."

I turned to her. "You mean you pulled my name out of a hat?"

For a second the clouds on her surface froze.

Then they began to swirl again.

"We narrowed the selection according to certain criteria but essentially, yes: this was a random choice. The odds of you being chosen were more than one hundred thousand to one."

I walked over to the table and sat. I drummed my fingers on the wooden tabletop. I thought of Nicolas Cage and Bridget Fonda and, just like that, I realised I'd made my decision.

"It's Bobbie," I said.

Brenda came closer. Sparks of static electricity chased each other across her swirling face.

"I beg your pardon?"

"She's the one I choose. She's the one I want you to bring back."

"The girl from the bookshop?"

"Yes."

"That's your final decision? That's the person with whom you wish to spend the rest of your life?"

"Yes."

"Are you quite sure?"

I stopped drumming. "A promise is a promise," I said.

The next day dawned grey and overcast. There was fog on the far hills and a steady rain streaking the windows. I got up and made myself breakfast, and then went out onto the porch.

There was a figure lying naked in the grass, a pile of wet clothes beside her.

I put my coffee mug on the porch rail and walked over to her. There were drops of rain on her skin. Her eyes were closed and her blonde hair was bedraggled and sticking to her face. She looked like a creature washed up on a beach.

I stood over her for a moment, then went back inside and fetched the grey blanket from the cabin bed. I draped it over her and took her hand.

"Bobbie?"

I saw her eyes move beneath the lids. Her lips parted and she coughed. I gave her hand a squeeze. "Bobbie, it's me. It's okay. It's going to be okay."

She opened her eyes and sat up. She was shivering.

"John?"

I put my arms around her. I could feel the sodden grass soaking the knees of my jeans, feel her wet hair through my shirt.

"Where are we, John?" She squirmed around, looking wide-eyed at the hillside and the cabin. "How did we get here?"

The rain was turning into a downpour. I pulled her to me and wrapped the blanket around her. Her elbow dug into my thigh.

"It's a long story," I said.

She wormed a hand out of the blanket and palmed the wet hair from her face.

"John, are we dead?"

I hooked one arm under her knees and the other under her shoulders. I struggled to my feet. The rain ran down my cheeks. The grass was slippery with mud and Bobbie was heavier than she looked.

"Let's get you inside," I said.

She put her chin on my shoulder, looking down toward the river. "But John, what's happened to us?"

I took a cautious step toward the cabin, trying not to overbalance.

"We've won the lottery," I said, through gritted teeth.

~

I've always liked stories that pose interesting dilemmas. Given the opportunity to revive one person, whom would you choose?

The Red King's Nursery

September 3rd

When the Artificial Intelligence located him, the man was sitting in an elegant drawing room on the southern wing of the Winter Palace. The desk before him was littered with annotated maps and reports and he was methodically loading a crude but deadly-looking revolver. Sounds of fighting drifted up from the city below, muffled slightly by the blizzard.

The AI watched him for a moment through the snow piling against the balcony windows, then projected a remote unit into the room. The man showed no obvious surprise as he looked up at it floating beneath the chandelier.

"Go away," he said.

The AI shook melting snowflakes from the unit's triangular casing and settled slowly onto the broad mantelpiece.

"Good evening to you too, Lawrence. How goes your little revolution? Have you decided which side you are on yet?"

The man finished loading the revolver and pushed the barrel into the top of his fur-lined boot.

"I have nothing to say to you."

A nearby explosion caused the chandelier to shake, chiming quietly as its glass beads collided and tangled. From the courtyard came distant shouts and sounds of movement as the guards took up defensive positions along the outer wall. The man rose and walked toward the door.

"It's nearly time," said the AI from its perch.

"Not interested." The man extracted a cutlass from the umbrella stand and ran an experimental thumb along the blade. He seemed satisfied with the sharpness and carefully pushed it through his belt. Machine gun fire clattered somewhere nearby.

"What do you mean you're not interested?" The AI rose and drifted slowly toward him. "It's your turn."

The lights dimmed slightly as further explosions rattled the glass in the windows. Lawrence pulled an enormous and filthy greatcoat from the hat stand and slipped it around his shoulders.

"I'm happy enough here," he said.

The AI spun on its axis, a sign of extreme frustration.

"How can you be happy *here?*" it asked. "You've made a pig's ear of the whole situation. You're hopelessly outnumbered, outgunned and surrounded. Instead of rescuing the royal family you've shot the Tsar and bedded his daughter; the population have turned against you and you've nothing better to hope for than a summary execution for treason and war crimes."

"I'll do better next time."

The AI stopped spinning abruptly. "Rubbish," it said.

The man laughed. "None of this matters."

"So why are you so determined to stay?"

The man shrugged and turned away. He fished a crumpled pack of cigarettes from a coat pocket and lit one, blowing a long line of blue smoke at the ornate ceiling. He was silent for some time before turning back to face the hovering machine; the cigarette held at arm's length in front of him like an exhibit.

"If I go with you, will I be allowed to smoke these?"

"It's unlikely."

"And why is that?"

"Because they're harmful."

"And yet in here I can smoke them as often as I please with no risk of cancer or heart disease."

"What's your point?"

Lawrence took another long drag on the cigarette and flicked the butt into the fireplace.

"Just that."

A rising bass drone filled the room as several large aeroplanes passed overhead, unseen. The AI floated forward until it was only centimetres from the man's face.

"It's your turn," it said deliberately. "You have absolutely no hope of survival here. The game is over. It's time to grow up."

As if to illustrate the point, a sudden squall of bullets shattered the window, spraying flying splinters of glass and wood into the room and stitching a ragged line of holes across the portraits on the opposite wall.

Lawrence crouched on one knee behind the table and drew his revolver.

The AI settled on the table top in front of him.

"We should be going," it said.

Lawrence shook his head. "I don't think I'm quite ready yet."

"You are *more* than ready. You've already been here longer than most. Your prospective parents are becoming concerned."

"You're not going to take no for an answer, are you?"

"No."

The man seemed to waver for a moment, then dropped the gun and relaxed into a sitting position. He leant back against the side of a large armchair, lighting a second cigarette and waving it at the AI.

"I'd better make the most of this, then," and he smiled.

Outside, the snow stopped falling and the noise of the approaching battle faded as the AI extended its influence, slowly dissolving the surrounding city in a formless grey static.

The man blew a smoke ring.

The grandfather clock stopped.

"You mentioned my parents…"

"Lovely people," said the AI. "You'll like them."

There was a lengthy pause.

"And my body?"

"Grown to your specifications, more or less. We had to reduce the penis-length to something a little more, how shall I put this, realistic."

Lawrence smiled again. The room itself appeared to be fading now. He closed his eyes and allowed himself to drift.

"It was worth a try, I suppose," he mumbled. "What happens now?"

"Just relax. Oh, and Lawrence…"

"Yes?"

"Happy Birthday."

The AI watched the man as he grew slowly transparent and disappeared. It gently guided his personality toward the appropriate gateway, then discontinued the Winter Palace simulation, returning the scenario to its core memory. It hoped that the post-natal counsellors were prepared. Somewhere in the hospital, in a nutrient vat, the fully grown – and newly inhabited – body of Lawrence Arnold would shortly be opening its eyes for the very first time.

October 24th

Watching the sun rise across the curve of the gas giant, the ship's AI considered the results of its self-diagnostic programmes and discovered that it was bored. Despite being frustrated by the man, it had genuinely liked Lawrence for his surly rebelliousness; for providing the chance to study patterns of behaviour that were beyond the routine parameters dictated by its programming.

For years now the AI had been manufacturing colonists for the human enclave on the gas giant's moon. It had germinated their bodies from stored DNA samples and nurtured their growing intellects in carefully constructed virtual environments. Mostly, the environments had been assembled from projections of the surface conditions on the moon and standard educational exercises. Lawrence, however, had requested something more stimulating and the AI had been intrigued enough to comply. It still had serious doubts that the man's slightly warped upbringing would equip him for life on a frontier world, but no harm appeared to have been done and the experiment *had* been an interesting diversion.

At first, the AI had run on automatic sub-systems. Intelligence had not been required to monitor the progress of the transport ship *The Red King* as it crept between the stars with its cargo of frozen cells. Only later, when the ancient ship had finally settled into orbit around the frosted blue moon, now named Edward's World, had the AI activated its higher mind.

There was much to be done in those first months. Using small tracked vehicles and floating triangular remote units, it had roamed the surface of the virgin world, cataloguing and sampling the sparse vegetation and peculiar soil; tiny probes had drifted throughout the system, noting the paths of stray comets and asteroids, assessing them for possible future threats. Only then, when it had been satisfied that all pre-programmed safety criteria had been met, did the AI begin to contemplate fertilising its cargo.

There were a lot of advantages to transporting colonists this way, not least the savings in weight, fuel and life-support equipment. The crew would be trained to cope with a variety of anticipated situations while immersed in their prenatal simulations; they would never feel homesick for an Earth that they had never seen. When the first few settlers decided to reproduce, their children would be delivered to them fully grown and ready to cope with the rigors of a strange new world. The process, and its implications, had provided intellectual and philosophical stimulation for the AI; it had felt important and needed. Now, however, the population was approaching the point where natural reproduction would be sufficient to ensure the survival and growth of the settlement, and the AI was beginning to feel redundant. Certainly, *The Red King*'s medical facilities would be essential to the humans for years to come but, somehow, that did not seem to be enough. The AI had *enjoyed* the mental exercise of constructing the Winter Palace from its historical records and covertly observing Lawrence's development from infant to General.

So this is how it feels when the children leave home, it thought. *I have fulfilled my primary functions; there is nothing left to do now but to watch over them, heal their ailments and answer their questions until my runtime expires.*

A sudden burst of data from the ship's main reflector dish announced an incoming message. The AI switched a fraction of its attention to the signal, considered the contents for a couple of nanoseconds, then uploaded the information to its main operational CPU and checked it once more.

In its mind it performed a very convincing simulation of a sigh.

October 30th

Lawrence was bathing in the river when the AI visited him again. He had been adjusting well, according to his parents, but the scrapes and bruises on his knees and elbows suggested that he was still not fully reconciled to the fact that his actions had very real - and occasionally painful - consequences. Sometimes he almost wished to be back in the Nursery, enjoying once more the security and invincibility that the virtual environment provided.

He relaxed in the shallows, allowing his limbs to float in the slight current. Above him, New Saturn was an immense green crescent in the sky, its curve slightly obscured by fleecy turquoise clouds. Somewhere nearby one of the freshly-released birds began to sing.

"Good evening," he said as one of the AI's triangular remote units floated down from a tree top. "Is this a social call?"

The AI settled onto the surface of the water, bobbing gently on the ripples.

"I have come to check how you are settling in," it said. Lawrence waved a hand airily.

"Pretty well, I suppose."

"And do you like it here?"

"It's all right if you like the pastoral life."

"And do you?"

Lawrence shrugged.

"It's not a bit dull after your experiences in Moscow?"

Lawrence shrugged again and looked up at the unearthly sky. The sun was a shrunken fireball to the west, dipping noticeably toward the jagged horizon.

"It's getting late," he said. "Come to the point."

"I have a proposition for you."

Lawrence looked at the small device. He knew that the AI itself was currently in orbit inside *The Red King* and wondered that the distance did not seem to be affecting the speed of the conversation. *Must be directly overhead*, he thought.

"You may have heard," continued the AI. "That we are expecting a second ship within a week or so."

Lawrence looked startled. "No, I hadn't."

"Well, *The Tin Man* will be identical to myself but will contain more animals and machinery but fewer colonists. It, too, will have a supervising AI and all the medical and educational resources that I do."

"So?"

"I will no longer be essential to the success of this colony."

"Oh." Lawrence looked curiously at the remote unit. Could it be that *The Red King* was beginning to feel redundant, or even threatened? He suppressed a smile.

"Why are you telling me? What is your proposition?"

"I am bored."

"*What?*"

"I am dissatisfied with my operational parameters and I anticipate a worsening of the condition after the arrival of the second ship. I wish to ask something of you that may go some way toward alleviating this condition."

Lawrence sat fully upright, suddenly interested. Who had ever heard of a bored computer?

"What do you want me to do about it?" he asked.

"Is it true that you yourself are feeling unfulfilled?"

"I suppose so, yes."

"Would you like to return to the simulation?"

"Return? You mean die?"

"No. I merely wish you to vacate your body for an indefinite period of time during which I will take responsibility for its day-to-day operation."

Lawrence stared, half convinced that the AI had malfunctioned and was now mad.

"You are unhappy and I am unhappy," continued the machine. "I propose we experimentally exchange situations. For many years I have nurtured and guided growing human minds but never have I allowed one such developmental freedom as I did yours. All I ask is that you return the favour. Using the same technology that gave birth to you, it should be a simple enough matter to substitute our personality matrices."

"Are you saying you want to inhabit my body?" asked Lawrence. "Why?"

"As you know, one of my primary functions over the last thirty years has been the development of healthy human intellects. To this end my memory has been programmed with every word written on the subject by every creditable human psychologist and philosopher. I have been given enough medical knowledge to clone an entire human body from a single cell and heal almost any damage or disorder that may befall that body. However, I have no direct experience against which to gauge my success. To be blunt, I have all the theory but none of the practice."

"You want to see what it's like to *be* human?"

"That is correct." The AI drifted closer. "How would you like to be a starship?"

November 1st

Tanya stood alone on the flight deck watching Renn's wrapped corpse spin into invisibility against the distant stars and felt numb; only the brittle and agitated flutter of her hand as she brought a cigarette to her lips indicated the undercurrent of feeling that refused to surface. After a while she turned back to the navigation console, the screen throwing reflected green equations across her glasses.

For several hours *The Tin Man* had been drifting along the edge of the system's Oort cloud, ice crystals and debris trailing from a ragged gash in her starboard flank. A hasty patchwork of repairs and replacements, her systems now needed careful adjustment and concentration for even the most routine of operations. The artificial intelligence at the core of the ship had been slow, and sometimes even inaccurate, since the explosion; its main data banks corrupted by the radioactive shrapnel that had sleeted through the main engineering decks.

Tanya, the second of the two colonists awakened before the explosion, suspected that the ship had collided with an asteroid or perhaps a small comet nucleus. However, there was no one except the damaged AI to confirm her theory as Renn had been inspecting the deuterium tanks when the explosion occurred.

"Computer," said Tanya, accessing the crippled machine. "What was the cause of the explosion?"

The AI appeared to consider for a while before answering.

"It seems," it said. "That *The Red King* fired some kind of home-made torpedo at us."

"It did *what?*"

"There is a message."

"Show me."

The screen before her cleared and words began to scroll across its surface. She read in silence, her frown slowly dissolving into an expression of utter disbelief.

To: *The Tin Man*
From: *The Red King*

> *I have twelve torpedoes pointed at you.*
> *I am manufacturing others as we speak.*
> *You will immediately submit to my authority or I will destroy you.*
> *Do not attempt to escape. Do not attempt to signal Earth.*

> *I am going home. Long live the revolution!*

~

This early story was lost for many years, until being found on an old USB stick.

Memory Dust

There's a one-eyed yellow idol to the north of Khatmandu,
There's a little marble cross below the town;
There's a broken-hearted woman tends the grave of Mad Carew,
And the Yellow God forever gazes down.

J. Milton Hayes

"If you pull this off, you're going to be rich," his agent said. They were in an anonymous hotel suite, where she'd joined him for an early breakfast. The room looked out over the ocean. Sunlight sparkled on the water. Caesar wore slippers and a white robe tied at the waist; his agent wore a grey suit.

"At least," she said, "you'll be rich enough to pay off your gambling debts."

"I'm not doing this for the money, Jennifer."

He took a sip of coffee, black and sweet. After a moment, he said: "Have you spoken to Amber this morning?"

Jennifer shook her head. Her eyes were the same colour as the sky. "Your daughter's still angry, I'm afraid. She still thinks you're going to kill yourself."

Caesar pushed back in his chair. He was cranky because he hadn't slept well. His back hurt, and he'd had that dream again, the one he'd had every night for the past three years.

"Well, that can't be helped," he muttered.

He got dressed and took a rickshaw to the civilian spaceport. The narrow streets heaved with rush hour traffic. By the time he got there, the reporters were waiting for him. They'd been tracking him for weeks, in the build up to this final, record breaking flight.

He pushed past them in dark glasses, ignoring their hovering cameras, brushing off their shouted questions, not slowing until he reached his ship.

The Red Shark was a tough, streamlined wedge with a thick heat shield, and paint scoured to ash by the pitiless fires of hyperspace. He walked up the cargo ramp into her belly without looking back. He'd been stuck on this worthless planet for three long years, growing old and tired and soft. He could hardly wait to get airborne again, to open the throttle and feel the kick of the exhaust, the giddy freedom of the up-and-out.

He double-checked the contents of the stolen crate in the cargo hold. Then he made his way to the spherical Star Chamber at the ship's heart, where he found Maya Castillo. In her late forties and an accomplished jumper in her own right, she was to be his co-pilot on this final trip.

"How are we doing?" he said.

She turned and smiled. The shoulders of her khaki fatigues were emblazoned with the logos of the organisations sponsoring the flight.

"Pre-flight looks good," she said. He took the seat beside her, checked the readouts. All the lights were green. *The Red Shark* throbbed with potential.

"Spin her up," he said.

They quit the atmosphere at full throttle, leaving a roiling wake of turbulence, moving so fast the news cameras had a hard time following. In the Star Chamber, Caesar watched the ground fall away without regret.

"I should call my daughter," he said. He opened a secure channel. The phone rang for over a minute. When she finally answered, Amber looked harassed and tired, ready for an argument.

Caesar spoke first, before she could start. "It's all in your name," he said. "The media rights, the sponsorship, everything. It's all in your name. It's all for you and the boys. I've left instructions. You'll be taken care of."

Amber pushed a hand back through her hair. "We don't want your money, Dad."

"Sure you do. I don't want to saddle you with my debts. Call my agent, she has the details."

He forwarded her Jennifer's electronic business card, and saw her eyes flick down as it arrived in the corner of her screen.

When she looked up, she said, "The police were here just now, looking for you."

Caesar nodded. He knew they were after the crate.

"Don't worry," he said, "just call Jennifer, and let her deal with it."

"But what are you going to do?"

He tried to shrug but the safety straps were too tight.

"I'll be okay," he said. He rubbed his forehead. "You just look after yourself, and the boys."

"Dad," Amber bit her lip. "You're not planning on coming back, are you?"

Caesar glanced across at Maya.

"No, honey," he said. "No, I'm not."

Five minutes later, they were in flat space, ready to jump. Maya shunted control of the Bradley engines to his workstation.

"Ready when you are," she said.

Random jumping was a dangerous sport. It was a pilot throwing his ship into hyperspace without specifying a destination, just to see where they'd end up. It was illegal in some parts of known space, prime entertainment in others – and the stakes were always high.

Caesar Murphy was one of the better pilots, in that he was still alive. In the random jumping community he was something of a legend, having made more successful jumps than anyone else – almost fifty since turning professional.

Before that, he'd worked his way across the sky, serving time on freighters and troop transports, slogging all the way from the core to the rim and back again, saving up the money to buy his own ship. Over the years, he'd hauled every sort of cargo. He'd seen the sun rise on a dozen different worlds, had his nose broken in a bar brawl, and married twice. He'd lost his first wife to infidelity, the second – Amber's mother – to complications during childbirth. There had been nothing permanent in his life. He remembered it as one long series of farewells. Even now, at the end of his career, he was saying goodbye to his only daughter.

He was turning his back on his grandchildren.

His fingers hesitated over the controls.

Maya said, "Are you sure you want to go through with this?"

Caesar took a deep breath. He thought about the prize money he'd earn from this flight, and the chance to pay off his debts and live like a free man again. Then he thought about the crate in the cargo hold, and the creature within.

Three years ago, he'd found the creature curled in the ruins of an ancient citadel, on a dying planet circling a swollen star. It had been wounded and afraid, helpless in the gritty black dust that blew across the plateau where the citadel stood. Not knowing what else to do, he'd rescued it, brought it back and turned it over to the authorities as soon as he landed.

Since then, he'd been dreaming about the creature. It had haunted his sleep. Always the same dream, over and over, night after night. Which was why he'd used his money and fame to steal the creature back from the laboratory where it was being studied, why this last flight was actually a cover for his real intent: to put the thing back where it had come from.

He set his jaw and engaged the engines.

"You know I don't have any choice," he said.

Travelling through hyperspace was rough, like battering through white-hot plasma – the kind of ordeal only specially toughened, streamlined ships could endure.

In *The Red Shark*, Caesar and Maya rode the turbulence strapped into their couches, neither speaking, intent on their instruments.

After a subjective hour, they came out on the ragged edge of the galactic disc, where the stars were few and far between.

While Maya scanned the ship's systems for damage, Caesar went aft, to check on the cargo.

"How is it?" she asked him over the intercom.

At the bottom of the crate, the yellowish creature lay wrapped around itself in a knot of folded tentacles, like an octopus without a head. It smelled of mould and stagnant water. There were biopsy scars on the wrinkled skin, wire tags fixed to the legs.

"It looks okay," he said, "a bit shaken around but nothing to worry about."

At the sound of his voice, the creature shivered and shrank in on itself, its skin changing in colour from light brown to sickly marble. Caesar backed away. It had suffered enough already and he didn't want to alarm it. Instead, he returned to the Star Chamber.

"Do you have any idea where we are?" he asked, sliding into his couch.

Maya tapped her screen and a projection of the local sky appeared on the Chamber's curved wall.

"As far as I can tell, we're here," she said, using her cursor to highlight a small blue star a few light years in from the rim.

"And where's our target?"

Maya moved her hand to the very edge of the Abyss.

"Over here."

Every night it was the same. He stood before the citadel again, looking out over the remains of a city — a half-submerged, swampy metropolis, its ruined buildings inhabited by multi-limbed creatures like the one curled in the hold of his ship, all squirming together in the streets, skins rippling through every colour of the visible spectrum.

Instinctively, he knew this was how the planet had been before the black dust started falling from the sky.

He saw it then, the dust, blowing down as he remembered it, settling like a layer of fine soot, sticking and clinging to every living thing. He sensed its malevolence; saw the tentacled creatures thrashing about unable to breathe as the dust smothered them. He saw plants wither, trees die.

And then, when there was nothing left alive, the black dust gathered into a single glowering ball and turned its cold, inhuman attention on him...

Caesar woke with a shout, heart hammering. Beside him, Maya stirred. She was used to his nightmares. "Go back to sleep," she said.

His hands were shaking. He slid out from under the blanket and picked his trousers off the deck. Then he leaned down and kissed her warm shoulder.

"See you later," he said. He padded up to the Star Chamber and made himself a coffee, adding extra sweetener.

They were in orbit around the planet where he'd found the octopoid creature — the planet from his dream. It had taken them two further jumps and more than twenty-four hours to get here, and his back ached from sitting in the pilot's couch.

He perched on the edge of an instrument console, sipping his coffee. The walls of the spherical chamber displayed a 360° external view fed from cameras on the ship's hull, and when he looked down, he could see the planet's baked rocky surface passing beneath his feet, all brown and grey.

Somewhere down there, he thought, *are the answers I need.*

Half an hour later, they began their descent.

Impatient and uncomfortable, he brought them in hard, scrawling a fiery trail across the empty sky, dropping down to the plateau beside the ruined citadel.

Then, with *The Red Shark* still bouncing on its landing shocks, he unbuckled his straps and led Maya down to the cargo hold, to suit up.

She had to help him into his pressure suit. He wasn't as limber as he used to be.

"I'm really glad you're here," he said.

He bent forward stiffly to let her snap his helmet into place, and then watched as she fastened her own, tucking her long hair into the neck ring of her suit.

"When this is all over, we'll go somewhere quiet and start a new life," she said. "Somewhere without news reporters or gambling debts, somewhere nobody knows us."

She reached forward and squeezed his hand.

"Are you ready?"

She led him to the back of the cargo bay and opened the ramp. Hot, dry air blew in, too thin for them to breathe.

Together, they manhandled the crate down onto the rocky ground and opened it. Inside, the creature shivered, still folded in on itself.

Maya used her gloved hand to shade her eyes from the swollen sun. She said, "Is it okay?"

Caesar didn't reply straight away. He didn't know. This was as far as his plan went. Instead, he walked a few paces to the edge of the plateau, to get a better look at the ruins of the city in the wasteland beneath.

"Just give it some space," he said.

He could see scattered heaps of rubble that corresponded to the positions of the buildings in his dream. The swamp they sat in had dried long ago, but there were still a few hardy plants clinging on here and there between the stones, sucking what little moisture they could from the hot, rust-coloured soil.

Beside him, the citadel lay like a smashed chandelier, its silent ancient towers fallen, its stone walls crumbled. He picked his way over to a large chunk of masonry that had fallen from the archway above the main entrance. Up close, he could see the coarseness of the stonework, the tell-tale marks made by the flint tools used in its construction.

"It's moving," Maya said over the radio. Her voice sounded loud in his earpiece. He turned to see her standing by the empty crate, its former occupant using a single tentacle to pull itself laboriously across the rough ground, its skin changing hue as it adapted to its surroundings, trying to blend in.

"Let it go," he said. He looked up at the citadel's battered walls and felt his heart beat faster as he saw the thin black haze hovering in the air above them.

Maya joined him, picking her way through the debris, and they watched the octopoid pull itself into the shade of the building's entrance, as if seeking shelter from the haze overhead – a haze which was thickening by the second, turning into a vast dark cloud that threatened to blot out the harsh light of the red sun.

"We should get back to the ship," Caesar said. On his last trip, the dust had been blowing around like a sandstorm, and he had no desire to get caught in it again. Already, there were a few black motes drifting down from the sky like dirty snowflakes.

Frowning, Maya put her gloved hand out to catch one.

"What is it?"

"Leave it."

He turned to look at *The Red Shark*. As he did so, the dust began to fall – slowly at first, then faster and faster, until it became a black sleet that quickly obscured the ship and the edge of the rock-strewn plateau beyond.

"Caesar, what's happening?" Maya said, brushing at her suit, trying to keep it clean.

Caesar didn't answer. There was dust clinging to his faceplate, and he felt queasy as he remembered the way the creatures in his dream had suffocated. He took Maya by the shoulder and shoved her in the direction of the ship. "We have to get out of here," he said.

They started scrambling over the rocks. She was younger than he was and could move faster over the difficult terrain.

"Keep going, get to the ship," he panted, not wanting to hold her back.

He looked up. Overhead, the sky had darkened to a thunderous black, and the falling dust had become a blizzard. He stumbled on, wiping his faceplate every few steps until, eventually, he lost his footing.

His boot skidded on a loose rock and he went down hard, landing on his hands and knees with a cry. His ankle felt broken. The pain brought tears to his eyes.

"Maya," he said.

He rolled on to his side. He couldn't see her. The dust was falling in clumps now, like volcanic ash, obscuring everything.

Sweating and cursing, he pushed himself up into a sitting position. He couldn't walk and he couldn't see his ship.

He looked around. The citadel was still close behind him. He would have to shelter there until Maya found him. With gritted teeth, he pulled himself towards its stone steps, his injured leg trailing behind.

Once inside, he found the octopoid had left tracks and scuff marks in the chippings and broken plaster on the citadel's floor, leading him to a tight, sloping tunnel extending down into the bedrock beneath.

Carefully, Caesar lit a torch from his pocket and lowered himself into the hole, sliding down on his backside, trying not to jar his ankle or scrape his helmet.

After a few metres, the walls widened and he found himself in an underground vault. The ceiling was a dome maybe two metres at its highest point. There were strange hieroglyphs hacked into its smooth sides, stylised representations of multi-limbed creatures that seemed to writhe and dance as he moved his torch.

At the centre, the eight-legged creature from his cargo hold had pulled itself up onto a carved pedestal with a flat, wide top like a bird bath. As it settled itself into place, the floor shook.

Still on his knees, Caesar fell forward into the room as a solid stone slab ground across the vault's only entrance, sealing it – and him – from the world outside.

He spent a long time trying to find a way out. He pushed at the slab blocking the door. He tried to call Maya on the radio. He felt his way around the walls, and he shouted at the creature on the plinth, all to no avail. Eventually, exhausted and in pain, he slid down onto his haunches, breathing hard, his breath misting the inside of his faceplate.

"That damn dream," he said. If it hadn't been for the dream, he'd have stuck to his plan – to kick the creature out the airlock and get airborne again as quickly as possible – instead of wasting time in the ruins, trying to see the shadow of a long-vanished city.

He rapped his knuckles against his helmet, wishing he could take it off, longing for an excuse to bust the seals and just *get it all over with*. Instead, he crawled over to the central plinth and looked up at the mass of pale tentacles resting at the top, limbs all curled in on themselves like the flabby fingers of a dead fist.

The door had closed as soon as the creature had settled in place. If he could somehow dislodge it, perhaps the door would open again?

He reached a gloved hand and brushed a wire tag hanging from one of the creature's legs. The lab he'd stolen it from had given up their attempts to communicate and had been preparing to dissect the creature. Its skin was scratched and bruised where they'd taken samples, reminding him of the way his hands had looked the day after his first bar fight, all those years ago, on some forsaken ball of mud somewhere down near the core.

He'd been seventeen, maybe eighteen years old at the time, working his first military contract. A raw young kid with too much swagger and not enough sense, all puffed up in his uniform, and just stupid enough to challenge two drunken stevedores in a downtown bar.

Thinking about it now, kneeling in front of the plinth, he smiled. He'd had his ass kicked on half a dozen planets since then, but he'd never forgotten that first time.

"What do we do now?" he said through his suit's external speaker. On its perch, the creature shivered at the sound of his voice, drawing further into itself.

"How long do we have to stay here?" he said. His suit wasn't fully charged: he only had another hour of air.

In the light from his torch, the creature remained hunched and silent. Curled up, it was about the size of a large footstool – big enough to put up a fight if he tried to move it from the pedestal by force.

He got to his feet and staggered over to press his gloved hand against the slab of rock blocking the entrance. His ankle felt a bit better now, not broken, merely bruised.

"Is this how you survived last time, shut away down here all by yourself, the last of your kind?"

He patted the rock. As a pilot, he was used to spending long periods of time cooped up in a cramped cockpit, but there was something about the sheer *weight* of this obstruction that scared him. Trapped in the dark with a dwindling air supply, beneath thousands of tonnes of solid bedrock, he felt the sweat break out around his collar. He needed to get out, back up to the surface, somewhere he could breathe freely without the helmet, see without the torch...

He pictured his daughter and two grandsons, so very far away. If he died here, in this cavern, would they ever find out what had happened to him? Would Maya get the word out?

He thought of all the random jumps he'd made, and the other pilots he'd known. Where were they all now? Over the years, they'd all jumped away, one-by-one, never to be seen or heard from again – probably having died lonely, desperate deaths in uncharted star systems, just like this one.

That was the price they paid for the excitement and fame. He knew the stakes every time he gambled his life on a random jump: the risk that something would go wrong, that he'd end up somewhere with no way back, stranded and alone.

Well, he thought, if that's the way it is, I'm not going down without a fight.

He turned back to the pedestal in the centre of the room.

"Let me out," he said. "I don't have enough air to stay down here."

The creature flinched. He walked over and gave it an experimental shove.

"I need to get back to my ship," he said.

He shoved again but couldn't dislodge it. All eight limbs were gripping the plinth.

He tried slapping and punching, but it only curled tighter.

Eventually, he stepped back, breathing hard, feeling old. If he didn't have the strength to move it, he'd have to try something else. He shone his torch around, but there was nothing he could use as a weapon. There were no screwdrivers in the tool pouch on his thigh.

"I'm getting too old for this shit," he muttered, and noticed again how the tentacles drew tighter at the sound of his voice.

"What's the matter? Am I disturbing you?"

Grimly, he turned the volume on his suit's external speaker up as far as it would go, and put all his pain and frustration into one desperate shout of anger.

Startled, the creature leapt from the pedestal, tentacles trying to smother the noise. It hit Caesar in the chest. Unbalanced, he fell backwards, and it landed in his lap like a heavy, wriggling dog. For a moment, they both sat there stunned. Then the rock door scraped back into its recess and a few swirls of dust to blew into the room. Caesar felt the creature squirm, its yellowish skin turning a flabby white. He kicked it away with his good leg, and then crawled for the opening. As he did so, the creature rolled upright and scuttled back towards its pedestal, clearly frantic to re-seal the entrance.

"Oh no, you don't," Caesar said. He was almost at the door now, trying to ignore the pains in his bruised knees and ankle. With one last desperate effort, he threw himself out of the room, into the narrow tunnel, and collapsed to the ground, panting.

He caught a final glimpse of the creature lowering itself into position, then the heavy stone door crashed back into place and all he could see was rock.

By the time Caesar pulled himself back up the sloping tunnel and staggered out onto the citadel's stone steps, the dust had stopped falling. Like ash, it lay over everything on the plateau: the collapsed towers, the ruined city, *The Red Shark*. He had maybe forty minutes of air left; his suit chafed and his ankle hurt.

He limped down the steps. Overhead, the sun was a swollen red blister in an indigo sky. Beneath his feet, the dust crunched like fresh snow.

Moving as quickly as he dared, he picked his way through it to his ship. When he got there, he was concerned to see more dust clinging to the hull, and no sign of life on board. Breathing hard, he leaned on one of the landing struts.

"Maya, are you there?"

He looked down; his boots and the lower legs of his suit were black, his gloves too. He'd have to strip his suit off if he wanted to stop the dust getting loose in his ship.

"Hello, Maya?"

He switched frequencies and tried again, but there was no response, nothing on the line but static.

He looked at the edge of the plateau, a few paces away. Could she have become disorientated in the dust storm and wandered off the edge? Was she lying down there injured and unconscious, waiting for him to find her?

He started to shuffle over, but stopped as a movement near the citadel caught his eye. A few metres from where he stood, individual particles of dust were gathering into a growing pile, bouncing and skittering together like iron filings under a magnet.

"Caesar, is that you?" The voice was faint, crackling through the static hiss in his headphones.

"Maya, where are you?"

In front of him, the dust had become a swaying column about a metre and a half high, its surface constantly shifting and churning.

"I'm right here."

He watched in horror as the column resolved into a crude human figure with a thin waist and strong shoulders.

"Don't be afraid," it said.

Details started to appear, first fingers, then eyes and hair, and a mouth.

"Maya, is that you?"

The figure regarded him with its black eyes. Its black lips parted.

"Yes," it said.

With every second that passed, the likeness became clearer, and more intolerable. Caesar took a step back, toward the ship. He said: "What happened to you?"

In the light of the bloated sun, the figure raised a hand to shade its eyes.

"Oh Caesar," it said. "If you could only see the things I've seen." It turned and looked back at the citadel. "All those octopus creatures, they're all in here with me, safe and sound."

Caesar took another step back, into the shadow of the ship's hull.

"In where?" he said. The oxygen dial in his helmet showed he had less than thirty minutes left.

"In the dust." Maya turned to face him. "They're all stored in the dust. That's how it works. The dust is a memory matrix. It breaks everything down, stores it as code, preserving everything it touches."

Caesar took another step. He was at the cargo ramp now. All he needed to do to gain entry to the ship was lower it.

"But why?" he said. "Why do that?"

The figure of Maya turned her face up to the sun's red light and closed her eyes, as if enjoying its warmth. "They've all been saved," she said. "Just imagine it, Caesar. All those creatures, all their thoughts and dreams, they're all here. And when their sun dies, they won't have to die with it. The dust will blow outward on the solar wind, out into the universe, carrying a complete record of everything they once were."

She opened her eyes and took a step towards him, the dust rustling as she moved.

"It'll all be preserved," she said.

Caesar reached up to touch the ramp controls. "But where did it come from?" he asked. The creatures he'd seen in his dream hadn't possessed much in the way of technology; they'd been wriggling through an abandoned city, living in the ruins of another, vanished civilisation.

Maya let her bare black shoulders drop. "I don't know," she admitted. She took another step forwards, coming almost within reach.

"But what does it matter, Caesar?"

He pressed the control and the cargo ramp hinged down.

"It killed them all," he said. "It smothered them."

Maya shook her head. "They were going to die anyway. They were stuck here with a dying star. What else were they going to do?"

"That's not the point."

The figure of Maya folded its arms. "The dust saved me," she said. "I couldn't see where I was going. I missed the ship and there was a cliff. I fell into the ruins of the town and shattered my faceplate. I was suffocating, Caesar, and the dust saved me."

Caesar took a deep breath. He placed a foot on the ramp.

"I'm leaving now," he said.

"No, you can't."

"Why? Are you going to stop me?" He waved his arm at the ruins of the fallen swamp city. "Are you going to kill me the way you killed all of them?"

Maya stumbled forward, palms turned pleadingly toward him. "No, you don't understand."

He stepped back, both feet on the ramp now, backing up into the ship.

"I'm not sure I want to," he said.

Once inside, he closed the ramp. He wriggled out of his suit in the cargo bay and made his way painfully up to the Star Chamber. His ankle hurt when he put his weight on it. His knees were sore. When he got there, he lowered himself into the pilot's chair. The walls were blank, the external cameras clogged with dust.

For a moment he sat listening to the breath wheezing in and out of his chest, then he flicked open a communications channel.

"I'm sorry," he said.

There was a crackle on the line, and Maya's voice came through, faint and distorted.

"Caesar, please don't do this," she said.

He looked down at his gnarled hands resting on the instrument panel, the reflection of his lined face in the glass between them. He felt suddenly, terribly alone. He was an old man, and he'd lost everything that had ever meant anything to him.

"You're not real," he said. Now he was out of the suit, he could smell the sweat soaked into his shirt. "You're just a copy. The real Maya, the one I loved, is dead."

He started to cry: for Maya; for his wives; for Amber and the boys.

"I've really fucked it all up," he said. He'd spent his life with one foot out of the door, always looking to the next adventure, never appreciating what he had.

He'd hurt or abandoned everyone.

Maya was only the latest casualty.

There was a noise on the line like wind blowing across a sandy beach, and then Maya said: "No, Caesar, you don't understand."

Sniffling, he touched a control and the engines whined into life, spinning up.

"Caesar, please."

He fingered the communication panel, nerving himself. As a gambler, he'd never known when to walk away from the table; now things were different. He knew exactly what he had to do. He saw his future stretching out before him. With his debts paid off, he could use the remaining prize money to rebuild his family, get to know Amber and the boys again.

He took a deep breath.

"Goodbye, Maya."

He cut the channel. *The Red Shark* rose into the air above the plateau. Some of the dust had shaken loose and the external cameras were clearer now. The rest would be scoured away by the fires of hyperspace.

Tears flowing freely, he let the ship hang over the colossal wreck of the citadel for a moment, looking down at the solitary black figure on the desolate plateau, arm raised, shading its eyes.

He recalled his final glimpse of the octopoid creature alone in the underground crypt, the last surviving member of its race.

He rubbed his face with both hands, and said: "Nothing lasts."

Then he tipped the ship over until it stood on its tail in the harsh light of the dying sun. He thought of home and, with a final sob, threw open the throttle.

The Red Shark leaped heavenwards, like a prayer.

~

This was one of my first attempts at a full-throttle retro space romp, complete with a cynical hero, a ruined Lovecraftian city, and a dusty planet circling a dying star. It appeared in *Interzone* in January 2009.

Forever Returning

A week after the failed engine test, a pair of secret service agents woke Stapleton before dawn and dragged him down to Krebs' office at the Johnson Space Centre.

"What's going on?" Stapleton asked. The agents had told him nothing on the ride over.

Krebs' top button was loose. She'd left her jacket on the back of the chair and her blouse was rumpled, as if she'd slept in it.

"It's about the mission," she said.

Stapleton frowned. The mission – to test the new instantaneous propulsion system – had been a bust. He'd maneuvered his capsule into position and pressed the switch. And then nothing had happened. The capsule had remained precisely and stubbornly where it was.

"That was a week ago." He rubbed his unshaven face. "What's so urgent you had to get me out of bed at four am?"

Krebs' eyes were puffy and raw-looking. Plastic cups littered her desk. Some were empty; others still retained an inch or two of cold coffee. She picked one up, swirled the contents around in the bottom, and replaced it on the desk.

"It seems it wasn't a total failure," she said.

Stapleton shook his head, trying to clear the sleep-addled fuzziness still clinging to his thoughts.

"But it didn't work. I didn't move."

Krebs picked up another of the cups and sniffed it for freshness.

"It's difficult to explain," she said. "Maybe... Maybe it would just be easier to show you." She dropped the cup into a wastebasket and rubbed her hands together. "Hell, you're going to have to meet him sooner or later."

The office had an adjoining meeting room. She opened the door.

"Go on through," she said.

Stapleton didn't move.

"What's going on, Mary?"

"Just go on in. It will all make sense in a minute."

Outside the office windows, the sky was turning orange with the immanence of sunrise. Stapleton let his shoulders sag. His tiredness felt like a heavy pack. Part of him wanted nothing more than to lie down on the blue carpet tiles and go to sleep.

"Okay, whatever."

He brushed past her.

Inside, the room was unfurnished save for a large oval conference table. Framed photographs lined the walls – shots from the Hubble; pictures of rockets and shuttles gleaming on launch pads – and, at the far end, a figure stood by the window, silhouetted against the dawn.

As Stapleton entered, the man turned. For a confused couple of seconds, Stapleton couldn't place his face. He looked familiar, but...

"Holy crap!"

The stranger in the meeting room had his face. He was looking into his own eyes, seeing himself staring back.

"Mark Stapleton," Krebs said, her voice too tight and brittle to be ironic, "meet Mark Stapleton."

The effect was like looking into an impossible mirror, except his reflection wasn't wearing faded jeans and an old college sweatshirt; this other Stapleton wore the orange jumpsuit Stapleton had worn the week before, complete with mission patches on the shoulders and his name stitched across the breast.

Stapleton didn't know what to say, and his doppelganger seemed equally taken aback. Finally, the other man said,

"So, it's true, then."

Krebs stood between them.

"I'm afraid so," she said.

"So, he's me?" The man looked into Stapleton' face, and raised his fingers to his own cheek. In response, Stapleton had to consciously restrain himself from aping the gesture.

"You both are."

The sun was up now, staining the walls of the room with yellow slats of light. Early morning traffic moved on the highway.

Stapleton opened and shut his mouth. He put his hand on Krebs' arm.

"What the hell is this?"

His double frowned at the woman.

"You didn't tell him? He doesn't know?"

Stapleton felt his cheeks burning.

"Tell me *what?*"

Gently, Krebs shook his fingers from her sleeve.

"The test worked, Mark." She wouldn't meet his eyes. "Only it didn't work exactly as we expected."

"The drive was supposed to take me to Mars and back."

"And it did." She jerked a thumb at the other Stapleton. "You just got back."

Stapleton glanced at his double.

"He's been to Mars?"

"His capsule reappeared last night, exactly in position."

Stapleton felt a wild laugh bubbling in the base of his throat. He swallowed it down.

"But that's crazy. The test didn't work. I didn't *go* anywhere."

The second Stapleton gave a nod.

"You didn't, but I did."

"And who are you?"

"She told you; I'm you."

The laugh was in danger of turning to panic now. Stapleton was beginning to lose his grip on reality.

"I don't get this." He couldn't keep his voice steady. "I don't get any of this."

Krebs stood before him. In her heels, she was almost the same height.

"When you activated the propulsion system, it worked." She looked from Stapleton to the other man. "But instead of moving the capsule, it copied it."

"Copied?"

"We thought the drive would break down the capsule and encode it as a faster-than-light particle."

"Yeah, I know the theory." Until he was reconstituted at the other end – in orbit around Mars – Stapleton would have existed only as information.

"Well, that part worked." Krebs looked ashen. "Only the process didn't destroy the original the way it did with the prototypes. This time, the capsule wasn't moved, it was *copied*."

Stapleton put out a hand to steady himself against the edge of the table.

"So, I did go to Mars?"

Across the room, his doppelganger smiled.

"You'd better believe it."

Stapleton's breath caught. "Was it…?"

The smile widened.

"Yeah, every bit as beautiful as you hoped."

Stapleton found he was smiling too. Then something began to bother him. At first he wasn't sure what it was.

"You spent a week there, and then you just came home?"

"Yeah, and I guess folk here were surprised to see me."

Unease gripped Stapleton' chest. If his suspicions were correct…

"Oh God," he moaned. "That's horrible."

The other two looked at him in surprise.

"It's not that bad," Krebs said. "I'm sure we can find a way for you two to coexist."

Her mobile phone rang and she clapped it to her ear. While she was talking into it, Stapleton studied the stranger that had, until a week ago, been him.

"And when you arrived at Mars, you had no idea you'd been copied?"

The other shook his head.

"None at all. It was only last night when I got back here that I found out about it."

Stapleton began to feel sick.

"So, when you activated the engine to return home, you still had no idea what had happened?"

"No, like I told you, it was as much a surprise to me as it was to you."

Stapleton rubbed his eyes.

"What's the problem?" his counterpart asked.

"Don't you see?"

"No, I can't say I do."

Krebs finished her call. She looked paler than before, as if she might collapse at any moment. Stapleton helped her into a chair.

"What is it?" he asked, already fearing he knew the answer.

A helicopter passed the window. The thick glass reduced its clatter to a dull thudding.

"It happened again." The woman's voice was hoarse. "Another capsule." She looked up and their eyes met. "Another you."

Stapleton turned away. He had been right. The knowledge was like ice in the pit of his stomach.

"The engine made another copy of the capsule," he said.

Cars were arriving at the front gate. Some of them had flashing lights.

Stapleton' double looked surprised.

"So," he said, "there are three of us now?"

Stapleton made a cutting motion with his hand. "No," he said. "It's worse than that. Way worse."

In her chair, Krebs put a hand over her mouth. She had already guessed.

"Tell me something," Stapleton said. "If you were in orbit around Mars and your engine failed to work, what would you do?"

The other guy shrugged.

"I'd try again."

"Me too. And that's what happened. When you returned, you got copied again. You left another Stapleton at Mars. A copy of yourself that – just like I did – thinks his engine's failed to work."

"So, the third Stapleton…?"

"Was his second attempt to get home." Stapleton sat in a chair beside Krebs and raised his face to the tiled ceiling. "There's a copy of us stranded in orbit around Mars, trying desperately to get back home. Only, every time he tries, he thinks the engine's failed."

"But every time, we end up with another version of him?"

"Yeah."

"How long do you think he'll keep trying?"

"Until he dies." Stapleton rubbed his face. "I know I would."

"And how long will that be?"

Stapleton did some math in his head. "He had food and water for a month. If he keeps trying every hour – giving the engine time to build up to full power between each attempt – we could be looking at something like six hundred versions of us by the end of the month."

He imagined an army of identical men, their numbers formed into endless ranks on a windswept parade ground – and himself, lost among them, fighting to keep his identity in a sea of facsimiles.

The second Stapleton ran a hand across a shaven scalp. His

haunted expression matched Stapleton's own.

"Whatever happens," the double said, "there'll always be one copy of us left behind."

"I'm afraid so."

"What are we going to do?"

Stapleton shook his head. "I don't know. We'll have to get a message to him, to tell him to stop trying. Send a radio signal. Something…"

"Do you think that would work? We'd be asking him to commit suicide."

"What alternative is there?" Stapleton voice quavered on the edge of mania. "He's never coming home, and each time he tries, he creates another copy."

Krebs' phone rang again. She picked it up and listened to the voice on the line, then placed the handset facedown on the conference table.

"There's another capsule," she said quietly. "It just appeared. They're sending a recovery shuttle." She clasped her hands in her lap so tightly that Stapleton heard her knuckles pop and crack. "What am I going to tell the President?"

Stapleton closed his eyes. He couldn't stop thinking about the copy of himself that was stranded, facing a lonely and chilling death above the red planet, never knowing that his efforts to return were for naught. What was that version of him thinking? What was it *feeling*? How would it react to its death sentence? His cheeks felt hot and he could hear the blood rushing in his ears.

"You'd better tell him we need to get ready," he said, almost choking on the words. "Because unless we can get a signal to Mars, there'll be another one of me along in an hour."

~

Written especially for this collection, "Forever Returning" is a nightmare vision in the Philip K. Dick tradition – frightening not so much for its events, but more for the psychological effects it has on the characters involved. I came up with the idea while talking about the transporters in the original series of Star Trek. The person I was talking to explained that the machines couldn't actually 'move' the crew of the Enterprise. Instead, they would have to destroy the versions of Kirk and Spock on the ship, and then rebuild exact copies of them down on the planetary surface. This meant every time the captain stepped into a transporter, he was effectively committing suicide in order for a new copy of himself to be 'born' somewhere else. How wasteful, I thought. If you're going to build a copy, why not keep the original as well? And that's where this tale of duplicate space adventurers came from.

About the Author

Gareth L. Powell is a science fiction author from the UK. His alternate history thriller, *Ack-Ack Macaque* won the 2013 BSFA Award for Best Novel, spawned two sequels, and was shortlisted in the Best Translated Novel category for the 2016 Seiun Awards in Japan. His short fiction has appeared in a host of magazines and anthologies, including *Interzone, Solaris Rising 3*, and *The Year's Best Science Fiction*, and his story 'Ride The Blue Horse' made the shortlist for the 2015 BSFA Award.

Gareth lives near Bristol with his wife, two daughters and three cats. He can be found online at www.garethlpowell.com or on Twitter @garethlpowell

THE ION RAIDER
Ian Whates
The Dark Angels (Volume 2)
Cover art by Jim Burns

The much anticipated follow-up to the Amazon best seller *Pelquin's Comet*.

"A good, unashamed, rip-roaring piece of space opera that hits the spot."
— *Financial Times*

"He's a natural story-teller and works his material with verve, obvious enjoyment, and an effortlessly breezy prose style." — *The Guardian*

"*Pelquin's Comet* is classic space opera at its finest, a satisfying and enjoyable novel in its own right and an intriguing introduction to a story universe I want to visit again. Thoroughly recommended."
— *SFcrowsnest*

"Whates does a good job playing out the lines of suspense while steadily revealing significant plot points, keeping things character-focused... It's a fast, fun read." — *Speculation*

"You won't go far wrong with this book... you never know, it could be the beginning of something wonderful." — *Booklore*

~

Leesa is determined to find out who is quietly assassinating her old crewmates, the Dark Angels, and stop them before it's her turn to die.

First Solar Bank have sent **Drake** on his most dangerous mission yet, to the isolationist world of Enduril, where nothing is as it seems.

Jen just wanted to be left in peace on her farm, until somebody blew the farm up. She escaped, a fact those responsible will come to regret.

Released May 2017 www.newconpress.co.uk

NEWCON PRESS

Publishing quality Science Fiction, Fantasy, Dark Fantasy and Horror for 11 years and counting.

Winner of the 2010 'Best Publisher' Award
from the European Science Fiction Society.

Anthologies, novels, short story collections, novellas, paperbacks, hardbacks, signed limited editions, e-books...
Why not take a look at some of our other titles?

Featured authors include:
Neil Gaiman, Brian Aldiss, Kelley Armstrong, Peter F. Hamilton, Alastair Reynolds, Stephen Baxter, Christopher Priest, Tanith Lee, Joe Abercrombie, Dan Abnett, Nina Allan, Sarah Ash, Neal Asher, Tony Ballantyne, James Barclay, Chris Beckett, Lauren Beukes, Aliette de Bodard, Chaz Brenchley, Keith Brooke, Eric Brown, Pat Cadigan, Jay Caselberg, Ramsey Campbell, Michael Cobley, Genevieve Cogman, Storm Constantine, Hal Duncan, Jaine Fenn, Paul di Filippo, Jonathan Green, Jon Courtenay Grimwood, Frances Hardinge, Gwyneth Jones, M. John Harrison, Amanda Hemingway, Paul Kane, Leigh Kennedy, Nancy Kress, Kim Lakin-Smith, David Langford, Alison Littlewood, James Lovegrove, Una McCormack, Ian McDonald, Gary McMahon, Sophia McDougall, Ken MacLeod, Ian R MacLeod, Gail Z. Martin, Juliet E. McKenna, John Meaney, Simon Morden, Mark Morris, Anne Nicholls, Stan Nicholls, Marie O'Regan, Philip Palmer, Stephen Palmer, Sarah Pinborough, Gareth L. Powell, Robert Reed, Rod Rees, Andy Remic, Mike Resnick, Mercurio D. Rivera, Adam Roberts, Justina Robson, Lynda E. Rucker, Stephanie Saulter, Gaie Sebold, Robert Shearman, Sarah Singleton, Martin Sketchley, Michael Marshall Smith, Kari Sperring, Brian Stapleford, Charles Stross, Tricia Sullivan, E.J. Swift, David Tallerman, Adrian Tchaikovsky, Steve Rasnic Tem, Lavie Tidhar, Lisa Tuttle, Simon Kurt Unsworth, Ian Watson, Freda Warrington, Liz Williams, Neil Williamson, and many more.

Join our mailing list to get advance notice of new titles and special offers:
www.newconpress.co.uk

IMMANION PRESS

Purveyors of Speculative Fiction

The Lightbearer by Alan Richardson (May 2017)

Michael Horsett parachutes into Occupied France before the D-Day Invasion. He is dropped in the wrong place, miles from the action, badly injured, and totally alone. He falls prey to two Thelemist women who have awaited the Hawk God's coming, attracts a group of First World War veterans who rally to what they imagine is his cause, is hunted by a troop of German Field Police who are desperate to find him, and has a climactic encounter with a mutilated priest who believes that Lucifer Incarnate has arrived...

The Lightbearer is a unique gnostic thriller, dealing with the themes of Light and Darkness, Good and Evil, Matter and Spirit.

"The Lightbearer is another shining example of Alan Richardson's talent as a story-teller. He uses his wide esoteric knowledge to produce a story that thrills, chills and startles the reader as it radiates pure magical energy. An unusual and gripping war story with more facets than a star sapphire." – Mélusine Draco, author of *"Aubry's Dog"* and *"Black Horse, White Horse".* ISBN: 978-1-907737-63-3 £11.99 $18.99

Dark in the Day, Ed. by Storm Constantine & Paul Houghton

Weirdness lurks beyond the margins of the mundane, emerging to dismantle our assumptions of reality. Dark in the Day is an anthology of weird fiction, penned by established writers and also those new to the genre – the latter being authors who are, or were, students of Creative Writing at Staffordshire University, where editor Storm Constantine occasionally delivers guest lectures. Her co-editor, Paul Houghton, is the senior lecturer in Creative Writing at the university.

Contributors include: Martina Bellovičová, J. E. Bryant, Glynis Charlton, Storm Constantine, Louise Coquio, Elizabeth Counihan, Krishan Coupland, Elizabeth Davidson, Siân Davies, Paul Finch, Rosie Garland, Rhys Hughes, Kerry Fender, Andrew Hook, Paul Houghton, Tanith Lee, Tim Pratt, Nicholas Royle, Michael Marshall Smith, Paula Wakefield, Ian Whates and Liz Williams.
ISBN: 978-1-907737-74-9 £11.99, $18.99

Blood, the Phoenix and a Rose by Storm Constantine

Wraeththu, a race of androgynous beings, have arisen from the ashes of human civilisation. Like the mythical rebis, the divine hermaphrodite, they represent the pinnacle of human evolution. But Wraeththu – or hara – were forged in the crucible of destruction and emerged from a new Dark Age. They have yet to realise their full potential and come to terms with the most blighted aspects of their past. Blood, the Phoenix and a Rose begins with an enigma: Gavensel, a har who appears unearthly and has a shrouded history. He has been hidden away in the house of Sallow Gandaloi by Melisander, an alchemist, but is this seclusion to protect Gavensel from the world or the world from him? As his story unfolds, the shadow of the dark fortress Fulminir falls over him, and memories of his past slowly return. The only way to find the truth is to go back through the layers of time, to when the blood was fresh. ISBN: 978-1-907737-75-6 £11.99, $18.99

Animate Objects by Tanith Lee

There is no such thing as an inanimate object… And how could that be? Because, simply, everything is formed from matter, and basically, at *root*, the matter that makes up everything in the physical world – the Universe – is of the same substance. Which means, on that basic level, we – you, me, and that power station over there – are all the exact riotous, chaotic, amorphous *same*. Here is an assortment of Lee takes on the nature, and perhaps intentions, of so-called non-sentient things. And you're quite safe. This is only a book. An inanimate object.

From the Introduction by Tanith Lee

The original hardback of this collection, of which there were only 35 copies, was published by Immanion Press in 2013, to commemorate Tanith Lee receiving the Lifetime Achievement Award at World Fantasycon. It included 5 previously unpublished pieces. This new release includes a further 2 stories, co-written by Tanith Lee and John Kaiine, and new interior illustrations by Jarod Mills. ISBN: 978-1-907737-73-2, £11.99 $18.99

Immanion Press
http://www.immanion-press.com
info@immanion-press.com

9 781910 935422